The Soul of a People

H. Fielding

Copyright © 2017 Okitoks Press

All rights reserved.

ISBN: 1982049332

ISBN-13: 978-1982049331

Table of Contents

CHAPTER I 4
   LIVING BELIEFS 4
CHAPTER II 9
   HE WHO FOUND THE LIGHT—I 9
CHAPTER III 15
   HE WHO FOUND THE LIGHT—II 15
CHAPTER IV 19
   THE WAY TO THE GREAT PEACE 19
CHAPTER V 23
   WAR—I 23
CHAPTER VI 30
   WAR—II 30
CHAPTER VII 33
   GOVERNMENT 33
CHAPTER VIII 38
   CRIME AND PUNISHMENT 38
CHAPTER IX 43
   HAPPINESS 43
CHAPTER X 47
   THE MONKHOOD—I 47
CHAPTER XI 55
   THE MONKHOOD—II 55
CHAPTER XII 57
   PRAYER 57
CHAPTER XIII 60
   FESTIVALS 60
CHAPTER XIV 67
   WOMEN—I 67
   From a Man to a Girl. 73
CHAPTER XV 73
   WOMEN—II 73
CHAPTER XVI 80
   WOMEN—III 80
CHAPTER XVII 81
   DIVORCE 81
CHAPTER XVIII 86
   DRINK 86
CHAPTER XIX 88
   MANNERS 88
CHAPTER XX 91

'NOBLESSE OBLIGE'	91
CHAPTER XXI	98
ALL LIFE IS ONE	98
CHAPTER XXII	107
DEATH, THE DELIVERER	107
FOOTNOTE:	114
CHAPTER XXIII	114
THE POTTER'S WHEEL	114
FOOTNOTE:	121
CHAPTER XXIV	121
THE FOREST OF TIME	121
CHAPTER XXV	123
CONCLUSION	123
THE END	125

CHAPTER I

LIVING BELIEFS

'The observance of the law alone entitles to the right of belonging to my religion.'—
Saying of the Buddha.

For the first few years of my stay in Burma my life was so full of excitement that I had little care or time for any thought but of to-day. There was, first of all, my few months in Upper Burma in the King's time before the war, months which were full of danger and the exhilaration of danger, when all the surroundings were too new and too curious to leave leisure for examination beneath the surface. Then came the flight from Upper Burma at the time of the war, and then the war itself. And this war lasted four years. Not four years of fighting in Burma proper, for most of the Irrawaddy valley was peaceful enough by the end of 1889; but as the central parts quieted down, I was sent to the frontier, first on the North and then on the East by the Chin mountains; so that it was not until 1890 that a transfer to a more settled part gave me quiet and opportunity for consideration of all I had seen and known. For it was in those years that I gained most of whatever little knowledge I have of the Burmese people.

Months, very many months, I passed with no one to speak to, with no other companions but Burmese. I have been with them in joy and in sorrow, I have fought with them and against them, and sat round the camp-fire after the day's work and talked of it all. I have had many friends amongst them, friends I shall always honour; and I have seen them killed sometimes in our fights, or dead of fever in the marshes of the frontier. I have known them from the labourer to the Prime Minister, from the little neophyte just accepted into the faith to the head of all the Burmese religion. I have known their wives and daughters; have watched many a flirtation in the warm scented evenings; and have seen girls become wives and wives mothers while I have lived amongst them. So that although when the country settled down, and we built houses for ourselves and returned more to English modes of living, I felt that I was drifting away from them into the conventionality and ignorance of our official lives, yet I had in my memory much of what I had seen, much of what I had done, that I shall never forget. I felt that I had been—even if it were only for a time—behind the veil, where it is so hard to come.

In looking over these memories it seemed to me that there were many things I did not understand, acts of theirs and customs, which I had seen and noted, but of which I did not know the reason. We all know how hard it is to see into the heart even of our own people, those of our flesh and blood who are with us always, whose ways are our ways, and whose thoughts are akin to ours. And if this be so with them, it is ten thousand times harder with those whose ways are not our ways, and from whose thoughts we must be far apart. It is true that there are no dark places in the lives of the Burmese as there are in the lives of other Orientals. All is open to the light of day in their homes and in their religion, and their women are the freest in the world. Yet the barriers of a strange tongue and a strange religion, and of ways caused by another climate than ours, is so great that, even to those of us who have every wish and every opportunity to understand, it seems sometimes as if we should never know their hearts. It seems as if we should never learn more of their ways than just the outside—that curiously varied outside which is so deceptive, and which is so apt to prevent our understanding that they are men just as we are, and not strange creations from some far-away planet.

So when I settled down and sought to know more of the meaning of what I had seen, I thought that first of all I must learn somewhat of their religion, of that mainspring of many actions, which seemed sometimes admirable, sometimes the reverse, and nearly always foreign to my ideas. It is true that I knew they were Buddhists, that I recognized the yellow-robed monks as followers of the word of Gaudama the Buddha, and that I had a general acquaintance with the theory of their faith as picked up from a book or two—notably, Rhys Davids' 'Buddhism' and Bishop Bigandet's book—and from many inconsequent talks with the monks and others. But the knowledge was but superficial, and I was painfully aware that it did not explain much that I had seen and that I saw every day.

So I sent for more books, such books as had been published in English, and I studied them, and hoped thereby to attain the explanations I wanted; and as I studied, I watched as I could the doings of the people, that I might see the effects of causes and the results of beliefs. I read in these sacred books of the mystery of Dharma, of how a man has no soul, no consciousness after death; that to the Buddhist 'dead men rise up never,' and that those who go down to the grave are known no more. I read that all that survives is the effect of a man's actions, the evil effect, for good is merely negative, and that this is what causes pain and trouble to the next life. Everything changes, say the sacred books, nothing lasts even for a moment. It will be, and it has been, is the life of man. The life that lives tomorrow in the next incarnation is no more the life that died in the last than the flame we light in the lamp to-day is the same that went out yesternight. It is as if a stone were thrown into a pool—that is the life, the splash of the stone; all that remains, when the stone lies resting in the mud and weeds below the waters of forgetfulness, are the circles ever widening on the surface, and the ripples never dying, but only spreading farther and farther away. All this seemed to me a mystery such as I could not understand. But when I went to the people, I found that it was simple enough to them; for I found that they remembered their former lives often, that children, young children, could tell who they were before they died, and remember details of that former existence. As they grew older the remembrance grew fainter and fainter, and at length almost died away. But in many children it was quite fresh, and was believed in beyond possibility of a doubt by all the people. So I saw that the teachings of their sacred books and the thoughts of the people were not at one in this matter.

Again, I read that there was no God. Nats there were, spirits of great power like angels, and there was the Buddha (the just man made perfect), who had worked out for all men the way to reach surcease from evil; but of God I saw nothing. And because the Buddha had reached heaven (Nirvana), it would be useless to pray to him. For, having entered into his perfect rest, he could not be disturbed by the sharp cry of those suffering below; and if he heard, still he could not help; for each man must through pain and sorrow work out for himself his own salvation. So all prayer is futile.

Then I remembered I had seen the young mother going to the pagoda on the hilltop with a little offering of a few roses or an orchid spray, and pouring out her soul in passionate supplication to Someone—Someone unknown to her sacred books—that her firstborn might recover of his fever, and be to her once more the measureless delight of her life; and it would seem to me that she must believe in a God and in prayer after all.

So though I found much in these books that was believed by the people, and much that was to them the guiding influence of their lives, yet I was unable to trust to them altogether, and I was in doubt where to seek for the real beliefs of these people. If I went to their monks, their holy men, the followers of the great teacher, Gaudama, they referred me to their books as containing all that a Buddhist believed; and when I pointed out the discrepancies, they only shook their heads, and said that the people were an ignorant people and confused their beliefs in that way.

And when I asked what was a Buddhist, I was told that, to be a Buddhist, a man must be accepted into the religion with certain rites, certain ceremonies, he must become for a time a member of the community of the monks of the Buddha, and that a Buddhist was he who was so accepted, and who thereafter held by the teachings of the Buddha.

But when I searched the life of the Buddha, I could not find any such ceremonies necessary at all. So that it seemed that the religion of the Buddha was one religion, and the religion of the Buddhists another; but when I said so to the monks, they were horror-struck, and said that it was because I did not understand.

In my perplexity I fell back, as we all must, to my own thoughts and those of my own people; and I tried to imagine how a Burman would act if he came to England to search into the religion of the English and to know the impulses of our lives.

I saw how he would be sent to the Bible as the source of our religion, how he would be told to study that if he would know what we believed and what we did not—what it was that gave colour to our lives. I followed him in imagination as he took the Bible and studied it, and then went forth and watched our acts, and I could see him puzzled, as I was now puzzled when I studied his people.

I thought of him reading the New Testament, and how he would come to these verses:

'27. But I say unto you which hear, Love your enemies, do good to them which hate you,

'28. Bless them that curse you, and pray for them which despitefully use you.

'29. And unto him that smiteth thee on the one cheek offer also the other; and him that taketh away thy cloke forbid him not to take thy coat also.

'30. Give to every man that asketh of thee; and of him that taketh away thy goods ask them not again.'

He would read them again and again, these wonderful verses, that he was told the people and Church believed, and then he would go forth to observe the result of this belief. And what would he see? He would see this: A nation proud and revengeful, glorying in her victories, always at war, a conqueror of other peoples, a mighty hater of her enemies. He would find that in the public life of the nation with other nations there was no thought of this command. He would find, too, in her inner life, that the man who took a cloak was not forgiven, but was terribly punished—he used to be hanged. He would find—— But need I say what he would find? Those who will read this are those very people—they know. And the Burman would say at length to himself, Can this be the belief of this people at all? Whatever their Book may say, they do not think that it is good to humble yourself to your enemies—nay, but to strike hard back. It is not good to let the wrong-doer go free. They think the best way to stop crime is to punish severely. Those are their acts; the Book, they say, is their belief. Could they act one thing and believe another? Truly, *are* these their beliefs?

And, again, he would read how that riches are an offence to righteousness: hardly shall a rich man enter into the kingdom of God. He would read how the Teacher lived the life of the poorest among us, and taught always that riches were to be avoided.

And then he would go forth and observe a people daily fighting and struggling to add field to field, coin to coin, till death comes and ends the fight. He would see everywhere wealth held in great estimation; he would see the very children urged to do well, to make money, to struggle, to rise in the world. He would see the lives of men who have become rich held up as examples to be followed. He would see the ministers who taught the Book with fair incomes ranking themselves, not with the poor, but with the middle classes; he would see the dignitaries of the Church—the men who lead the way to heaven—among the wealthy of the land. And he would wonder. Is it true, he would say to himself, that these people believe that riches are an evil thing? Whence, then, come their acts, for their acts seem to show that they hold riches to be a good thing? What is to be accepted as their belief: the Book they say they believe, which condemns riches, or their acts, by which they show that they hold that wealth is a good thing—ay, and if used according to their ideas of right, a very good thing indeed?

So, it seemed to me, would a Burman be puzzled if he came to us to find out our belief; and as the Burman's difficulty in England was, *mutatis mutandis*, mine in Burma, I set to work to think the matter out. How were the beliefs of a people to be known, and why should there be such difficulties in the way? If I could understand how it was with us, it might help me to know how it was with them.

And I have thought that the difficulty arises from the fact that there are two ways of seeing a religion—from within and from without—and that these are as different as can possibly be. It is because we forget there are the two standpoints that we fall into error.

In every religion, to the believers in it, the crown and glory of their creed is that it is a revelation of truth, a lifting of the veil, behind which every man born into this mystery desires to look.

They are sure, these believers, that they have the truth, that they alone have the truth, and that it has come direct from where alone truth can live. They believe that in their religion alone lies safety for man from the troubles of this world and from the terrors and threats of the next, and that those alone who follow its teaching will reach happiness hereafter, if not here. They believe, too, that this truth only requires to be known to be understood and accepted of all men; that as the sun requires no witness of its warmth, so the truth requires no evidence of its truth.

It is to them so eternally true, so matchless in beauty, so convincing in itself, that adherents of all other creeds have but to hear it pronounced and they must believe. So, then, the question, How do you know that your faith is true? is as vain and foolish as the cry of the wind in an empty house. And if they be asked wherein lies their religion, they will produce their sacred books, and declare that in them is contained the whole matter. Here is the very word of truth, herein is told the meaning of all things, herein alone lies righteousness. This, they say, is their faith: that they believe in every line of it, this truth from everlasting to everlasting, and that its precepts, and none other, can be held by him who seeks to be a sincere believer. And to these believers the manifestation of their faith is that its believers attain salvation hereafter. But as that is in the next world, if the unbeliever ask what is the manifestation in this, the believers will answer him that the true mark and sign whereby a man may be known to hold the truth is the observance of certain forms, the performance of certain ceremonies, more or less mystical, more or less symbolical, of some esoteric meaning. That a man should be baptized, should wear certain marks on his forehead, should be accepted with certain rites, is generally the outward and visible sign of a believer, and the badge whereby others of the same faith have known their fellows.

It has never been possible for any religion to make the acts and deeds of its followers the test of their belief. And for these reasons: that it is a test no one could apply, and that if anyone were to attempt to apply it, there would soon be no Church at all. For to no one is it given to be able to observe in their entirety all the precepts of their prophet, whoever that prophet may be. All must fail, some more and some less, but generally more, and thus all would fall from the faith at some time or another, and there would be no Church left. And so another test has been made necessary. If from his weakness a man cannot keep these precepts, yet he can declare his belief in and his desire to keep them, and here is a test that can be applied. Certain rites have been instituted, and it has been laid down that those who by their submission to these rites show their belief in the truth and their desire to follow that truth as far as in them lies, shall be called the followers of the faith. So in time it has come about that these ceremonial rites have been held to be the true and only sign of the believer, and the fact that they were but to be the earnest of the beginning and living of a new life has become less and less remembered, till it has faded into nothingness. Instead of the life being the main thing, and being absolutely necessary to give value and emphasis to the belief, it has come to pass that it is the belief, and the acceptance of the belief, that has been held to hallow the life and excuse and palliate its errors.

Thus of every religion is this true, that its essence is a belief that certain doctrines are revelations of eternal truth, and that the fruit of this truth is the observance of certain forms. Morality and works may or may not follow, but they are immaterial compared with the other. This, put shortly, is the view of every believer.

But to him who does not believe in a faith, who views it from without, from the standpoint of another faith, the whole view is changed, the whole perspective altered. Those landmarks which to one within the circle seem to stand out and overtop the world are to the eyes of him without dwarfed often into insignificance, and other points rise into importance.

For the outsider judges a religion as he judges everything else in this world. He cannot begin by accepting it as the only revelation of truth; he cannot proceed from the unknown to the known, but the reverse. First of all, he tries to learn what the beliefs of the people really are, and then he judges from their lives what value this religion has to them. He looks to acts as proofs of beliefs, to lives as the ultimate effects of thoughts. And he finds out very quickly that the sacred books of a people can never be taken as showing more than approximately their real beliefs. Always through the embroidery of the new creed he will find the foundation of an older faith, of older faiths, perhaps, and below these, again, other beliefs that seem to be part of no system, but to be the outcome of the great fear that is in the world.

The more he searches, the more he will be sure that there is only one guide to a man's faith, to his soul, and that is not any book or system he may profess to believe, but the real system that he follows—that is to say, that a man's beliefs can be known even to himself from his acts only. For it is futile to say that a man believes in one thing and does another. That is not a belief at all. A man may cheat himself, and say it is, but in his heart he knows that it is not. A belief is not a proposition to be assented to, and then put away and forgotten. It is always in our minds, and for ever in our thoughts. It guides our every action, it colours our whole life. It is not for a day, but for ever. When we have learnt that a cobra's bite is death, we do not put the belief away in a pigeon-hole of our minds, there to rust for ever unused, nor do we go straightway and pick up the first deadly snake that we see. We remember it always; we keep it as a guiding principle of our daily lives.

A belief is a strand in the cord of our lives, that runs through every fathom of it, from the time that it is first twisted among the others till the time when that life shall end. And as it is thus impossible for the onlooker to accept from adherents of a creed a definition of what they really believe, so it is impossible for him to acknowledge the forms and ceremonies of which they speak as the real manifestations of their creed.

It seems to the onlooker indifferent that men should be dipped in water or not, that they should have their heads shaved or wear long hair. Any belief that is worth considering at all must have results more important to its believers, more valuable to mankind, than such signs as these. It is true that of the great sign of all, that the followers of a creed attain heaven hereafter, he cannot judge. He can only tell of what he sees. This may or may not be true; but surely, if it be true, there must be some sign of it here on earth beyond forms.

A religion that fits a soul for the hereafter will surely begin by fitting it for the present, he will think. And it will show that it does so otherwise than by ceremonies.

For forms and ceremonies that have no fruit in action are not marks of a living truth, but of a dead dogma. There is but little thought of forms to him whose heart is full of the teaching of his Master, who has His words within his heart, and whose soul is full of His love. It is when beliefs die, and love has faded into indifference, that forms are necessary, for to the living no monument is needed, but to the dead. Forms and ceremonies are but the tombs of dead truths, put up to their memory to recall to those who have never known them that they lived—and died—long ago.

And because men do not seek for signs of the living among the graveyards of the dead, so it is not among the ceremonies of religions that we shall find the manifestations of living beliefs.

It is from the standpoint of this outsider that I have looked at and tried to understand the soul of the Burmese people. When I have read or heard of a teaching of Buddhism, I have always taken it to the test of the daily life of the people to see whether it was a living belief or no. I have accepted just so much as I could find the people have accepted, such as they have taken into their hearts to be with them for ever. A teaching that has been but a teaching or theory, a vain breath of mental assent, has seemed to me of no value at all. The guiding principles of their lives, whether in accordance with the teaching of Buddhism or not, these only have seemed to me worthy of inquiry or understanding. What I have desired to know is not their minds, but their souls. And as this test of mine has obliged me to omit much that will be found among the dogmas of Buddhism, so it has led me to accept many things that have no place there at all. For I have thought that what stirs the heart of man is his religion, whether he calls it religion or not. That which makes the heart beat and the breath come quicker, love and hate, and joy and sorrow—that has been to me as worthy of record as his hopes of a future life. The thoughts that come into the mind of the ploughman while he leads his team afield in the golden glory of the dawn; the dreams that swell and move in the heart of the woman when she knows the great mystery of a new life; whither the dying man's hopes and fears are led—these have seemed to me the religion of the people as well as doctrines of the unknown. For are not these, too, of the very soul of the people?

CHAPTER II

HE WHO FOUND THE LIGHT—I

'He who pointed out the way to those that had lost it.'

Life of the Buddha.

The life-story of Prince Theiddatha, who saw the light and became the Buddha twenty-five centuries ago, has been told in English many times. It has been told in translations from the Pali, from Burmese, and from Chinese, and now everyone has read it. The writers, too, of these books have been men of great attainments, of untiring industry in searching out all that can be known of this life, of gifts such as I cannot aspire to. There is now nothing new to learn of those long past days, nothing fresh for me to tell, no discovery that can be made. Yet in thinking out what I have to say about the religion of the Burmese, I have found that I must tell again some of the life of the Buddha, I must rewrite this ten-times-told tale, of which I know nothing new. And the reason is this: that although I know nothing that previous writers have not known, although I cannot bring to

g like their knowledge, yet I have something to say that they have not
ive written of him as they have learned from books, whereas I want to
have learned from men. Their knowledge has been taken from the
records of the dead past, whereas mine is from the actualities of the living present.

I do not mean that the Buddha of the sacred books and the Buddha of the Burman's belief are different persons. They are the same. But as I found it with their faith, so I find it with the life of their teacher. The Burmese regard the life of the Buddha from quite a different standpoint to that of an outsider, and so it has to them quite a different value, quite a different meaning, to that which it has to the student of history. For to the writer who studies the life of the Buddha with a view merely to learn what that life was, and to criticise it, everything is very different to what it is to the Buddhist who studies that life because he loves it and admires it, and because he desires to follow it. To the former the whole detail of every portion of the life of the Buddha, every word of his teaching, every act of his ministry, is sought out and compared and considered. Legend is compared with legend, and tradition with tradition, that out of many authorities some clue to the actual fact may be found. But to the Buddhist the important parts in the great teacher's life are those acts, those words, that appeal directly to him, that stand out bravely, lit with the light of his own experiences and feelings, that assist him in living his own life. His Buddha is the Buddha he understands, and who understood and sympathized with such as him. Other things may be true, but they are matters of indifference.

To hear of the Buddha from living lips in this country, which is full of his influence, where the spire of his monastery marks every village, and where every man has at one time or another been his monk, is quite a different thing to reading of him in far countries, under other skies and swayed by other thoughts. To sit in the monastery garden in the dusk, in just such a tropic dusk as he taught in so many years ago, and hear the yellow-robed monk tell of that life, and repeat his teaching of love, and charity, and compassion—eternal love, perfect charity, endless compassion—until the stars come out in the purple sky, and the silver-voiced gongs ring for evening prayers, is a thing never to be forgotten. As you watch the starlight die and the far-off hills fade into the night, as the sounds about you still, and the calm silence of the summer night falls over the whole earth, you know and understand the teacher of the Great Peace as no words can tell you. A sympathy comes to you from the circle of believers, and you believe, too. An influence and an understanding breathes from the nature about you—the same nature that the teacher saw—from the whispering fig-trees and the scented champaks, and the dimly seen statues in the shadows of the shrines, that you can never gain elsewhere. And as the monks tell you the story of that great life, they bring it home to you with reflection and comment, with application to your everyday existence, till you forget that he of whom they speak lived so long ago, so very long ago, and your heart is filled with sorrow when you remember that he is dead, that he is entered into his peace.

I do not hope that I can convey much of this in my writing. I always feel the hopelessness of trying to put on paper the great thoughts, the intense feeling, of which Buddhism is so full. But still I can, perhaps, give something of this life as I have heard it, make it a little more living than it has been to us, catch some little of that spirit of sympathy that it holds for all the world.

Around the life of the Buddha has gathered much myth, like dust upon an ancient statue, like shadows upon the mountains far away, blurring detail here and there, and hiding the beauty. There are all sorts of stories of the great portents that foretold his coming: how the sun and the stars knew, and how the wise men prophesied. Marvels attended his birth, and miracles followed him in life and in death. And the appearance of the miraculous has even been heightened by the style of the chroniclers in telling us of his mental conflicts: by the personification of evil in the spirit Man, and of desire in his three beautiful daughters.

All the teacher's thoughts, all his struggles, are materialized into forms, that they may be more readily brought home to the reader, that they may be more clearly realized by a primitive people as actual conflicts.

Therefore at first sight it seems that of all creeds none is so full of miracle, so teeming with the supernatural, as Buddhism, which is, indeed, the very reverse of the truth. For to the supernatural Buddhism owes nothing at all. It is in its very essence opposed to all that goes beyond what we can see of earthly laws, and miracle is never used as evidence of the truth of any dogma or of any doctrine.

If every supernatural occurrence were wiped clean out of the chronicles of the faith, Buddhism would, even to the least understanding of its followers, remain exactly where it is. Not in one jot or tittle would it suffer in the authority of its teaching. The great figure of the teacher would even gain were all the tinsel of the miraculous swept from him, so that he stood forth to the world as he lived—would gain not only to our eyes, but even to theirs who believe in him. For the Buddha was no prophet. He was no messenger from any power above this world, revealing laws of that power. No one came to whisper into his ear the secrets of eternity, and to show him where truth lived. In no trance, in no vision, did he enter into the presence of the Unknown, and return from thence full of the wisdom of another world; neither did he teach the worship of any god, of any power. He breathed no threatenings of revenge for disobedience, of forgiveness for the penitent. He held out no everlasting hell to those who refused to follow him, no easily gained heaven to his believers.

He went out to seek wisdom, as many a one has done, looking for the laws of God with clear eyes to see, with a pure heart to understand, and after many troubles, after many mistakes, after much suffering, he came at last to the truth.

Even as Newton sought for the laws of God in the movement of the stars, in the falling of a stone, in the stir of the great waters, so this Newton of the spiritual world sought for the secrets of life and death, looking deep into the heart of man, marking its toil, its suffering, its little joys, with a soul attuned to catch every quiver of the life of the world. And as to Newton truth did not come spontaneously, did not reveal itself to him at his first call, but had to be sought with toil and weariness, till at last he reached it where it hid in the heart of all things, so it was with the prince. He was not born with the knowledge in him, but had to seek it as every other man has done. He made mistakes as other men do. He wasted time and labour following wrong roads, demonstrating to himself the foolishness of many thoughts. But, never discouraged, he sought on till he found, and what he found he gave as a heritage to all men for ever, that the way might be easier for them than it had been for him.

Nothing is more clear than this: that to the Buddhist his teacher was but a man like himself, erring and weak, who made himself perfect, and that even as his teacher has done, so, too, may he if he do but observe the everlasting laws of life which the Buddha has shown to the world. These laws are as immutable as Newton's laws, and come, like his, from beyond our ken.

And this, too, is another point wherein the parallel with Newton will help us: that just as when Newton discovered gravitation he was obliged to stop, for his knowledge of that did not lead him at once to the knowledge of the infinite, so when he had attained the laws of righteousness, Gaudama the Buddha also stopped, because here his standing-ground failed. It is not true, that which has been imputed to the Buddha by those who have never tried to understand him—that he denied some power greater than ourselves; that because he never tried to define the indefinite, to confine the infinite within the corners of a phrase, therefore his creed was materialistic. We do not say of Newton that he was an atheist because when he taught us of gravity he did not go further and define to us in equations Him who made gravity; and as we understand more of the Buddha, as we search into life and consider his teaching, as we try to think as he thought, and to see as he saw, we understand that he stopped as Newton stopped, because he had come to the end of all that he could see, not because he declared that he knew all things, and that beyond his knowledge there was nothing.

No teacher more full of reverence, more humble than Gaudama the Buddha ever lived to be an example to us through all time. He tells us of what he knows; of what he knows not he is silent. Of the laws that he can see, the great sequences of life to death, of evil to sorrow, of goodness to happiness, he tells in burning words. Of the beginning and the end of the world, of the intentions and the ways of the great Unknown, he tells us nothing at all. He is no prophet, as we understand the word, but a man; and all that is divine in him beyond what there is in us is that he hated the darkness and sought the light, sought and was not dismayed, and at last he found.

And yet nothing could be further from the truth than to call the Buddha a philosopher and Buddhism a philosophy. Whatever he was, he was no philosopher. Although he knew not any god, although he rested his claims to be heard upon the fact that his teachings were clear and understandable, that you were not required to believe, but only to open your eyes and see, and 'his delight was in the contemplation of unclouded truth,' yet he was far from a philosopher. His was not an appeal to our reason, to our power of putting two and two together and making five of them; his teachings were no curious designs woven with words, the counters of his thought. He appealed to the heart, not to the brain; to our feelings, not to our power of arranging these feelings. He drew men to him by love and reverence, and held them so for ever. Love and charity and compassion, endless compassion, are the foundations of his teachings; and his followers believe in him because they have seen in him the just man made perfect, and because he has shown to them the way in which all men may become even as he is.

He was a prince in a little kingdom in the Northeast of India, the son of King Thudoodana and his wife Maia. He was strong, we are told, and handsome, famous in athletic exercises, and his father looked forward to the time when he should be grown a great man, and a leader of armies. His father's ambition for him was that he should be a great conqueror, that he should lead his troops against the neighbouring kings and overcome them, and in time make for himself a wide-stretching empire. India was in those days, as in many later ones, split up into little kingdoms, divided from each other by no natural boundary, overlooked by no sovereign power, and always at war. And the king, as fathers are, was full of dreams that this son of his should subdue all India to himself, and be the glory of his dynasty, and the founder of a great race.

Everything seemed to fall in with the desire of the king. The prince grew up strong and valiant, skilled in action, wise in counsel, so that all his people were proud of him. Everything fell in with the desire of the king except the prince himself, for instead of being anxious to fight, to conquer other countries, to be a great leader of armies, his desires led him away from all this. Even as a boy he was meditative and given to religious musings, and as he grew up he became more and more confirmed in his wish to know of sacred things, more and more an inquirer into the mysteries of life.

He was taught all the faith of those days, a faith so old that we do not know whence it came. He was brought up to believe that life is immortal, that no life can ever utterly die. He was taught that all life is one; that there is not one life of the beasts and one life of men, but that all life was one glorious unity, one great essence coming from the Unknown. Man is not a thing apart from this world, but of it. As man's body is but the body of beasts, refined and glorified, so the soul of man is but a higher stage of the soul of beasts. Life is a great ladder. At the bottom are the lower forms of animals, and some way up is man; but all are climbing upwards for ever, and sometimes, alas! falling back. Existence is for each man a great struggle, punctuated with many deaths; and each death ends one period but to allow another to begin, to give us a new chance of working up and gaining heaven.

He was taught that this ladder is very high, that its top is very far away, above us, out of our sight, and that perfection and happiness lie up there, and that we must strive to reach them. The greatest man, even the greatest king, was farther below perfection than an animal was below him. We are very near the beasts, but very far from heaven. So he was taught to remember that even as a very great prince he was but a weak and erring soul, and that unless he lived well, and did honest deeds, and was a true man, instead of rising he might fall.

This teaching appealed to the prince far more than all the urging of his father and of the courtiers that he should strive to become a great conqueror. It entered into his very soul, and his continual thought was how he was to be a better man, how he was to use this life of his so that he should gain and not lose, and where he was to find happiness.

All the pomp and glory of the palace, all its luxury and ease, appealed to him very little. Even in his early youth he found but little pleasure in it, and he listened more to those who spoke of holiness than to those who spoke of war. He desired, we are told, to become a hermit, to cast off from him his state and dignity, and to put on the yellow garments of a mendicant, and beg his bread wandering up and down upon the world, seeking for peace.

This disposition of the prince grieved his parents very much. That their son, who was so full of promise, so brave and so strong, so wise and so much beloved by everyone, should become a mendicant clad in unclean garments, begging his daily food from house to house, seemed to them a horrible thing. It could never be permitted that a prince should disgrace himself in this way. Every effort must be taken to eradicate such ideas; after all, it was but the melancholy of youth, and it would pass. So stringent orders were given to distract his mind in every way from solemn thoughts, to attempt by a continued round of pleasure and luxury to attract him to more worldly things. And when he was eighteen he was married to his cousin Yathodaya, in the hope that in marriage and paternity he might forget his desire to be a hermit, might feel that love was better than wisdom. And if Yathodaya had been other than she was—who can tell?—perhaps after all the king might have succeeded; but it was not to be so. For to Yathodaya, too, life was a very solemn thing, not to be thrown away in laughter and frivolity, but to be used as a great gift worthy of all care. To the prince in his trouble there came a kindred soul, and though from the palace all the teachers of religion, all who would influence the prince against the desires of his father, were banished, yet Yathodaya more than made up to him for all he had lost. For nearly ten years they lived together there such a life as princes led in those days in the East, not, perhaps, so very different from what they lead now.

And all that time the prince had been gradually making up his mind, slowly becoming sure that life held something better than he had yet found, hardening his determination that he must leave all that he had and go out into the world looking for peace. Despite all the efforts of the king his father, despite the guards and his young men companions, despite the beauty of the dancing-girls, the mysteries of life came home to him, and he was afraid. It is a beautiful story told in quaint imagery how it was that the knowledge of sickness and of death came to him, a horror stalking amid the glories of his garden. He learnt, and he understood, that he too would grow old, would fall sick, would die. And beyond death? There was the fear, and no one could allay it. Daily he grew more and more discontented with his life in the palace, more and more averse to the pleasures that were around him. Deeper and deeper he saw through the laughing surface to the depths that lay beneath. Silently all these thoughts ripened in his mind, till at last the change came. We are told that the end came suddenly, the resolve was taken in a moment. The lake fills and fills until at length it overflows, and in a night the dam is broken, and the pent-up waters are leaping far towards the sea.

As the prince returned from his last drive in his garden with resolve firmly established in his heart, there came to him the news that his wife had borne to him a son. Wife and child, his cup of desire was now full. But his resolve was unshaken. 'See, here is another tie, alas! a new and stronger tie that I must break,' he said; but he never wavered.

That night the prince left the palace. Silently in the dead of night he left all the luxury about him, and went out secretly with only his faithful servant, Maung San, to saddle for him his horse and lead him forth. Only before he left he looked in cautiously to see Yathodaya, the young wife and mother. She was lying asleep, with one hand upon the face of her firstborn, and the prince was afraid to go further. 'To see him,' he said, 'I must remove the hand of his mother, and she may awake; and if she awake, how shall I depart? I will go, then, without seeing my son. Later on, when all these passions are faded from my heart, when I am sure of myself, perhaps then I shall be able to see him. But now I must go.'

So he went forth very silently and very sadly, and leapt upon his horse—the great white horse that would not neigh for fear of waking the sleeping guards—and the prince and his faithful noble Maung San went out into the night. He was only twenty-eight when he fled from all his world, and what he sought was this: 'Deliverance for men from the misery of life, and the knowledge of the truth that will lead them unto the Great Peace.'

This is the great renunciation.

I have often talked about this with the monks and others, often heard them speak about this great renunciation, of this parting of the prince and his wife.

'You see,' said a monk once to me, 'he was not yet the Buddha, he had not seen the light, only he was desirous to look for it. He was just a prince, just a man like any other man, and he was very fond of his wife. It is very hard to resist a woman if she loves you and cries, and if you love her. So he was afraid.'

And when I said that Yathodaya was also religious, and had helped him in his thoughts, and that surely she would not have stopped him, the monk shook his head.

'Women are not like that,' he said.

And a woman said to me once: 'Surely she was very much to be pitied because her husband went away from her and her baby. Do you think that when she talked religion with her husband she ever thought that it would cause him to leave her and go away for ever? If she had thought that, she would never have done as she did. A woman would never help anything to sever her husband from her, not even religion. And when after ten years a baby had come to her! Surely she was very much to be pitied.' This woman made me understand that the highest religion of a woman is the true love of her husband, of her children; and what is it to her if she gain the whole world, but lose that which she would have?

All the story of Yathodaya and her dealings with her husband is full of the deepest pathos, full of passionate protest against her loss, even in order that her husband and all the world should gain. She would have held him, if she could, against the world, and deemed that she did well. And so, though it is probable that it was a great deal owing to Yathodaya's help, to her sympathy, to her support in all his difficulties, that Gaudama came to his final resolve to leave the world and seek for the truth, yet she acted unwittingly of what would be the end.

'She did not know,' said the woman. 'She helped her husband, but she did not know to what. And when she was ill, when she was giving birth to her baby, then her husband left her. Surely she was very much to be pitied.'

And so Yathodaya, the wife of the Prince Gaudama, who became the Buddha, is held in high honour, in great esteem, by all Buddhists. By the men, because she helped her husband to his resolve to seek for the truth, because she had been his great stay and help when everyone was against him, because if there had been no Yathodaya there had been perchance no Buddha. And by the women—I need not say why she is honoured by all women. If ever there was a story that appealed to woman's heart, surely it is this: her love, her abandonment, her courage, her submission when they met again in after-years, her protest against being sacrificed upon the altar of her husband's religion. Truly, it is all of the very essence of humanity. Whenever the story of the Buddha comes to be written, then will be written also the story of the life of Yathodaya his wife. If one is full of wisdom and teaching, the other is full of suffering and teaching also. I cannot write it here. I have so much to say on other matters that there is no room. But some day it will be written, I trust, this old message to a new world.

CHAPTER III

HE WHO FOUND THE LIGHT—II

'He who never spake but good and wise words, he who was the light of the world, has found too soon the Peace.'—*Lament on the death of the Buddha.*

The prince rode forth into the night, and as he went, even in the first flush of his resolve, temptation came to him. As the night closed behind he remembered all he was leaving: he remembered his father and his mother; his heart was full of his wife and child.

'Return!' said the devil to him. 'What seek you here? Return, and be a good son, a good husband, a good father. Remember all that you are leaving to pursue vain thoughts. You, a great man—you might be a great king, as your father wishes—a mighty conqueror of nations. The night is very dark, and the world before you is very empty.'

The prince's heart was full of bitterness at the thought of those he loved, of all that he was losing. Yet he never wavered. He would not even turn to look his last on the great white city lying in a silver dream behind him. He set his face upon his way, trampling beneath him every worldly consideration, despising a power that was but vanity and illusion; he went on into the dark.

Presently he came to a river, the boundary of his father's kingdom, and here he stopped. Then the prince turned to Maung San, and told him that he must return. Beyond the river lay for the prince the life of a holy man, who needed neither servant nor horse, and Maung San must return. All his prayers were in vain; his supplications that he might be allowed to follow his master as a disciple; his protestations of eternal faith. No, he must return; so Maung San went back with the horse, and the prince was alone.

As he waited there alone by the river, alone in the dark waiting for the dawn ere he could cross, alone with his own fears and thoughts, doubt came to him again. He doubted if he had done right, whether he should ever find the light, whether, indeed, there was any light to find, and in his doubt and distress he asked for a sign. He desired that it might be shown to him whether all his efforts would be in vain or not, whether he should ever win in the struggle that was before him. We are told that the sign came to him, and he knew that, whatever happened, in the end all would go well, and he would find that which he sought.

So he crossed the river out of his father's kingdom into a strange country, and he put on the garment of a recluse, and lived as they did.

He sought his bread as they did, going from house to house for the broken victuals, which he collected in a bowl, retiring to a quiet spot to eat.

The first time he collected this strange meal and attempted to eat, his very soul rose against the distastefulness of the mess. He who had been a prince, and accustomed to the very best of everything, could not at first bring himself to eat such fare, and the struggle was bitter. But in the end here, too, he conquered. 'Was I not aware,' he said, with bitter indignation at his weakness, 'that when I became a recluse I must eat such food as this? Now is the time to trample upon the appetite of nature.' He took up his bowl, and ate with a good appetite, and the fight had never to be fought again.

So in the fashion of those days he became a seeker after truth. Men, then, when they desired to find holiness, to seek for that which is better than the things of this world, had to begin their search by an utter repudiation of all that which the world holds good. The rich and worldly wore handsome garments, they would wear rags; those of the world were careful of their personal appearance, they would despise it; those of the world were cleanly, the hermits were filthy; those of the world were decent, and had a care for outward observances, and so hermits had no care for either decency or modesty. The world was evil, surely, and therefore all that the world held good was surely evil too. Wisdom was to be sought in the very opposites of the conventions of men.

The prince took on him their garments, and went to them to learn from all that which they had learnt. He went to all the wisest hermits of the land, to those renowned for their wisdom and holiness; and this is what they taught him, this is all the light they gave to him who came to them for light. 'There is,' they said, 'the soul and the body of man, and they are enemies; therefore, to punish the soul, you must destroy and punish the body. All that the body holds good is evil to the soul.' So they purified their souls by ceremonies and forms, by torture and starvation, by nakedness and contempt of decency, by nameless abominations. And the young prince studied all their teaching, and essayed to follow their example, and he found it was all of no use. Here he could find no way to happiness, no raising of the soul to higher planes, but, rather, a degradation towards the beasts. For self-punishment is just as much a submission to the flesh as luxury and self-indulgence. How can you forget the body, and turn the soul to better thoughts, if you are for ever torturing that body, and thereby keeping it in memory? You can keep your lusts just as easily before your eyes by useless punishment as by indulgence. And how can you turn your mind to meditation and thought if your body is in suffering? So the prince soon saw that here was not the way he wanted. His soul revolted from them and their austerities, and he left them. As he fathomed the emptiness of his counsellors of the palace, so he fathomed the emptiness of the teachers of the cave and monastery. If the powerful and wealthy were ignorant, wisdom was not to be found among the poor and feeble, and he was as far from it as when he left the palace. Yet he did not despair. Truth was somewhere, he was sure; it must be found if only it be looked for with patience and sincerity, and he would find it. Surely there was a greater wisdom than mere contempt of wealth and comfort, surely a greater happiness than could be found in self-torture and hysteria. And so, as he could find no one to teach him, he went out into the forest to look for truth there. In the great forest where no one comes, where the deer feed and the tiger creeps, he would seek what man could not give him. They would know, those great trees that had seen a thousand rains, and outlived thirty generations of men; they would know, those streams that flashed from the far snow summits; surely the forest and the hills, the dawn and the night, would have something to tell him of the secrets of the world. Nature can never lie, and here, far away from the homes of men, he would learn the knowledge that men could not give him. With a body purified by abstinence, with a heart attuned by solitude, he would listen as the winds talked to the mountains in the dusk, and understand the beckoning of the stars. And so, as many others did then and afterwards, he left mankind and went to Nature for help. For six years he lived so in the fastnesses of the hills.

We are told but very little of those six years, only that he was often very lonely, often very sad with the remembrance of all whom he had left. 'Think not,' he said many years later to a favourite disciple—'think not that I, though the Buddha, have not felt all this even as any other of you. Was I not alone when I was seeking for wisdom in the wilderness? And yet what could I have gained by wailing and lamentation either for myself or for others? Would it have brought to me any solace from my loneliness? Would it have been any help to those I had left?'

We are told that his fame as a solitary, as a a man who communed with Nature, and subdued his own lower feelings, was so great that all men knew of it. His fame was as a 'bell hung in the canopy of the skies,' that all nations heard; and many disciples came to him. But despite all his fame among men, he himself knew that he had not yet come to the truth. Even the great soul of Nature had failed to tell him what he desired. The truth was as far off as ever, so he thought, and to those that came to him for wisdom he had nothing to teach. So, at the end of six years, despairing of finding that which he sought, he entered upon a great fast, and he pushed it to such an extreme that at length he fainted from sheer exhaustion and starvation.

When he came to himself he recognised that he had failed again. No light had shone upon his dimmed eyes, no revelation had come to him in his senselessness. All was as before, and the truth—the truth, where was that?

For this man was no inspired teacher. He had no one to show him the way he should go; he was tried with failure, with failure after failure. He learnt as other men learn, through suffering and mistake. Here was his third failure. The rich had failed him, and the poor; even the voices of the hills had not told him of what he would know; the radiant finger of dawn had pointed to him no way to happiness. Life was just as miserable, as empty, as meaningless, as before.

All that he had done was in vain, and he must try again, must seek out some new way, if he were ever to find that which he sought.

He rose from where he lay, and took his bowl in his hands and went to the nearest village, and ate heartily and drank, and his strength came back to him, and the beauty he had lost returned.

And then came the final blow: his disciples left him in scorn.

'Behold,' they said to each other, 'he has lived through six years of mortification and suffering in vain. See, now, he goes forth and eats food, and assuredly he who does this will never attain wisdom. Our master's search is not after wisdom, but worldly things; we must look elsewhere for the guidance that we seek.'

They departed, leaving him to bear his disappointment alone, and they went into the solitude far away, to continue in their own way and pursue their search after their own method. He who was to be the Buddha had failed, and was alone.

To the followers of the Buddha, to those of our brothers who are trying to follow his teachings and emulate his example to attain a like reward, can there be any greater help than this: amid the failure and despair of our own lives to remember that the teacher failed, even as we are doing? If we find the way dark and weary, if our footsteps fail, if we wander in wrong paths, did not he do the same? And if we find we have to bear sufferings alone, so had he; if we find no one who can comfort us, neither did he; as we know in our hearts that we stand alone, to fight with our own hands, so did he. He is no model of perfection whom it is hopeless for us to imitate, but a man like ourselves, who failed and fought, and failed and fought again, and won. And so, if we fail, we need not despair. Did not our teacher fail? What he has done, we can do, for he has told us so. Let us be up again and be of good heart, and we, too, shall win in the end, even as he did. The reward will come in its own good time if we strive and faint not.

Surely this comes home to all of our hearts—this failure of him who found the light. That he should have won—ah, well, that is beautiful; but that he should have failed—and failed, that is what comes home to us, because we too have failed many times. Can you wonder that his followers love him? Can you wonder that his teaching has come home to them as never did teaching elsewhere? I do not think it is hard to see why: it is simply because he was a man as we are. Had he been other than a man, had truth been revealed to him from the beginning, had he never fought, had he never failed, do you think that he would have held the love of men as he does? I fear, had it been so, this people would have lacked a soul.

His disciples left him, and he was alone. He went away to a great grove of trees near by—those beautiful groves of mango and palm and fig that are the delight of the heart in that land of burning, flooding sunshine—and there he slept, defeated, discredited, and abandoned; and there the truth came to him.

There is a story of how a young wife, coming to offer her little offerings to the spirit of the great fig-tree, saw him, and took him for the spirit, so beautiful was his face as he rose.

There are spirits in all the great trees, in all the rivers, in all the hills—very beautiful, very peaceful, loving calm and rest.

The woman thought he was the spirit come down to accept her offering, and she gave it to him—the cup of curdled milk—in fear and trembling, and he took it. The woman went away again full of hope and joy, and the prince remained in the grove. He lived there for forty-nine days, we are told, under the great fig-tree by the river. And the fig-tree has become sacred for ever because he sat there and because there he found the truth. We are told of it all in wonderful trope and imagery—of his last fight over sin, and of his victory.

There the truth came to him at last out of his own heart. He had sought for it in men and in Nature, and found it not, and, lo! it was in his own heart.

When his eyes were cleared of imaginings, and his body purified by temperance, then at last he saw, down in his own soul, what he had sought the world over for. Every man carries it there. It is never dead, but lives with our life, this light that we seek. We darken it, and turn our faces from it to follow strange lights, to pursue vague glimmers in the dark, and there, all the time, is the light in each man's own heart. Darkened it may be, crusted over with our ignorance and sin, but never dead, never dead, always burning brightly for us when we care to seek for it.

The truth for each man is in his own soul. And so it came at last, and he who saw the light went forth and preached it to all the world. He lived a long life, a life full of wonderful teaching, of still more marvellous example. All the world loved him.

He saw again Yathodaya, she who had been his wife; he saw his son. Now, when passion was dead in him, he could do these things. And Yathodaya was full of despair, for if all the world had gained a teacher, she had lost a husband. So it will be for ever. This is the difference between men and women. She became a nun, poor soul! and her son—his son—became one of his disciples.

I do not think it is necessary for me to tell much more of his life. Much has been told already by Professor Max Müller and other scholars, who have spared no pains to come to the truth of that life. I do not wish to say more. So far, I have written to emphasize the view which, I think, the Burmese take of the Buddha, and how he came to his wisdom, how he loved, and how he died.

He died at a great age, full of years and love. The story of his death is most beautiful. There is nowhere anything more wonderful than how, at the end of that long good life, he entered into the Great Peace for which he had prepared his soul.

'Ananda,' he said to his weeping disciple, 'do not be too much concerned with what shall remain of me when I have entered into the Peace, but be rather anxious to practise the works that lead to perfection; put on those inward dispositions that will enable you also to reach the everlasting rest.'

And again:

'When I shall have left life and am no more seen by you, do not believe that I am no longer with you. You have the laws that I have found, you have my teachings still, and in them I shall be ever beside you. Do not, therefore, think that I have left you alone for ever.'

And before he died:

'Remember,' he said, 'that life and death are one. Never forget this. For this purpose have I gathered you together; for life and death are one.'

And so 'the great and glorious teacher,' he who never spoke but good and wise words, he who has been the light of the world, entered into the Peace.

CHAPTER IV

THE WAY TO THE GREAT PEACE

'Come to Me: I teach a doctrine which leads to deliverance from all the miseries of life.'—*Saying of the Buddha.*

To understand the teaching of Buddhism, it must be remembered that to the Buddhist, as to the Brahmin, man's soul is eternal.

In other faiths and other philosophies this is not so. There the soul is immortal; it cannot die, but each man's soul appeared newly on his birth. Its beginning is very recent.

To the Buddhist the beginning as well as the end is out of our ken. Where we came from we cannot know, but certainly the soul that appears in each newborn babe is not a new thing. It has come from everlasting, and the present life is merely a scene in the endless drama of existence. A man's identity, the sum of good and of evil tendencies, which is his soul, never dies, but endures for ever. Each body is but a case wherein the soul is enshrined for the time.

And the state of that soul, whether good predominate in it or evil, is purely dependent on that soul's thoughts and actions in time past.

Men are not born by chance wise or foolish, righteous or wicked, strong or feeble. A man's condition in life is the absolute result of an eternal law that as a man sows so shall he reap; that as he reaps so has he sown.

Therefore, if you find a man's desires naturally given towards evil, it is because he has in his past lives educated himself to evil. And if he is righteous and charitable, long-suffering and full of sympathy, it is because in his past existence he has cultivated these virtues; he has followed goodness, and it has become a habit of his soul.

Thus is every man his own maker. He has no one to blame for his imperfections but himself, no one to thank for his virtues but himself. Within the unchangeable laws of righteousness each man is absolutely the creator of himself and of his own destiny. It has lain, and it lies, within each man's power to determine what manner of man he shall be. Nay, it not only lies within his power to do so, but a man *must* actually mould himself. There is no other way in which he can develop.

Every man has had an equal chance. If matters are somewhat unequal now, there is no one to blame but himself. It is within his power to retrieve it, not perhaps in this short life, but in the next, maybe, or the next.

Man is not made perfect all of a sudden, but takes time to grow, like all valuable things. You might as well expect to raise a teak-tree in your garden in a night as to make a righteous man in a day. And thus not only is a man the sum of his passions, his acts and his thoughts, in past time, but he is in his daily life determining his future—what sort of man he shall be. Every act, every thought, has its effect, not only upon the outer world, but upon the inner soul. If you follow after evil, it becomes in time a habit of your soul. If you follow after good, every good act is a beautifying touch to your own soul.

Man is as he has made himself; man will be as he makes himself. This is a very simple theory, surely. It is not at all difficult to understand the Buddhist standpoint in the matter. It is merely the theory of evolution applied to the soul, with this difference: that in its later stages it has become a deliberate and a conscious evolution, and not an unconscious one.

And the deduction from this is also simple. It is true, says Buddhism, that every man is the architect of himself, that he can make himself as he chooses. Now, what every man desires is happiness. As a man can form himself as he will, it is within his power to make himself happy, if he only knows how. Let us therefore carefully consider what happiness is, that we may attain it; what misery is, that we may avoid it.

It is a commonplace of many religions, and of many philosophies—nay, it is the actual base upon which they have been built, that this is an evil world.

Judaism, indeed, thought that the world was really a capital place, and that it was worth while doing well in order to enjoy it. But most other faiths thought very differently. Indeed, the very meaning of most religions and philosophies has been that they should be refuges from the wickedness and unhappiness of the world. According to them the world has been a very weary world, full of wickedness and of deceit, of war and strife, of untruth and of hate, of all sorts of evil.

The world has been wicked, and man has been unhappy in it.

'I do not know that any theory has usually been propounded to explain why this is so. It has been accepted as a fact that man is unhappy, accepted, I think, by most faiths over the world. Indeed, it is the belief that has been, one thinks, the cause of faiths. Had the world been happy, surely there had been no need of religions. In a summer sea, where is the need of havens? It is a generally-accepted fact, accepted, as I have said, without explanation. But the Buddhist has not been contented to leave it so. He has thought that it is in the right explanation of this cardinal fact that lies all truth. Life suffers from a disease called misery. He would be free from it. Let us, then, says the Buddhist, first discover the cause of this misery, and so only can we understand how to cure it.' It is this explanation which is really the distinguishing tenet of Buddhism, which differentiates it from all other faiths and all philosophies.

The reason, says Buddhism, why men are unhappy is that they are alive. Life and sorrow are inseparable—nay, they are one and the same thing. The mere fact of being alive is a misery. When you have clear eyes and discern the truth, you shall see this without a doubt, says the Buddhist. For consider, What man has ever sat down and said:

'Now am I in perfect happiness; just as I now am would I like to remain for ever and for ever without change'? No man has ever done so. What men desire is change. They weary of the present, and desire the future; and when the future comes they find it no better than the past. Happiness lies in yesterday and in to-morrow, but never in to-day. In youth we look forward, in age we look back. What is change but the death of the present? Life is change, and change is death, so says the Buddhist. Men shudder at and fear death, and yet death and life are the same thing—inseparable, indistinguishable, and one with sorrow. We men who desire life are as men athirst and drinking of the sea. Every drop we drink of the poisoned sea of existence urges on men surely to greater thirst still. Yet we drink on blindly, and say that we are athirst.

This is the explanation of Buddhism. The world is unhappy because it is alive, because it does not see that what it should strive for is not life, not change and hurry and discontent and death, but peace—the Great Peace. There is the goal to which a man should strive.

See now how different it is from the Christian theory. In Christianity there are two lives—this and the next. The present is evil, because it is under the empire of the devil—the world, the flesh, and the devil. The next will be beautiful, because it is under the reign of God, and the devil cannot intrude.

But Buddhism acknowledges only one life—an existence that has come from the forever, that may extend to the forever. If this life is evil, then is all life evil, and happiness can live but in peace, in surcease from the troubles of this weary world. If, then, a man desire happiness—and in all faiths that is the desired end—he must strive to attain peace. This, again, is not a difficult idea to understand. It seems to me so simple that, when once it has been listened to, it may be understood by a child. I do not say believed and followed, but understood. Belief is a different matter. 'The law is deep; it is difficult to know and to believe it. It is very sublime, and can be comprehended only by means of earnest meditation,' for Buddhism is not a religion of children, but of men.

This is the doctrine that has caused Buddhism to be called pessimism. Taught, as we have been taught, to believe that life and death are antagonistic, that life in the world to come is beautiful, that death is a horror, it seems to us terrible to think that it is indeed our very life itself that is the evil to be eradicated, and that life and death are the same. But to those that have seen the truth, and believed it, it is not terrible, but beautiful. When you have cleansed your eyes from the falseness of the flesh, and come face to face with truth, it is beautiful. 'The law is sweet, filling the heart with joy.'

To the Buddhist, then, the end to be obtained is the Great Peace, the mighty deliverance from all sorrow. He must strive after peace; on his own efforts depends success or failure.

When the end and the agent have been determined, there remains but to discover the means, the road whereby the end may be reached. How shall a man so think and so act that he shall come at length unto the Great Peace? And the answer of Buddhism to this question is here: good deeds and good thoughts—these are the gate wherein alone you may enter into the way. Be honourable and just, be kind and compassionate, truth-loving and averse to wrong—this is the beginning of the road that leads unto happiness. Do good to others, not in order that they may do good to you, but because, by doing so, you do good to your own soul. Give alms, and be charitable, for these things are necessary to a man. Above all, learn love and sympathy. Try to feel as others feel, try to understand them, try to sympathize with them, and love will come. Surely he was a Buddhist at heart who wrote: 'Tout comprendre, c'est tout pardonner.' There is no balm to a man's heart like love, not only the love others feel towards him, but that he feels towards others. Be in love with all things, not only with your fellows, but with the whole world, with every creature that walks the earth, with the birds in the air, with the insects in the grass. All life is akin to man. Man's life is not apart from other life, but of it, and if a man would make his heart perfect, he must learn to sympathize with and understand all the great world about him. But he must always remember that he himself comes first. To make others just, you must yourself be just; to make others happy, you must yourself be happy first; to be loved, you must first love. Consider your own soul, to make it lovely. Such is the teaching of Buddha. But if this were all, then would Buddhism be but a repetition of the commonplaces of all religions, of all philosophies. In this teaching of righteousness is nothing new. Many teachers have taught it, and all have learnt in the end that righteousness is no sure road to happiness, to peace. Buddhism goes farther than this. Honour and righteousness, truth and love, are, it says, very beautiful things, but are only the beginning of the way; they are but the gate. In themselves they will never bring a man home to the Great Peace. Herein lies no salvation from the troubles of the world. Far more is required of a man than to be righteous. Holiness alone is not the gate to happiness, and all that have tried have found it so. It alone will not give man surcease from pain. When a man has so purified his heart by love, has so weaned himself from wickedness by good acts and deeds, then he shall have eyes to see the further way that he should go. Then shall appear to him the truth that it is indeed life that is the evil to be avoided; that life is sorrow, and that the man who would escape evil and sorrow must escape from life itself—not in death. The death of this life is but the commencement of another, just as, if you dam a stream in one direction, it will burst forth in another. To take one's life now is to condemn one's self to longer and more miserable life hereafter. The end of misery lies in the Great Peace. A man must estrange himself from the world, which is sorrow. Hating struggle and fight, he will learn to love peace, and to so discipline his soul that the world shall appear to him clearly to be the unrest which it is. Then, when his heart is fixed upon the Great Peace, shall his soul come to it at last. Weary of the earth, it shall come into the haven where there are no more storms, where there is no more struggle, but where reigns unutterable peace. It is not death, but the Great Peace.

'Ever pure, and mirror bright and even,

Life among the immortals glides away;

Moons are waning, generations changing,

Their celestial life flows everlasting,

Changeless 'midst a ruined world's decay.'

This is Nirvana, the end to which we must all strive, the only end that there can be to the trouble of the world. Each man must realize this for himself, each man will do so surely in time, and all will come into the haven of rest. Surely this is a simple faith, the only belief that the world has known that is free from mystery and dogma, from ceremony and priestcraft; and to know that it is a beautiful faith you have but to look at its believers and be sure. If a people be contented in their faith, if they love it and exalt it, and are never ashamed of it, and if it exalts them and makes them happy, what greater testimony can you have than that?

It will seem that indeed I have compressed the teaching of this faith into too small a space—this faith about which so many books have been written, so much discussion has taken place. But I do not think it is so. I cannot see that even in this short chapter I have left out anything that is important in Buddhism. It is such a simple faith that all may be said in a very few words. It would be, of course, possible to refine on and gloze over certain points of the teaching. Where would be the use? The real proof of the faith is in the results, in the deeds that men do in its name. Discussion will not alter these one way or another.

CHAPTER V

WAR—I

'Love each other and live in peace.'

Saying of the Buddha.

This is the Buddhist belief as I have understood it, and I have written so far in order to explain what follows. For my object is not to explain what the Buddha taught, but what the Burmese believe; and this is not quite the same thing, though in nearly every action of their life the influence of Buddhism is visible more or less strongly. Therefore I propose to describe shortly the ideas of the Burmese people upon the main objects of life; and to show how much or how little Buddhism has affected their conceptions. I will begin with courage.

I think it will be evident that there is no quality upon which the success of a nation so much depends as upon its courage. No nation can rise to a high place without being brave; it cannot maintain its independence even; it cannot push forward upon any path of life without courage. Nations that are cowards must fail.

I am aware that the courage of a nation depends, as do its other qualities, upon many things: its situation with regard to other nations, its climate, its food, its occupations. It is a great subject that I cannot go into. I wish to take all such things as I find them, and to discuss only the effect of the religion upon the courage of the people, upon its fighting capabilities. That religion may have a very serious effect one way or the other, no one can doubt. I went through the war of annexation, from 1885 to 1889, and from it I will draw my examples.

When we declared war in Upper Burma, and the column advanced up the river in November, 1885, there was hardly any opposition. A little fight there was at the frontier fort of Minhla, but beyond that nothing. The river that might have been blocked was open; the earthworks had no cannon, the men no guns. Such a collapse was never seen. There was no organization, no material, no money. The men wanted officers to command and teach them; the officers wanted authority and ability to command. The people looked to their rulers to repel the invaders; the rulers looked to the people. There was no common intelligence or will between them. Everything was wanting; nothing was as it should be. And so Mandalay fell without a shot, and King Thibaw, the young, incapable, kind-hearted king, was taken into captivity.

That was the end of the first act, brief and bloodless. For a time the people were stupefied. They could not understand what had happened; they could not guess what was going to happen. They expected that the English would soon retire, and that then their own government would reorganize itself. Meanwhile they kept quiet.

It is curious to think how peaceful the country really was from November, 1885, till June, 1886. Then the trouble came. The people had by that time, even in the wild forest villages, begun to understand that we wanted to stay, that we did not intend going away unless forced to. They felt that it was of no further use looking to Mandalay for help. We had begun, too, to consider about collecting taxes, to interfere with the simple machinery of local affairs, to show that we meant to govern. And as the people did not desire to be governed—certainly not by foreigners, at least—they began to organize resistance. They looked to their local leaders for help, and, as too often these local governors were not very capable men, they sought, as all people have done, the assistance of such men of war as they could find—brigands, and freelances, and the like—and put themselves under their orders. The whole country rose, from Bhamo to Minhla, from the Shan Plateau to the Chin Mountains. All Upper Burma was in a passion of insurrection, a very fury of rebellion against the usurping foreigners. Our authority was confined to the range of our guns. Our forts were attacked, our convoys ambushed, our steamers fired into on the rivers. There was no safety for an Englishman or a native of India, save within the lines of our troops, and it was soon felt that these troops were far too few to cope with the danger. To overthrow King Thibaw was easy, to subdue the people a very different thing.

It is almost impossible to describe the state of Upper Burma in 1886. It must be remembered that the central government was never very strong—in fact, that beyond collecting a certain amount of taxes, and appointing governors to the different provinces, it hardly made itself felt outside Mandalay and the large river towns. The people to a great extent governed themselves. They had a very good system of village government, and managed nearly all their local affairs. But beyond the presence of a governor, there was but little to attach them to the central government. There was, and is, absolutely no aristocracy of any kind at all. The Burmese are a community of equals, in a sense that has probably never been known elsewhere. All their institutions are the very opposite to feudalism. Now, feudalism was instituted to be useful in war. The Burmese customs were instituted that men should live in comfort and ease during peace; they were useless in war. So the natural leaders of a people, as in other countries, were absent. There were no local great men; the governors were men appointed from time to time from Mandalay, and usually knew nothing of their charges; there were no rich men, no large land-holders—not one. There still remained, however, one institution that other nations have made useful in war, namely, the organization of religion. For Buddhism is fairly well organized—certainly much better than ever the government was. It has its heads of monasteries, its Gaing-dauks, its Gaing-oks, and finally the Thathanabaing, the head of the Burmese Buddhism. The overthrow of King Thibaw had not injured any of this. This was an organization in touch with the whole people, revered and honoured by every man and woman and child in the country. In this terrible scene of anarchy and confusion, in this death peril of their nation, what were the monks doing?

We know what religion can do. We have seen how it can preach war and resistance, and can organize that war and resistance. We know what ten thousand priests preaching in ten thousand hamlets can effect in making a people almost unconquerable, in directing their armies, in strengthening their determination. We remember La Vendée, we remember our Puritans, and we have had recent experience in the Soudan. We know what Christianity has done again and again; what Judaism, what Mahommedanism, what many kinds of paganism, have done.

To those coming to Burma in those days, fresh from the teachings of Europe, remembering recent events in history, ignorant of what Buddhism means, there was nothing more surprising than the fact that in this war religion had no place. They rode about and saw the country full of monasteries; they saw the monasteries full of monks, whom they called priests; they saw that the people were intensely attached to their religion; they had daily evidence that Buddhism was an abiding faith in the hearts of the people. And yet, for all the assistance it was to them in the war, the Burmese might have had no faith at all.

And the explanation is, that the teachings of the Buddha forbid war. All killing is wrong, all war is hateful; nothing is more terrible than this destroying of your fellow-man. There is absolutely no getting free of this commandment. The teaching of the Buddha is that you must strive to make your own soul perfect. This is the first of all things, and comes before any other consideration. Be pure and kind-hearted, full of charity and compassion, and so you may do good to others. These are the vows the Buddhist monks make, these are the vows they keep; and so it happened that all that great organization was useless to the patriot fighter, was worse than useless, for it was against him. The whole spectacle of Burma in those days, with the country seething with strife, and the monks going about their business calmly as ever, begging their bread from door to door, preaching of peace, not war, of kindness, not hatred, of pity, not revenge, was to most foreigners quite inexplicable. They could not understand it. I remember a friend of mine with whom I went through many experiences speaking of it with scorn. He was a cavalry officer, 'the model of a light cavalry officer'; he had with him a squadron of his regiment, and we were trying to subdue a very troubled part of the country.

We were camping in a monastery, as we frequently did—a monastery on a hill near a high golden pagoda. The country all round was under the sway of a brigand leader, and sorely the villagers suffered at his hands now that he had leapt into unexpected power. The villages were half abandoned, the fields untilled, the people full of unrest; but the monasteries were as full of monks as ever; the gongs rang, as they ever did, their message through the quiet evening air; the little boys were taught there just the same; the trees were watered and the gardens swept as if there were no change at all—as if the king were still on his golden throne, and the English had never come; as if war had never burst upon them. And to us, after the very different scenes we saw now and then, saw and acted in, these monks and their monasteries were difficult to understand. The religion of the Buddha thus professed was strange.

'What is the use,' said my friend, 'of this religion that we see so many signs of? Suppose these men had been Jews or Hindus or Mussulmans, it would have been a very different business, this war. These yellow-robed monks, instead of sitting in their monasteries, would have pervaded the country, preaching against us and organizing. No one organizes better than an ecclesiastic. We should have had them leading their men into action with sacred banners, and promising them heaven hereafter when they died. They would have made Ghazis of them. Any one of these is a religion worth having. But what is the use of Buddhism? What do these monks do? I never see them in a fight, never hear that they are doing anything to organize the people. It is, perhaps, as well for us that they do not. But what is the use of Buddhism?'

So, or somewhat like this, spoke my friend, speaking as a soldier. Each of us speaks from our own standpoint. He was a brilliant soldier, and a religion was to him a sword, a thing to fight with. That was one of the first uses of a religion. He knew nothing of Buddhism; he cared to know nothing, beyond whether it would fight. If so, it was a good religion in its way. If not, then not.

Religion meant to him something that would help you in your trouble, that would be a stay and a comfort, a sword to your enemies and a prop for yourself. Though he was himself an invader, he felt that the Burmans did no wrong in resisting him. They fought for their homes, as he would have fought; and their religion, if of any value, should assist them. It should urge them to battle, and promise them peace and happiness if dying in a good cause. His faith would do this for him. What was Buddhism doing? What help did it give to its believers in their extremity? It gave none. Think of the peasant lying there in the ghostly dim-lit fields waiting to attack us at the dawn. Where was his help? He thought, perhaps, of his king deported, his village invaded, his friends killed, himself reduced to the subject of a far-off queen. He would fight—yes, even though his faith told him not. There was no help there. His was no faith to strengthen his arm, to straighten his aim, to be his shield in the hour of danger.

If he died, if in the strife of the morning's fight he were to be killed, if a bullet were to still his heart, or a lance to pierce his chest, there was no hope for him of the glory of heaven. No, but every fear of hell, for he was sinning against the laws of righteousness—

'Thou shalt take no life.' There is no exception to that at all, not even for a patriot fighting for his country. 'Thou shalt not take the life even of him who is the enemy of thy king and nation.' He could count on no help in breaking the everlasting laws that the Buddha has revealed to us. If he went to his monks, they could but say: 'See the law, the unchangeable law that man is subject to. There is no good thing but peace, no sin like strife and war.' That is what the followers of the great teacher would tell the peasant yearning for help to strike a blow upon the invaders. The law is the same for all. There is not one law for you and another for the foreigner; there is not one law to-day and another to-morrow. Truth is for ever and for ever. It cannot change even to help you in your extremity. Think of the English soldier and the Burmese peasant. Can there be anywhere a greater contrast than this?

Truly this is not a creed for a soldier, not a creed for a fighting-man of any kind, for what the soldier wants is a personal god who will always be on his side, always share his opinions, always support him against everyone else. But a law that points out unalterably that right is always right, and wrong always wrong, that nothing can alter one into the other, nothing can ever make killing righteous and violence honourable, that is no creed for a soldier. And Buddhism has ever done this. It never bent to popular opinion, never made itself a tool in the hands of worldly passion. It could not. You might as well say to gravity, 'I want to lift this stone; please don't act on it for a time,' as expect Buddhism to assist you to make war. Buddhism is the unalterable law of righteousness, and cannot ally itself with evil, cannot ever be persuaded that under any circumstances evil can be good.

The Burmese peasant had to fight his own fight in 1885 alone. His king was gone, his government broken up, he had no leaders. He had no god to stand beside him when he fired at the foreign invaders; and when he lay a-dying, with a bullet in his throat, he had no one to open to him the gates of heaven.

Yet he fought—with every possible discouragement he fought, and sometimes he fought well. It has been thrown against him as a reproach that he did not do better. Those who have said this have never thought, never counted up the odds against him, never taken into consideration how often he did well.

Here was a people—a very poor people of peasants—with no leaders, absolutely none; no aristocracy of any kind, no cohesion, no fighting religion. They had for their leaders outlaws and desperadoes, and for arms old flint-lock guns and soft iron swords. Could anything be expected from this except what actually did happen? And yet they often did well, their natural courage overcoming their bad weapons, their passionate desire of freedom giving them the necessary impulse.

In 1886, as I have said, all Burma was up. Even in the lower country, which we held for so long, insurrection was spreading fast, and troops and military police were being poured in from India.

There is above Mandalay a large trading village—a small town almost—called Shemmaga. It is the river port for a large trade in salt from the inner country, and it was important to hold it. The village lay along the river bank, and about the middle of it, some two hundred yards from the river, rises a small hill. Thus the village was a triangle, with the base on the river, and the hill as apex. On the hill were some monasteries of teak, from which the monks had been ejected, and three hundred Ghurkas were in garrison there. A strong fence ran from the hill to the river like two arms, and there were three gates, one just by the hill, and one on each end of the river face.

Behind Shemmaga the country was under the rule of a robber chief called Maung Yaing, who could raise from among the peasants some two hundred or three hundred men, armed mostly with flint-locks. He had been in the king's time a brigand with a small number of followers, who defied or eluded the local authorities, and lived free in quarters among the most distant villages. Like many a robber chief in our country and elsewhere, he was liked rather than hated by the people, for his brutalities were confined to either strangers or personal enemies, and he was open-handed and generous. We look upon things now with different eyes to what we did two or three hundred years ago, but I dare say Maung Yaing was neither better nor worse than many a hero of ours long ago. He was a fairly good fighter, and had a little experience fighting the king's troops; and so it was very natural, when the machinery of government fell like a house of cards, and some leaders were wanted, that the young men should crowd to him, and put themselves under his orders. He had usually with him forty or fifty men, but he could, as I have said, raise five or six times as many for any particular service, and keep them together for a few days. He very soon discovered that he and his men were absolutely no match for our troops. In two or three attempts that he made to oppose the troops he was signally worsted, so he was obliged to change his tactics. He decided to boycott the enemy. No Burman was to accept service under him, to give him information or supplies, to be his guide, or to assist him in any way. This rule Maung Yaing made generally known, and he announced his intention of enforcing it with rigour. He did so. There was a head man of a village near Shemmaga whom he executed because he had acted as guide to a body of troops, and he cut off all supplies from the interior, lying on the roads, and stopping all men from entering Shemmaga. He further issued a notice that the inhabitants of Shemmaga itself should leave the town. They could not move the garrison, therefore the people must move themselves. No assistance must be given to the enemy. The villagers of Shemmaga, mostly small traders in salt and rice, were naturally averse to leaving. This trade was their only means of livelihood, the houses their only homes, and they did not like the idea of going out into the unknown country behind. Moreover, the exaction by Maung Yaing of money and supplies for his men fell most heavily on the wealthier men, and on the whole they were not sorry to have the English garrison in the town, so that they could trade in peace. Some few left, but most did not, and though they collected money, and sent it to Maung Yaing, they at the same time told the English officer in command of Maung Yaing's threats, and begged that great care should be taken of the town, for Maung Yaing was very angry. When he found he could not cause the abandonment of the town, he sent in word to say that he would burn it. Not three hundred foreigners, nor three thousand, should protect these lazy, unpatriotic folk from his vengeance. He gave them till the new moon of a certain month, and if the town were not evacuated by that time he declared that he would destroy it. He would burn it down, and kill certain men whom he mentioned, who had been the principal assistants of the foreigners. This warning was quite public, and came to the ears of the English officer almost at once. When he heard it he laughed.

He had three hundred men, and the rebels had three hundred. His were all magnificently trained and drilled troops, men made for war; the Burmans were peasants, unarmed, untrained. He was sure he could defeat three thousand of them, or ten times that number, with his little force, and so, of course, he could if he met them in the open; no one knew that better, by bitter experience, than Maung Yaing. The villagers, too, knew, but nevertheless they were stricken with fear, for Maung Yaing was a man of his word. He was as good as his threat.

One night, at midnight, the face of the fort where the Ghurkas lived on the hill was suddenly attacked. Out of the brushwood near by a heavy fire was opened upon the breastwork, and there was shouting and beating of gongs. So all the Ghurkas turned out in a hurry, and ran to man the breastwork, and the return fire became hot and heavy. In a moment, as it seemed, the attackers were in the village. They had burst in the north gate by the river face, killed the Burmese guard on it, and streamed in. They lit torches from a fire they found burning, and in a moment the village was on fire. Looking down from the hill, you could see the village rushing into flame, and in the lurid light men and women and children running about wildly. There were shouts and screams and shots. No one who has never heard it, never seen it, can know what a village is like when the enemy has burst in at night. Everyone is mad with hate, with despair, with terror. They run to and fro, seeking to kill, seeking to escape being killed. It is impossible to tell one from another. The bravest man is dismayed. And the noise is like a great moan coming out of the night, pierced with sharp cries. It rises and falls, like the death-cry of a dying giant. It is the most terrible sound in the world. It makes the heart stop.

To the Ghurkas this sight and sound came all of a sudden, as they were defending what they took to be a determined attack on their own position. The village was lost ere they knew it was attacked. And two steamers full of troops, anchored off the town, saw it, too. They were on their way up country, and had halted there that night, anchored in the stream. They were close by, but could not fire, for there was no telling friend from foe.

Before the relief party of Ghurkas could come swarming down the hill, only two hundred yards, before the boats could land the eager troops from the steamers, the rebels were gone. They went through the village and out of the south gate. They had fulfilled their threat and destroyed the town. They had killed the men they had declared they would kill. The firing died away from the fort side, and the enemy were gone, no one could tell whither, into the night.

Such a scene of desolation as that village was next day! It was all destroyed—every house. All the food was gone, all furniture, all clothes, everything, and here and there was a corpse in among the blackened cinders. The whole countryside was terror-stricken at this failure to defend those who had depended on us.

I do not think this was a particularly gallant act, but it was a very able one. It was certainly war. It taught us a very severe lesson—more severe than a personal reverse would have been. It struck terror in the countryside. The memory of it hampered us for very long; even now they often talk of it. It was a brutal act—that of a brigand, not a soldier.

But there was no want of courage. If these men, inferior in number, in arms, in everything, could do this under the lead of a robber chief, what would they not have done if well led, if well trained, if well armed?

Of desperate encounters between our troops and the insurgents I could tell many a story. I have myself seen such fights. They nearly always ended in our favour—how could it be otherwise?

There was Ta Te, who occupied a pagoda enclosure with some eighty men, and was attacked by our mounted infantry. There was a long fight in that hot afternoon, and very soon the insurgents' ammunition began to fail, and the pagoda was stormed. Many men were killed, and Ta Te, when his men were nearly all dead, and his ammunition quite expended, climbed up the pagoda wall, and twisted off pieces of the cement and threw them at the troops. He would not surrender—not he—and he was killed. There were many like him. The whole war was little affairs of this kind—a hundred, three hundred, of our men, and much the same, or a little more, of theirs. They only once or twice raised a force of two thousand men. Nothing can speak more forcibly of their want of organization than this. The whole country was pervaded by bands of fifty or a hundred men, very rarely amounting to more than two hundred, never, I think, to five hundred, armed men, and no two bands ever acted in concert.

It is probable that most of the best men of the country were against us. It is certain, I think, that of those who openly joined us and accompanied us in our expedition, very, very few were other than men who had some private grudge to avenge, or some purpose to gain, by opposing their own people. Of such as these you cannot expect very much.

And yet there were exceptions—men who showed up all the more brilliantly because they were exceptions—men whom I shall always honour. There were two I remember best of all. They are both dead now.

One was the eldest son of the hereditary governor of a part of the country called Kawlin. It is in the north-west of Upper Burma, and bordered on a semi-independent state called Wuntho. In the troubles that occurred after the deposition of King Thibaw, the Prince of Wuntho thought that he would be able to make for himself an independent kingdom, and he began by annexing Kawlin. So the governor had to flee, and with him his sons, and naturally enough they joined our columns when we advanced in that direction, hoping to be replaced. They were replaced, the father as governor under the direction of an English magistrate, and the son as his assistant. They were only kept there by our troops, and upheld in authority by our power against Wuntho. But they were desired by many of their own people, and so, perhaps, they could hardly be called traitors, as many of those who joined us were. The father was a useless old man, but his son, he of whom I speak, was brave and honourable, good tempered and courteous, beyond most men whom I have met. It was well known that he was the real power behind his father. It was he who assisted us in an attempt to quell the insurrections and catch the raiders that troubled our peace, and many a time they tried to kill him, many a time to murder him as he slept.

There was a large gang of insurgents who came across the Mu River one day, and robbed one of his villages, so a squadron of cavalry was sent in pursuit. We travelled fast and long, but we could not catch the raiders. We crossed the Mu into unknown country, following their tracks, and at last, being without guides, we camped that night in a little monastery in the forest. At midnight we were attacked. A road ran through our camp, and there was a picket at each end of the road, and sentries were doubled.

It was just after midnight that the first shot was fired. We were all asleep when a sudden volley was poured into the south picket, killing one sentry and wounding another. There was no time to dress, and we ran down the steps as we were (in sleeping dresses), to find the men rapidly falling in, and the horses kicking at their pickets. It was pitch-dark. The monastery was on a little cleared space, and there was forest all round that looked very black. Just as we came to the foot of the steps an outbreak of firing and shouts came from the north, and the Burmese tried to rush our camp from there; then they tried to rush it again from the south, but all their attempts were baffled by the steadiness of the pickets and the reinforcements that were running up. So the Burmese, finding the surprise ineffectual, and that the camp could not be taken, spread themselves about in the forest in vantage places, and fired into the camp. Nothing could be seen except the dazzling flashes from their guns as they fired here and there, and the darkness was all the darker for those flashes of flame, that cut it like swords. It was very cold. I had left my blanket in the monastery, and no one was allowed to ascend, because there, of all places, the bullets flew thickest, crushing through the mat walls, and going into the teak posts with a thud. There was nothing we could do. The men, placed in due order about the camp, fired back at the flashes of the enemy's guns. That was all they had to fire at. It was not much guide. The officers went from picket to picket encouraging the men, but I had no duty; when fighting began my work as a civilian was at a standstill. I sat and shivered with cold under the monastery, and wished for the dawn. In a pause of the firing you could hear the followers hammering the pegs that held the foot-ropes of the horses. Then the dead and wounded were brought and put near me, and in the dense dark the doctor tried to find out what injuries the men had received, and dress them as well as he could. No light dare be lit. The night seemed interminable. There were no stars, for a dense mist hung above the trees. After an hour or two the firing slackened a little, and presently, with great caution, a little lamp, carefully shrouded with a blanket, was lit. A sudden burst of shots that came splintering into the posts beside us caused the lamp to be hurriedly put out; but presently it was lit again, and with infinite caution one man was dressed. At last a little very faint silver dawn came gleaming through the tree-tops—the most beautiful sight I ever saw—and the firing stopped. The dawn came quickly down, and very soon we were able once more to see what we were about, and count our losses.

Then we moved out. We had hardly any hope of catching the enemy, we who were in a strange country, who were mounted on horses, and had a heavy transport, and they who knew every stream and ravine, and had every villager for a spy. So we moved back a march into a more open country, where we hoped for better news, and two days later that news came.

CHAPTER VI

WAR—II

'Never in the world does hatred cease by hatred. Hatred ceases by love.'—*Dammapada*.

We were encamped at a little monastery in some fields by a village, with a river in front. Up in the monastery there was but room for the officers, so small was it, and the men were camped beneath it in little shelters. It was two o'clock, and very hot, and we were just about to take tiffin, when news came that a party of armed men had been seen passing a little north of us. It was supposed they were bound to a village known to be a very bad one—Laka—and that they would camp there. So 'boot and saddle' rang from the trumpets, and in a few moments later we were off, fifty lances. Just as we started, his old Hindostani Christian servant came up to my friend, the commandant, and gave him a little paper. 'Put it in your pocket, sahib,' he said. The commandant had no time to talk, no time even to look at what it could be. He just crammed it into his breast-pocket, and we rode on. The governor's son was our guide, and he led us through winding lanes into a pass in the low hills. The road was very narrow, and the heavy forest came down to our elbows as we passed. Now and again we crossed the stream, which had but little water in it, and the path would skirt its banks for awhile. It was beautiful country, but we had no time to notice it then, for we were in a hurry, and whenever the road would allow we trotted and cantered. After five or six miles of this we turned a spur of the hills, and came out into a little grass-glade on the banks of the stream, and at the far end of this was the village where we expected to find those whom we sought. They saw us first, having a look-out on a high tree by the edge of the forest; and as our advanced guard came trotting into the open, he fired. The shot echoed far up the hills like an angry shout, and we could see a sudden stir in the village—men running out of the houses with guns and swords, and women and children running, too, poor things! sick with fear. They fired at us from the village fence, but had no time to close the gate ere our sowars were in. Then they escaped in various ways to the forest and scrub, running like madmen across the little bit of open, and firing at us directly they reached shelter where the cavalry could not come. Of course, in the open they had no chance, but in the dense forest they were safe enough. The village was soon cleared, and then we had to return. It was no good to wait. The valley was very narrow, and was commanded from both its sides, which were very steep and dense with forest. Beyond the village there was only forest again. We had done what we could: we had inflicted a very severe punishment on them; it was no good waiting, so we returned. They fired on us nearly all the way, hiding in the thick forest, and perched on high rocks. At one place our men had to be dismounted to clear a breastwork, run up to fire at us from. All the forest was full of voices—voices of men and women and even children—cursing our guide. They cried his name, that the spirits of the hills might remember that it was he who had brought desolation to their village. Figures started up on pinnacles of cliff, and cursed him as he rode by. Us they did not curse; it was our guide.

And so after some trouble we got back. That band never attacked us again.

As we were dismounting, my friend put his hand in his pocket, and found the little paper. He took it out, looked at it, and when his servant came up to him he gave the paper back with a curious little smile full of many thoughts. 'You see,' he said, 'I am safe. No bullet has hit me.' And the servant's eyes were dim. He had been very long with his master, and loved him, as did all who knew him. 'It was the goodness of God,' he said—'the great goodness of God. Will not the sahib keep the paper?' But the sahib would not. 'You may need it as well as I. Who can tell in this war?' And he returned it.

And the paper? It was a prayer—a prayer used by the Roman Catholic Church, printed on a sheet of paper. At the top was a red cross. The paper was old and worn, creased at the edges; it had evidently been much used, much read. Such was the charm that kept the soldier from danger.

The nights were cold then, when the sun had set, and after dinner we used to have a camp-fire built of wood from the forest, to sit round for a time and talk before turning in. The native officers of the cavalry would come and sit with us, and one or two of the Burmans, too. We were a very mixed assembly. I remember one night very well—I think it must have been the very night after the fight at Laka, and we were all of us round the fire. I remember there was a half-moon bending towards the west, throwing tender lights upon the hills, and turning into a silver gauze the light white mist that lay upon the rice-fields. Opposite to us, across the little river, a ridge of hill ran down into the water that bent round its foot. The ridge was covered with forest, very black, with silver edges on the sky-line. It was out of range for a Burmese flint-gun, or we should not have camped so near it. On all the other sides the fields stretched away till they ended in the forest that gloomed beyond. I was talking to the governor's son (our guide of the fight at Laka) of the prospects of the future, and of the intentions of the Prince of Wuntho, in whose country Laka lay. I remarked to him how the Burmans of Wuntho seemed to hate him, of how they had cursed him from the hills, and he admitted that it was true. 'All except my friends,' he said, 'hate me. And yet what have I done? I had to help my father to get back his governorship. They forget that they attacked us first.'

He went on to tell me of how every day he was threatened, of how he was sure they would murder him some time, because he had joined us. 'They are sure to kill me some time,' he said. He seemed sad and depressed, not afraid.

So we talked on, and I asked him about charms. 'Are there not charms that will prevent you being hurt if you are hit, and that will not allow a sword to cut you? We hear of invulnerable men. There were the Immortals of the King's Guard, for instance.'

And he said, yes, there were charms, but no one believed in them except the villagers. He did not, nor did men of education. Of course, the ignorant people believed in them. There were several sorts of charms. You could be tattooed with certain mystic letters that were said to insure you against being hit, and there were certain medicines you could drink. There were also charms made out of stone, such as a little tortoise he had once seen that was said to protect its wearer. There were mysterious writings on palm-leaves. There were men, he said vaguely, who knew how to make these things. For himself, he did not believe in them.

I tried to learn from him then, and I have tried from others since, whether these charms have any connection with Buddhism. I cannot find that they have. They are never in the form of images of the Buddha, or of extracts from the sacred writings. There is not, so far as I can make out, any religious significance in these charms; mostly they are simply mysterious. I never heard that the people connect them with their religion. Indeed, all forms of enchantment and of charms are most strictly prohibited. One of the vows that monks take is never to have any dealings with charms or with the supernatural, and so Buddhism cannot even give such little assistance to its believers as to furnish them with charms. If they have charms, it is against their faith; it is a falling away from the purity of their teachings; it is simply the innate yearning of man to the supernatural, to the mysterious. Man's passions are very strong, and if he must fight, he must also have a charm to protect him in fight. If his religion cannot give it him, he must find it elsewhere. You see that, as the teachings of the Buddha have never been able to be twisted so as to permit war directly, neither have they been able to assist indirectly by furnishing charms, by making the fighter bullet-proof. And I thought then of the little prayer and the cross that were so certain a defence against hurt.

We talked for a long time in the waning moonlight by the ruddy fire, and at last we broke up to go to bed. As we rose a voice called to us across the water from the little promontory. In the still night every word was as clear as the note of a gong.

'Sleep well,' it cried—'sleep well—sle-e-ep we-l-l.'

We all stood astonished—those who did not know Burmese wondering at the voice; those who did, wondering at the meaning. The sentries peered keenly towards the sound.

'Sleep well,' the voice cried again; 'eat well. It will not be for long. Sleep well while you may.'

And then, after a pause, it called the governor's son's name, and 'Traitor, traitor!' till the hills were full of sound.

The Burman turned away.

'You see,' he said, 'how they hate me. What would be the good of charms?'

The voice was quiet, and the camp sank into stillness, and ere long the moon set, and it was quite dark.

He was a brave man, and, indeed, there are many brave men amongst the Burmese. They kill leopards with sticks and stones very often, and even tigers. They take their frail little canoes across the Irrawaddy in flood in a most daring way. They in no way want for physical courage, but they have never made a cult of bravery; it has never been a necessity to them; it has never occurred to them that it is the prime virtue of a man. You will hear them confess in the calmest way, 'I was afraid.' We would not do that; we should be much more afraid to say it. And the teaching of Buddhism is all in favour of this. Nowhere is courage—I mean aggressive courage—praised. No soldier could be a fervent Buddhist; no nation of Buddhists could be good soldiers; for not only does Buddhism not inculcate bravery, but it does not inculcate obedience. Each man is the ruler of his life, but the very essence of good fighting is discipline, and discipline, subjection, is unknown to Buddhism. Therefore the inherent courage of the Burmans could have no assistance from their faith in any way, but the very contrary: it fought against them.

There is no flexibility in Buddhism. It is a law, and nothing can change it. Laws are for ever and for ever, and there are no exceptions to them. The law of the Buddha is against war—war of any kind at all—and there can be no exception. And so every Burman who fought against us knew that he was sinning. He did it with his eyes open; he could never imagine any exception in his favour. Never could he in his bivouac look at the stars, and imagine that any power looked down in approbation of his deeds. No one fought for him. Our bayonets and lances were no keys to open to him the gates of paradise; no monks could come and close his dying eyes with promises of rewards to come. He was sinning, and he must suffer long and terribly for this breach of the laws of righteousness.

If such be the faith of the people, and if they believe their faith, it is a terrible handicap to them in any fight; it delivers them bound into the hands of the enemy. Such is Buddhism.

But it must never be forgotten that, if this faith does not assist the believer in defence, neither does it in offence. What is so terrible as a war of religion? There can never be a war of Buddhism.

No ravished country has ever borne witness to the prowess of the followers of the Buddha; no murdered men have poured out their blood on their hearthstones, killed in his name; no ruined women have cursed his name to high Heaven. He and his faith are clean of the stain of blood. He was the preacher of the Great Peace, of love, of charity, of compassion, and so clear is his teaching that it can never be misunderstood. Wars of invasion the Burmese have waged, that is true, in Siam, in Assam, and in Pegu. They are but men, and men will fight. If they were perfect in their faith, the race would have died out long ago. They have fought, but they have never fought in the name of their faith. They have never been able to prostitute its teachings to their own wants. Whatever the Burmans have done, they have kept their faith pure. When they have offended against the laws of the Buddha they have done so openly. Their souls are guiltless of hypocrisy—for whatever that may avail them. They have known the difference between good and evil, even if they have not always followed the good.

CHAPTER VII

GOVERNMENT

'Fire, water, storms, robbers, rulers—these are the five great evils.'—*Burmese saying.*

It would be difficult, I think, to imagine anything worse than the government of Upper Burma in its later days. I mean by 'government' the king and his counsellors and the greater officials of the empire. The management of foreign affairs, of the army, the suppression of greater crimes, the care of the means of communication, all those duties which fall to the central government, were badly done, if done at all. It must be remembered that there was one difficulty in the way—the absence of any noble or leisured class to be entrusted with the greater offices. As I have shown in another chapter, there was no one between the king and the villager—no noble, no landowner, no wealthy or educated class at all. The king had to seek for his ministers among the ordinary people, consequently the men who were called upon to fill great offices of state were as often as not men who had no experience beyond the narrow limits of a village.

The breadth of view, the knowledge of other countries, of other thoughts, that comes to those who have wealth and leisure, were wanting to these ministers of the king. Natural capacity many of them had, but that is not of much value until it is cultivated. You cannot learn in the narrow precincts of a village the knowledge necessary to the management of great affairs; and therefore in affairs of state this want of any noble or leisured class was a very serious loss to the government of Burma. It had great and countervailing advantages, of which I will speak when I come to local government, but that it was a heavy loss as far as the central government goes no one can doubt. There was none of that check upon the power of the king which a powerful nobility will give; there was no trained talent at his disposal. The king remained absolutely supreme, with no one near his throne, and the ministers were mere puppets, here to-day and gone to-morrow. They lived by the breath of the king and court, and when they lost favour there was none to help them. They had no faction behind them to uphold them against the king. It can easily be understood how disastrous all this was to any form of good government. All these ministers and governors were corrupt; there was corruption to the core.

When it is understood that hardly any official was paid, and that those who were paid were insufficiently paid, and had unlimited power, there will be no difficulty in seeing the reason. In circumstances like this all people would be corrupt. The only securities against bribery and abuse of power are adequate pay, restricted authority, and great publicity. None of these obtained in Burma any more than in the Europe of five hundred years ago, and the result was the same in both. The central government consisted of the king, who had no limit at all to his power, and the council of ministers, whose only check was the king. The executive and judicial were all the same: there was no appeal from one to the other. The only appeal from the ministers was to the king, and as the king shut himself up in his palace, and was practically inaccessible to all but high officials, the worthlessness of this appeal is evident. Outside Mandalay the country was governed by *wuns* or governors. These were appointed by the king, or by the council, or by both, and they obtained their position by bribery. Their tenure was exceedingly insecure, as any man who came and gave a bigger bribe was likely to obtain the former governor's dismissal and his own appointment. Consequently the usual tenure of office of a governor was a year. Often there were half a dozen governors in a year; sometimes a man with strong influence managed to retain his position for some years. From the orders of the governor there was an appeal to the council. This was in some matters useful, but in others not so. If a governor sentenced a man to death—all governors had power of life and death—he would be executed long before an appeal could reach the council. Practically no check was possible by the palace over distant governors, and they did as they liked. Anything more disastrous and fatal to any kind of good government than this it is impossible to imagine. The governors did what they considered right in their own eyes, and made as much money as they could, while they could. They collected the taxes and as much more as they could get; they administered the laws of Manu in civil and criminal affairs, except when tempted to deviate therefrom by good reasons; they carried out orders received from Mandalay, when these orders fell in with their own desires, or when they considered that disobedience might be dangerous. It is a Burmese proverb that officials are one of the five great enemies of mankind, and there was, I think (at all events in the latter days of the kingdom) good reason to remember it. And yet these officials were not bad men in themselves; on the contrary, many of them were men of good purpose, of natural honesty, of right principles. In a well-organized system they would have done well, but the system was rotten to the core.

It may be asked why the Burmese people remained quiet under such a rule as this; why they did not rise and destroy it, raising a new one in its place; how it was that such a state of corruption lasted for a year, let alone for many years.

The answer is this: However bad the government may have been, it had the qualities of its defects. If it did not do much to help the people, it did little to hinder them. To a great extent it left them alone to manage their own affairs in their own way. Burma in those days was like a great untended garden, full of weeds, full of flowers too, each plant striving after its own way, gradually evolving into higher forms. Now sometimes it seems to me to be like an old Dutch garden, with the paths very straight, very clean swept, with the trees clipped into curious shapes of bird and beast, tortured out of all knowledge, and many of the flowers mown down. The Burmese government left its people alone; that was one great virtue. And, again, any government, however good, however bad, is but a small factor in the life of a people; it comes far below many other things in importance. A short rainfall for a year is more disastrous than a mad king; a plague is worse than grasping governors; social rottenness is incomparably more dangerous than the rottenest government.

And in Burma it was only the supreme government, the high officials, that were very bad. It was only the management of state affairs that was feeble and corrupt; all the rest was very good. The land laws, the self-government, the social condition of the people, were admirable. It was so good that the rotten central government made but little difference to the people, and it would probably have lasted for a long while if not attacked from outside. A greater power came and upset the government of the king, and established itself in his place; and I may here say that the idea that the feebleness or wrong-doing of the Burmese government was the cause of the downfall is a mistake. If the Burmese government had been the best that ever existed, the annexation would have happened just the same. It was a political necessity for us.

The central government of a country is, as I have said, not a matter of much importance. It has very little influence in the evolution of the soul of a people. It is always a great deal worse than the people themselves—a hundred years behind them in civilization, a thousand years behind them in morality. Men will do in the name of government acts which, if performed in a private capacity, would cover them with shame before men, and would land them in a gaol or worse. The name of government is a cloak for the worst passions of manhood. It is not an interesting study, the government of mankind.

A government is no part of the soul of the people, but is a mere excrescence; and so I have but little to say about this of Burma, beyond this curious fact—that religion had no part in it. Surely this is a very remarkable thing, that a religion having the hold upon its followers that Buddhism has upon the Burmese has never attempted to grasp the supreme authority and use it to its ends.

It is not quite an explanation to say that Buddhism is not concerned with such things; that its very spirit is against the assumption of any worldly power and authority; that it is a negation of the value of these things. Something of this sort might be said of other religions, and yet they have all striven to use the temporal power.

I do not know what the explanation is, unless it be that the Burmese believe their religion and other people do not. However that may be, there is no doubt of the fact. Religion had nothing whatever—absolutely nothing in any way at all—to do with government. There are no exceptions. What has led people to think sometimes that there were exceptions is the fact that the king confirmed the Thathanabaing—the head of the community of monks—after he had been elected by his fellow-monks. The reason of this was as follows: All ecclesiastical matters—I use the word 'ecclesiastical' because I can find no other—were outside the jurisdiction of civil limits. By 'ecclesiastical' I mean such matters as referred to the ownership and habitation of monasteries, the building of pagodas and places of prayer, the discipline of the monkhood. Such questions were decided by ecclesiastical courts under the Thathanabaing.

Now, it was necessary sometimes, as may be understood, to enforce these decrees, and for that reason to apply to civil power. Therefore there must be a head of the monks acknowledged by the civil power as head, to make such applications as might be necessary in this, and perhaps some other such circumstances.

It became, therefore, the custom for the king to acknowledge by order the elect of the monks as Thathanabaing for all such purposes. That was all. The king did not appoint him at all.

Any such idea as a monk interfering in the affairs of state, or expressing an opinion on war or law or finance, would appear to the Burmese a negation of their faith. They were never led away by the idea that good might come of such interference. This terrible snare has never caught their feet. They hold that a man's first duty is to his own soul. Never think that you can do good to others at the same time as you injure yourself, and the greatest good for your own heart is to learn that beyond all this turmoil and fret there is the Great Peace—so great that we can hardly understand it, and to reach it you must fit yourself for it. The monk is he who is attempting to reach it, and he knows that he cannot do that by attempting to rule his fellow-man; that is probably the very worst thing he could do. And therefore the monkhood, powerful as they were, left all politics alone. I have never been able to hear of a single instance in which they even expressed an opinion either as a body or as individuals on any state matter.

It is true that, if a governor oppressed his people, the monks would remonstrate with him, or even, in the last extremity, with the king; they would plead with the king for clemency to conquered peoples, to rebels, to criminals; their voice was always on the side of mercy. As far as urging the greatest of all virtues upon governors and rulers alike, they may be said to have interfered with politics; but this is not what is usually understood by religion interfering in things of state. It seems to me we usually mean the reverse of this, for we are of late beginning to regard it with horror. The Burmese have always done so. They would think it a denial of all religion.

And so the only things worth noting about the government of the Burmese were its exceeding badness, and its disconnection with religion. That it would have been a much stronger government had it been able to enlist on its side all the power of the monkhood, none can doubt. It might even have been a better government; of that I am not sure. But that such a union would have meant the utter destruction of the religion, the debasing of the very soul of the people, no one who has tried to understand that soul can doubt. And a soul is worth very many governments.

But when you left the central government, and came down to the management of local affairs, there was a great change. You came straight down from the king and governor to the village and its headman. There were no lords, no squires, nor ecclesiastical power wielding authority over the people.

Each village was to a very great extent a self-governing community composed of men free in every way. The whole country was divided into villages, sometimes containing one or two hamlets at a little distance from each other—offshoots from the parent stem. The towns, too, were divided into quarters, and each quarter had its headman. These men held their appointment-orders from the king as a matter of form, but they were chosen by their fellow-villagers as a matter of fact. Partly this headship was hereditary, not from father to son, but it might be from brother to brother, and so on. It was not usually a very coveted appointment, for the responsibility and trouble were considerable, and the pay small. It was 10 per cent. on the tax collections. And with this official as their head, the villagers managed nearly all their affairs. Their taxes, for instance, they assessed and collected themselves. The governor merely informed the headman that he was to produce ten rupees per house from his village. The villagers then appointed assessors from among themselves, and decided how much each household should pay. Thus a coolie might pay but four rupees, and a rice-merchant as much as fifty or sixty. The assessment was levied according to the means of the villagers. So well was this done, that complaints against the decisions of the assessors were almost unknown—I might, I think, safely say were absolutely unknown. The assessment was made publicly, and each man was heard in his own defence before being assessed. Then the money was collected. If by any chance, such as death, any family could not pay, the deficiency was made good by the other villagers in proportion. When the money was got in it was paid to the governor.

Crime such as gang-robbery, murder, and so on, had to be reported to the governor, and he arrested the criminals if he felt inclined, and knew who they were, and was able to do it. Generally something was in the way, and it could not be done. All lesser crime was dealt with in the village itself, not only dealt with when it occurred, but to a great extent prevented from occurring. You see, in a village anyone knows everyone, and detection is usually easy. If a man became a nuisance to a village, he was expelled. I have often heard old Burmans talking about this, and comparing these times with those. In those times all big crimes were unpunished, and there was but little petty crime. Now all big criminals are relentlessly hunted down by the police; and the inevitable weakening of the village system has led to a large increase of petty crime, and certain breaches of morality and good conduct. I remember talking to a man not long ago—a man who had been a headman in the king's time, but was not so now. We were chatting of various subjects, and he told me he had no children; they were dead.

'When were you married?' I asked, just for something to say, and he said when he was thirty-two.

'Isn't that rather old to be just married?' I asked. 'I thought you Burmans often married at eighteen and twenty. What made you wait so long?'

And he told me that in his village men were not allowed to marry till they were about thirty. 'Great harm comes,' he said, 'of allowing boys and girls to make foolish marriages when they are too young. It was never allowed in my village.'

'And if a young man fell in love with a girl?' I asked.

'He was told to leave her alone.'

'And if he didn't?'

'If he didn't, he was put in the stocks for one day or two days, and if that was no good, he was banished from the village.'

A monk complained to me of the bad habits of the young men in villages. 'Could government do nothing?' he asked. They used shameful words, and they would shout as they passed his monastery, and disturb the lads at their lessons and the girls at the well. They were not well-behaved. In the Burmese time they would have been punished for all this—made to draw so many buckets of water for the school-gardens, or do some road-making, or even be put in the stocks. Now the headman was afraid to do anything, for fear of the great government. It was very bad for the young men, he said.

All villages were not alike, of course, in their enforcement of good manners and good morals, but, still, in every village they were enforced more or less. The opinion of the people was very decided, and made itself felt, and the influence of the monastery without the gate was strong upon the people.

Yet the monks never interfered with village affairs. As they abstained from state government, so they did from local government. You never could imagine a Buddhist monk being a magistrate for his village, taking any part at all in municipal affairs. The same reasons that held them from affairs of the state held them from affairs of the commune. I need not repeat them. The monastery was outside the village, and the monk outside the community. I do not think he was ever consulted about any village matters. I know that, though I have many and many a time asked monks for their opinion to aid me in deciding little village disputes, I have never got an answer out of them. 'These are not our affairs,' they will answer always. 'Go to the people; they will tell you what you want.' Their influence is by example and precept, by teaching the laws of the great teacher, by living a life blameless before men, by preparing their souls for rest. It is a general influence, never a particular one. If anyone came to the monk for counsel, the monk would only repeat to him the sacred teaching, and leave him to apply it.

So each village managed its own affairs, untroubled by squire or priest, very little troubled by the state. That within their little means they did it well, no one can doubt. They taxed themselves without friction, they built their own monastery schools by voluntary effort, they maintained a very high, a very simple, code of morals, entirely of their own initiative.

All this has passed, or is passing away. The king has gone to a banishment far across the sea, the ministers are either banished or powerless for good or evil. It will never rise again, this government of the king, which was so bad in all it did, and only good in what it left alone. It will never rise again. The people are now part of the British Empire, subjects of the Queen. What may be in store for them in the far future no one can tell, only we may be sure that the past can return no more. And the local government is passing away, too. It cannot exist with a strong government such as ours. For good or for evil, in a few years it, too, will be gone.

But, after all, these are but forms; the soul is far within. In the soul there will be no change. No one can imagine even in the far future any monk of the Buddha desiring temporal power or interfering in any way with the government of the people. That is why I have written this chapter, to show how Buddhism holds itself towards the government. With us, we are accustomed to ecclesiastics trying to manage affairs of state, or attempting to grasp the secular power. It is in accordance with our ideals that they should do so. Our religious phraseology is full of such terms as lord and king and ruler and servant. Buddhism knows nothing of any of them. In our religion we are subject to the authority of deacons and priests and bishops and archbishops, and so on up to the Almighty Himself. But in Buddhism every man is free—free, subject to the inevitable laws of righteousness. There is no hierarchy in Buddhism: it is a religion of absolute freedom. No one can damn you except yourself; no one can save you except yourself. Governments cannot do it, and therefore it would be useless to try and capture the reins of government, even if you did not destroy your own soul in so doing. Buddhism does not believe that you can save a man by force.

As Buddhism was, so it is, so it will remain. By its very nature it abhors all semblance of authority. It has proved that, under temptation such as no other religion has felt, and resisted; it is a religion of each man's own soul, not of governments and powers.

CHAPTER VIII

CRIME AND PUNISHMENT

'Overcome anger by kindness, evil by good.'

Dammapada.

Not very many years ago an officer in Rangoon lost some currency notes. He had placed them upon his table overnight, and in the morning they were gone. The amount was not large. It was, if I remember rightly, thirty rupees; but the loss annoyed him, and as all search and inquiry proved futile, he put the matter in the hands of the police.

Before long—the very next day—the possession of the notes was traced to the officer's Burman servant, who looked after his clothes and attended on him at table. The boy was caught in the act of trying to change one of the notes. He was arrested, and he confessed.

He was very hard up, he said, and his sister had written asking him to help her. He could not do so, and he was troubling himself about the matter early that morning while tidying the room, and he saw the notes on the table, and so he took them. It was a sudden temptation, and he fell. When the officer learnt all this, he would, I think, have withdrawn from the prosecution and forgiven the boy; but it was too late. In our English law theft is not compoundable. A complaint of theft once made must be proved or disproved; the accused must be tried before a magistrate. There is no alternative. So the lad—he was only a lad—was sent up before the magistrate, and he again pleaded guilty, and his master asked that the punishment might be light. The boy, he said, was an honest boy, and had yielded to a sudden temptation. He, the master, had no desire to press the charge, but the reverse. He would never have come to court at all if he could have withdrawn from the charge. Therefore he asked that the magistrate would consider all this, and be lenient.

But the magistrate did not see matters in the same light at all. He would consider his judgment, and deliver it later on.

When he came into court again and read the judgment he had prepared, he said that he was unable to treat the case leniently. There were many such cases, he said. It was becoming quite common for servants to steal their employers' things, and they generally escaped. It was a serious matter, and he felt himself obliged to make an example of such as were convicted, to be a warning to others. So the boy was sentenced to six months' rigorous imprisonment; and his master went home, and before long had forgotten all about it.

But one day, as he was sitting in his veranda reading before breakfast, a lad came quickly up the stairs and into the veranda, and knelt down before him. It was the servant. As soon as he was released from gaol, he went straight to his old master, straight to the veranda where he was sure he would be sitting at that hour, and begged to be taken back again into his service. He was quite pleased, and sure that his master would be equally pleased, at seeing him again, and he took it almost as a matter of course that he would be reinstated.

But the master doubted.

'How can I take you back again?' he said. 'You have been in gaol.'

'But,' said the boy, 'I did very well in gaol. I became a warder with a cap white on one side and yellow on the other. Let the thakin ask.'

Still the officer doubted.

'I cannot take you back,' he repeated. 'You stole my money, and you have been in prison. I could not have you as a servant again.'

'Yes,' admitted the boy, 'I stole the thakin's money, but I have been in prison for it a long time—six months. Surely that is all forgotten now. I stole; I have been in gaol—that is the end of it.'

'No,' answered the master, 'unfortunately, your having been in gaol only makes matters much worse. I could forgive the theft, but the being in gaol—how can I forgive that?'

And the boy could not understand.

'If I have stolen, I have been in gaol for it. That is wiped out now,' he said again and again, till at last he went away in sore trouble of mind, for he could not understand his master, nor could his master understand him.

You see, each had his own idea of what was law, and what was justice, and what was punishment. To the Burman all these words had one set of meanings; to the Englishman they had another, a very different one. And each of them took his ideas from his religion. To all men the law here on earth is but a reflection of the heavenly law; the judge is the representative of his god. The justice of the court should be as the justice of heaven. Many nations have imagined their law to be heaven-given, to be inspired with the very breath of the Creator of the world. Other nations have derived their laws elsewhere. But this is of little account, for to the one, as to the other, the laws are a reflection of the religion.

And therefore on a man's religion depends all his views of law and justice, his understanding of the word 'punishment,' his idea of how sin should be treated. And it was because of their different religions, because their religions differed so greatly on these points as to be almost opposed, that the English officer and his Burman servant failed to understand each other.

For to the Englishman punishment was a degradation. It seemed to him far more disgraceful that his servant should have been in gaol than that he should have committed theft. The theft he was ready to forgive, the punishment he could not. Punishment to him meant revenge. It is the revenge of an outraged and injured morality. The sinner had insulted the law, and therefore the law was to make him suffer. He was to be frightened into not doing it again. That is the idea. He was to be afraid of receiving punishment. And again his punishment was to be useful as a warning to others. Indeed, the magistrate had especially increased it with that object in view. He was to suffer that others might be saved. The idea of punishment being an atonement hardly enters into our minds at all. To us it is practically a revenge. We do not expect people to be the better for it. We are sure they are the worse. It is a deterrent for others, not a healing process for the man himself. We punish A. that B. may be afraid, and not do likewise. Our thoughts are bent on B., not really on A. at all. As far as he is concerned, the process is very similar to pouring boiling lead into a wound. We do not wish or intend to improve him, but simply and purely to make him suffer. After we have dealt with him, he is never fit again for human society. That was in the officer's thought when he refused to take back his Burmese servant.

Now see the boy's idea.

Punishment is an atonement, a purifying of the soul from the stain of sin. That is the only justification for, and meaning of, suffering. If a man breaks the everlasting laws of righteousness and stains his soul with the stain of sin, he must be purified, and the only method of purification is by suffering. Each sin is followed by suffering, lasting just so long as to cleanse the soul—not a moment less, or the soul would not be white; not a moment more, or it would be useless and cruel. That is the law of righteousness, the eternal inevitable sequence that leads us in the end to wisdom and peace. And as it is with the greater laws, so it should, the Buddhist thinks, be with the lesser laws.

If a man steals, he should have such punishment and for such a time as will wean his soul from theft, as will atone for his sin. Just so much. You see, to him mercy is a falling short of what is necessary, a leaving of work half done, as if you were to leave a garment half washed. Excess of punishment is mere useless brutality. He recognizes no vicarious punishment. He cannot understand that A. should be damned in order to save B. This does not agree with his scheme of righteousness at all. It seems as futile to him as the action of washing one garment twice that another might be clean. Each man should atone for his own sin, *must* atone for his own sin, in order to be freed from it. No one can help him, or suffer for him. If I have a sore throat, it would be useless to blister you for it: that is his idea.

Consider this Burman. He had committed theft. That he admitted. He was prepared to atone for it. The magistrate was not content with that, but made him also atone for other men's sins. He was twice punished, because other men who escaped did ill. That was the first thing he could not understand. And then, when he had atoned both for his own sin and for that of others, when he came out of prison, he was looked upon as in a worse state than if he had never atoned at all. If he had never been in prison, his master would have forgiven his theft and taken him back, but now he would not. The boy was proud of having atoned in full, very full, measure for his sin; the master looked upon the punishment as inconceivably worse than the crime.

So the officer went about and told the story of his boy coming back, and expecting to be taken on again, as a curious instance of the mysterious working of the Oriental mind, as another example of the extraordinary way Easterns argue. 'Just to think,' said the officer, 'he was not ashamed of having been in prison!' And the boy? Well, he probably said nothing, but went away and did not understand, and kept the matter to himself, for they are very dumb, these people, very long-suffering, very charitable. You may be sure that he never railed at the law, or condemned his old master for harshness.

He would wonder why he was punished because other people had sinned and escaped. He could not understand that. It would not occur to him that sending him to herd with other criminals, that cutting him off from all the gentle influences of life, from the green trees and the winds of heaven, from the society of women, from the example of noble men, from the teachings of religion, was a curious way to render him a better man. He would suppose it was intended to make him better, that he should leave gaol a better man than when he entered, and he would take the intention for the deed. Under his own king things were not much better. It is true that very few men were imprisoned, fine being the usual punishment, but still, imprisonment there was, and so that would not seem to him strange; and as to the conduct of his master, he would be content to leave that unexplained. The Buddhist is content to leave many things unexplained until he can see the meaning. He is not fond of theories. If he does not know, he says so. 'It is beyond me,' he will say; 'I do not understand.' He has no theory of an occidental mind to explain acts of ours of which he cannot grasp the meaning; he would only not understand.

But the pity of it—think of the pity of it all! Surely there is nothing more pathetic than this: that a sinner should not understand the wherefore of his sentence, that the justice administered to him should be such as he cannot see the meaning of.

Certain forms of crime are very rife in Burma. The villages are so scattered, the roads so lonely, the amount of money habitually carried about so large, the people so habitually careless, the difficulty of detection so great, that robbery and kindred crimes are very common; and it is more common in the districts of the delta, long under our rule, than in the newly-annexed province in the north. Under like conditions the Burman is probably no more criminal and no less criminal than other people in the same state of civilization. Crime is a condition caused by opportunity, not by an inherent state of mind, except with the very, very few, the exceptional individuals; and in Upper Burma there is, now that the turmoil of the annexation is past, very little crime comparatively. There is less money there, and the village system—the control of the community over the individual—the restraining influence of public opinion is greater. But even during the years of trouble, the years from 1885 till 1890, when, in the words of the Burmese proverb, 'the forest was on fire and the wild-cat slapped his arm,' there were certain peculiarities about the criminals that differentiated them from those of Europe. You would hear of a terrible crime, a village attacked at night by brigands, a large robbery of property, one or two villagers killed, and an old woman tortured for her treasure, and you would picture the perpetrators as hardened, brutal criminals, lost to all sense of humanity, tigers in human shape; and when you came to arrest them—if by good luck you did so—you would find yourself quite mistaken. One, perhaps, or two of the ringleaders might be such as I have described, but the others would be far different. They would be boys or young men led away by the idea of a frolic, allured by the romance of being a free-lance for a night, very sorry now, and ready to confess and do all in their power to atone for their misdeeds.

Nothing, I think, was more striking than the universal confession of criminals on their arrest. Even now, despite the spread of lawyers and notions of law, in country districts accused men always confess, sometimes even they surrender themselves. I have known many such cases. Here is one that happened to myself only the other day.

A man was arrested in another jurisdiction for cattle theft; he was tried there and sentenced to two years' rigorous imprisonment. Shortly afterwards it was discovered that he was suspected of being concerned in a robbery in my jurisdiction, committed before his arrest. He was therefore transferred to the gaol near my court, and I inquired into the case, and committed him and four others for trial before the sessions judge for the robbery, which he admitted.

Now, it so happened that immediately after I had passed orders in the case I went out into camp, leaving the necessary warrants to be signed in my absence by my junior magistrate, and a mistake occurred by which the committal-warrant was only made out for the four. The other man being already under sentence for two years, it was not considered necessary to make out a remand-warrant for him. But, as it happened, he had appealed from his former sentence and he was acquitted, so a warrant of release arrived at the gaol, and, in absence of any other warrant, he was at once released.

Of course, on the mistake being discovered a fresh warrant was issued, and mounted police were sent over the country in search of him, without avail; he could not be found. But some four days afterwards, in the late afternoon, as I was sitting in my house, just returned from court, my servant told me a man wanted to see me. He was shown up into the veranda, and, lo! it was the very man I wanted. He had heard, he explained, that I wanted him, and had come to see me. I reminded him he was committed to stand his trial for dacoity, that was why I wanted him. He said that he thought all that was over, as he was released; but I explained to him that the release only applied to the theft case. And then we walked over half a mile to court, I in front and he behind, across the wide plain, and he surrendered to the guard. He was tried and acquitted on this charge also. Not, as the sessions judge said later, that he had any doubt that my friend and the others were the right men, but because he considered some of the evidence unsatisfactory, and because the original confession was withdrawn. So he was released again, and went hence a free man.

But think of him surrendering himself! He knew he had committed the dacoity with which he was charged: he himself had admitted it to begin with, and again admitted it freely when he knew he was safe from further trial. He knew he was liable to very heavy punishment, and yet he surrendered because he understood that I wanted him. I confess that I do not understand it at all, for this is no solitary instance. The circumstances, truly, were curious, but the spirit in which the man acted was usual enough. I have had dacoit leaders with prices on their heads walk into my camp. It was a common experience with many officers.

The Burmans often act as children do. Their crimes are the violent, thoughtless crimes of children; they are as little depraved by crime as children are. Who are more criminal than English boys? and yet they grow up decent, law-abiding men. Almost the only confirmed criminals have been made so by punishment, by that punishment which some consider is intended to uplift them, but which never does aught but degrade them. Instead of cleansing the garment, it tears it, and renders it useless for this life.

It is a very difficult question, this of crime and punishment. I have not written all this because I have any suggestion to make to improve it. I have not written it because I think that the laws of Manu, which obtained under the Burmese kings, and their methods of punishment, were any improvement on ours. On the contrary, I think they were much worse. Their laws and their methods of enforcing the law were those of a very young people. But, notwithstanding this, there was a spirit in their laws different from and superior to ours.

I have been trying to see into the soul of this people whom I love so well, and nothing has struck me more than the way they regard crime and punishment; nothing has seemed to me more worthy of note than their ideas of the meaning and end of punishment, of its scope and its limits. It is so very different from ours. As in our religion, so in our laws: we believe in mercy at one time and in vengeance at another. We believe in vicarious punishment and vicarious salvation; they believe in absolute justice—always the same, eternal and unchangeable as the laws of the stars. We purposely make punishment degrading; they think it should be elevating, that in its purifying power lies its sole use and justification. We believe in tearing a soiled garment; they think it ought to be washed.

Surely these are great differences, surely thoughts like these, engraven in the hearts of a young people, will lead, in the great and glorious future that lies before them, to a conception of justice, to a method of dealing with crime, very different from what we know ourselves. They are now very much as we were sixteen centuries ago, when the Romans ruled us. Now we are a greater people, our justice is better, our prisons are better, our morality is inconceivably better than Imperial Rome ever dreamt of. And so with these people, when their time shall come, when they shall have grown out of childhood into manhood, when they shall have the wisdom and strength and experience to put in force the convictions that are in their hearts, it seems to me that they will bring out of these convictions something more wonderful than we to-day have dreamt of.

CHAPTER IX

HAPPINESS

'The thoughts of his heart, these are the wealth of a man.'

Burmese saying.

As I have said, there was this very remarkable fact in Burma—that when you left the king, you dropped at once to the villager. There were no intermediate classes. There were no nobles, hereditary officers, great landowners, wealthy bankers or merchants.

Then there is no caste; there are no guilds of trade, or art, or science. If a man discovered a method of working silver, say, he never hid it, but made it common property. It is very curious how absolutely devoid Burma is of the exclusiveness of caste so universal in India, and which survives to a great extent in Europe. The Burman is so absolutely enamoured of freedom, that he cannot abide the bonds which caste demands. He will not bind himself with other men for a slight temporal advantage; he does not consider it worth the trouble. He prefers remaining free and poor to being bound and rich. Nothing is further from him than the feeling of exclusiveness. He abominates secrecy, mystery. His religion, his women, himself, are free; there are no dark places in his life where the light cannot come. He is ready that everything should be known, that all men should be his brothers.

And so all the people are on the same level. Richer and poorer there are, of course, but there are no very rich; there is none so poor that he cannot get plenty to eat and drink. All eat much the same food, all dress much alike. The amusements of all are the same, for entertainments are nearly always free. So the Burman does not care to be rich. It is not in his nature to desire wealth, it is not in his nature to care to keep it when it comes to him. Beyond a sufficiency for his daily needs money has not much value. He does not care to add field to field or coin to coin; the mere fact that he has money causes him no pleasure. Money is worth to him what it will buy. With us, when we have made a little money we keep it to be a nest-egg to make more from. Not so a Burman: he will spend it. And after his own little wants are satisfied, after he has bought himself a new silk, after he has given his wife a gold bangle, after he has called all his village together and entertained them with a dramatic entertainment—sometimes even before all this—he will spend the rest on charity.

    He will build a pagoda to the honour of the great teacher, where men may go to meditate on the great laws of existence. He will build a monastery school where the village lads are taught, and where each villager retires some time in his life to learn the great wisdom. He will dig a well or build a bridge, or make a rest-house. And if the sum be very small indeed, then he will build, perhaps, a little house—a tiny little house—to hold two or three jars of water for travellers to drink. And he will keep the jars full of water, and put a little cocoanut-shell to act as cup.

    The amount spent thus every year in charity is enormous. The country is full of pagodas; you see them on every peak, on every ridge along the river. They stand there as do the castles of the robber barons on the Rhine, only with what another meaning! Near villages and towns there are clusters of them, great and small. The great pagoda in Rangoon is as tall as St. Paul's; I have seen many a one not three feet high—the offering of some poor old man to the Great Name, and everywhere there are monasteries. Every village has one, at least; most have two or three. A large village will have many. More would be built if there was anyone to live in them, so anxious is each man to do something for the monks. As it is, more are built than there is actual need for.

    And there are rest-houses everywhere. Far away in the dense forests by the mountain-side you will find them, built in some little hollow by the roadside by someone who remembered his fellow-traveller. You cannot go five miles along any road without finding them. In villages they can be counted by tens, in towns by fifties. There are far more than are required.

    In Burmese times such roads and bridges as were made were made in the same way by private charity. Nowadays, the British Government takes that in hand, and consequently there is probably more money for rest-house building than is needed. As time goes on, the charity will flow into other lines, no doubt, in addition. They will build and endow hospitals, they will devote money to higher education, they will spend money in many ways, not in what we usually call charity, for that they already do, nor in missions, as whatever missions they may send out will cost nothing. Holy men are those vowed to extreme poverty. But as their civilization (*their* civilization, not any imposed from outside) progresses, they will find out new wants for the rich to supply, and they will supply them. That is a mere question of material progress.

    The inclination to charity is very strong. The Burmans give in charity far more in proportion to their wealth than any other people. It is extraordinary how much they give, and you must remember that all of this is quite voluntary. With, I think, two or three exceptions, such as gilding the Shwe Dagon pagoda, collections are never made for any purpose. There is no committee of appeal, no organized collection. It is all given straight from the giver's heart. It is a very marvellous thing.

    I remember long ago, shortly after I had come to Burma, I was staying with a friend in Toungoo, and I went with him to the house of a Burman contractor. We had been out riding, and as we returned my friend said he wished to see the contractor about some business, and so we rode to his house. He came out and asked us in, and we dismounted and went up the stairs into the veranda, and sat down. It was a little house built of wood, with three rooms. Behind was a little kitchen and a stable. The whole may have cost a thousand rupees. As my friend and the Burman talked of their business I observed the furniture. There was very little; three or four chairs, two tables and a big box were all I could see. Inside, no doubt, were a few beds and more chairs. While we sat, the wife and daughter came out and gave us cheroots, and I talked to them in my very limited Burmese till my friend was ready. Then we went away.

That contractor, so my friend told me as we went home, made probably a profit of six or seven thousand rupees a year. He spent on himself about a thousand of this; the rest went in charity. The great new monastery school, with the marvellous carved façade, just to the south of the town, was his, the new rest-house on the mountain road far up in the hills was his. He supported many monks, he gave largely to the gilding of the pagoda. If a theatrical company came that way, he subscribed freely. Soon he thought he would retire from contracting altogether, for he had enough to live on quietly for the rest of his life.

His action is no exception, but the rule. You will find that every well-to-do man has built his pagoda or his monastery, and is called 'school-builder' or 'pagoda-builder.' These are the only titles the Burman knows, and they always are given most scrupulously. The builder of a bridge, a well, or a rest-house may also receive the title of 'well-builder,' and so on, but such titles are rarely used in common speech. Even the builder of a long shed for water-jars may call himself after it if he likes, but it is only big builders who receive any title from their fellows. But the satisfaction to the man himself, the knowledge that he has done a good deed, is much the same, I think.

A Burman's wants are very few, such wants as money can supply—a little house, a sufficiency of plain food, a cotton dress for weekdays and a silk one for holidays, and that is nearly all.

They are still a very young people. Many wants will come, perhaps, later on, but just now their desires are easily satisfied.

The Burman does not care for a big house, for there are always the great trees and the open spaces by the village. It is far pleasanter to sit out of doors than indoors. He does not care for books. He has what is better than many books—the life of his people all about him, and he has the eyes to see it and the heart to understand it. He cares not to see with other men's eyes, but with his own; he cares not to read other men's thoughts, but to think his own, for a love of books only comes to him who is shut always from the world by ill-health, by poverty, by circumstance. When we are poor and miserable, we like to read of those who are happier. When we are shut in towns, we love to read of the beauties of the hills. When we have no love in our hearts, we like to read of those who have. Few men who think their own thoughts care much to read the thoughts of others, for a man's own thoughts are worth more to him than all the thoughts of all the world besides. That a man should think, that is a great thing. Very, very few great readers are great thinkers. And he who can live his life, what cares he for reading of the lives of other people? To have loved once is more than to have read all the poets that ever sang. So a Burman thinks. To see the moon rise on the river as you float along, while the boat rocks to and fro and someone talks to you—is not that better than any tale?

So a Burman lives his life, and he asks a great deal from it. He wants fresh air and sunshine, and the great thoughts that come to you in the forest. He wants love and companionship, the voice of friends, the low laugh of women, the delight of children. He wants his life to be a full one, and he wants leisure to teach his heart to enjoy all these things; for he knows that you must learn to enjoy yourself, that it does not always come naturally, that to be happy and good-natured and open-hearted requires an education. To learn to sympathize with your neighbours, to laugh with them and cry with them, you must not shut yourself away and work. His religion tells him that the first of all gifts is sympathy; it is the first step towards wisdom, and he holds it true. After that, all shall be added to you. He believes that happiness is the best of all things.

We think differently. We are content with cheerless days, with an absence of love, of beauty, of all that is valuable to the heart, if we can but put away a little money, if we can enlarge our business, if we can make a bigger figure in the world. Nay, we go beyond this: we believe that work, that drudgery, is a beautiful thing in itself, that perpetual toil and effort is admirable.

This we do because we do not know what to do with our leisure, because we do not know for what to seek, because we cannot enjoy. And so we go back to work, to feverish effort, because we cannot think, and see, and understand. 'Work is a means to leisure,' Aristotle told us long ago, and leisure, adds the Burman, is needed that you may compose your own soul. Work, no doubt, is a necessity, too, but not excess of it.

The necessary thing to a man is not gold, nor position, nor power, but simply his own soul. Nothing is worth anything to him compared with that, for while a man lives, what is the good of all these things if he have no leisure to enjoy them? And when he dies, shall they go down into the void with him? No; but a man's own soul shall go with and be with him for ever.

A Burman's ideas of this world are dominated by his religion. His religion says to him, 'Consider your own soul, that is the main thing.' His religion says to him, 'The aim of every man should be happiness.' These are the fundamental parts of his belief; these he learns from his childhood: they are born in him. He looks at all the world by their light. Later on, when he grows older, his religion says to him, 'And happiness is only to be found by renouncing the whole world.' This is a hard teaching. This comes to him slowly, or all Buddhists would be monks; but, meanwhile, if he does but remember the first two precepts, he is on the right path.

He does do this. Happiness is the aim he seeks. Work and power and money are but the means by which he will arrive at the leisure to teach his own soul. First the body, then the spirit; but with us it is surely first the body, and then the body again.

He often watches us with surprise. He sees us work and work and work; he sees us grow old quickly, and our minds get weary; he sees our sympathies grow very narrow, our ideas bent into one groove, our whole souls destroyed for a little money, a little fame, a little promotion, till we go home, and do not know what to do with ourselves, because we have no work and no sympathy with anything; and at last we die, and take down with us our souls—souls fit for nothing but to be driven for ever with a goad behind and a golden fruit in front.

But do not suppose that the Burmese are idle. Such a nation of workers was never known. Every man works, every woman works, every child works. Life is not an easy thing, but a hard, and there is a great deal of work to be done. There is not an idle man or woman in all Burma. The class of those who live on other men's labour is unknown. I do not think the Burman would care for such a life, for a certain amount of work is good, he knows. A little work he likes; a good deal of work he does, because he is obliged often to do so to earn even the little he requires. And that is the end. He is a free man, never a slave to other men, nor to himself.

Therefore I do not think his will ever make what we call a great nation. He will never try to be a conqueror of other peoples, either with the sword, with trade, or with religion. He will never care to have a great voice in the management of the world. He does not care to interfere with other people: he never believes interference can do other than harm to both sides.

He will never be very rich, very powerful, very advanced in science, perhaps not even in art, though I am not sure about that. It may be he will be very great in literature and art. But, however that may be, in his own idea his will be always the greatest nation in the world, because it is the happiest.

CHAPTER X

THE MONKHOOD—I

'Let his life be kindness, his conduct righteousness; then in the fulness of gladness he will make an end of grief.'—*Dammapada.*

During his lifetime, that long lifetime that remained to him after he had found the light, Gaudama the Buddha gathered round him many disciples. They came to learn from his lips of that truth which he had found, and they remained near him to practise that life which alone can lead unto the Great Peace.

From time to time, as occasion arose, the teacher laid down precepts and rules to assist those who desired to live as he did—precepts and rules designed to help his disciples in the right way. Thus there arose about him a brotherhood of those who were striving to purify their souls, and lead the higher life, and that brotherhood has lasted ever since, till you see in it the monkhood of to-day, for that is all that the monks are—a brotherhood of men who are trying to live as their great master lived, to purify their souls from the lust of life, to travel the road that reaches unto deliverance. Only that, nothing more.

There is no idea of priesthood about it at all, for by a priest we understand one who has received from above some power, who is, as it were, a representative on earth of God. Priests, to our thinking, are those who have delegated to them some of that authority of which God is the fountainhead. They can absolve from sin, we think; they can accept into the faith; they can eject from it; they can exhort with authority; they can administer the sacraments of religion; they can speed the parting soul to God; they can damn the parting soul to hell. A priest is one who is clothed with much authority and holiness.

But in Buddhism there is not, there cannot be, anything of all this. The God who lies far beyond our ken has delegated His authority to no one. He works through everlasting laws. His will is manifested by unchangeable sequences. There is nothing hidden about His laws that requires exposition by His agents, nor any ceremonies necessary for acceptance into the faith. Buddhism is a free religion. No one holds the keys of a man's salvation but himself. Buddhism never dreams that anyone can save or damn you but yourself, and so a Buddhist monk is as far away from our ideas of a priest as can be. Nothing could be more abhorrent to Buddhism than any claim of authority, of power, from above, of holiness acquired except by the earnest effort of a man's own soul.

These monks, who are so common all through Burma, whose monasteries are outside every village, who can be seen in every street in the early morning begging their bread, who educate the whole youth of the country, are simply men who are striving after good.

This is a difficult thing for us to understand, for our minds are bent in another direction. A religion without a priesthood seems to us an impossibility, and yet here it is so. The whole idea and thing of a priesthood would be repugnant to Buddhism.

It is a wonderful thing to contemplate how this brotherhood has existed all these many centuries, how it has always gained the respect and admiration of the people, how it has always held in its hands the education of the children, and yet has never aspired to sacerdotalism. Think of the temptation resisted here. The temptation to interfere in government was great, the temptation to arrogate to themselves priestly powers is far, far greater. Yet it has been always resisted. This brotherhood of monks is to-day as it was twenty-three centuries ago—a community of men seeking for the truth.

Therefore, in considering these monks, we must dismiss from our minds any idea of priesthood, any idea of extra human sanctity, of extra human authority. We must never liken them in any way to our priests, or even to our friars. I use the word monk, because it is the nearest of any English word I can find, but even that is not quite correct. I have often found this difficulty. I do not like to use the Burmese terms if I can help it, for this reason, that strange terms and names confuse us. They seem to lift us into another world—a world of people differing from us, not in habits alone, but in mind and soul. It is a dividing partition. It is very difficult to read a book speaking of people under strange terms, and feel that they are flesh and blood with us, and therefore I have, if possible, always used an English word where I can come anywhere near the meaning, and in this case I think monk comes closest to what I mean. Hermits they are not, for they live always in communities by villages, and they do not seclude themselves from human intercourse. Priests they are not, ministers they are not, clergymen they are not; mendicants only half describe them, so I use the word monk as coming nearest to what I wish to say.

The monks, then, are those who are trying to follow the teaching of Gaudama the Buddha, to wean themselves from the world, 'who have turned their eyes towards heaven, where is the lake in which all passions shall be washed away.' They are members of a great community, who are governed by stringent regulations—the regulations laid down in the Wini for observance by all monks. When a man enters the monkhood, he makes four vows—that he will be pure from lust, from desire of property, from the taking of any life, from the assumption of any supernatural powers. Consider this last, how it disposes once and for all of any desire a monk may have toward mysticism, for this is what he is taught:

'No member of our community may ever arrogate to himself extraordinary gifts or supernatural perfection, or through vainglory give himself out to be a holy man; such, for instance, as to withdraw into solitary places on pretence of enjoying ecstasies like the Ariahs, and afterwards to presume to teach others the way to uncommon spiritual attainments. Sooner may the lofty palm-tree that has been cut down become green again, than an elect guilty of such pride be restored to his holy station. Take care for yourself that you do not give way to such an excess.'

Is not this teaching the very reverse of that of all other peoples and religions? Can you imagine the religious teachers of any other religion being warned to keep themselves free from visions? Are not visions and trances, dreams and imaginations, the very proof of holiness? But here it is not so. These are vain things, foolish imaginations, and he who would lead the pure life must put behind him all such things as mere dram-drinking of the soul.

This is a most wonderful thing, a religion that condemns all mysticisms. It stands alone here amongst all religions, pure from the tinsel of miracle, either past, or present, or to come. And yet this people is, like all young nations, given to superstition: its young men dream dreams, its girls see visions. There are interpreters of dreams, many of them, soothsayers of all kinds, people who will give you charms, and foretell events for you. Just as it was with us not long ago, the mystery, *what is* beyond the world, exercises a curious fascination over them. Everywhere you will meet with traces of it, and I have in another chapter told some of the principal phases of these. But the religion has kept itself pure. No hysteric visions, no madman's dreams, no clever conjurer's tricks, have ever shed a tawdry glory on the monkhood of the Buddha. Amid all the superstition round about them they have remained pure, as they have from passion and desire. Here in the far East, the very home, we think, of the unnatural and superhuman, the very cradle of the mysterious and the wonderful, is a religion which condemns it all, and a monkhood who follow their religion. Does not this out-miracle any miracle?

With other faiths it is different: they hold out to those who follow their tenets and accept their ministry that in exchange for the worldly things which their followers renounce they shall receive other gifts, heavenly ones; they will be endued with power from above; they will have authority from on high; they will become the chosen messengers of God; they may even in their trances enter into His heaven, and see Him face to face.

Buddhism has nothing of all this to offer. A man must surrender all the world, with no immediate gain. There is only this: that if he struggle along in the path of righteousness, he will at length attain unto the Great Peace.

A monk who dreamed dreams, who said that the Buddha had appeared to him in a vision, who announced that he was able to prophesy, would be not exalted, but expelled. He would be deemed silly or mad; think of that—mad—for seeing visions, not holy at all! The boys would jeer at him; he would be turned out of his monastery.

A monk is he who observes purity and sanity of life. Hysteric dreams, the childishness of the mysterious, the insanity of the miraculous, are no part of that.

And so a monk has to put behind him everything that is called good in this life, and govern his body and his soul in strict temperance.

He must wear but yellow garments, ample and decent, but not beautiful; he must shave his head; he must have none but the most distant intercourse with women; he must beg his food daily in the streets; he must eat but twice, and then but a certain amount, and never after noon; he must take no interest in worldly affairs; he must own no property, must attend no plays or performances; 'he must eat, not to satisfy his appetite, but to keep his body alive; he must wear clothes, not from vanity, but from decency; he must live under a roof, not because of vainglory, but because the weather renders it necessary.' All his life is bounded by the very strictest poverty and purity.

There is no austerity. A monk may not over-eat, but he must eat enough; he must not wear fine clothes, but he must be decent and comfortable; he must not have proud dwellings, but he should be sheltered from the weather.

There is no self-punishment in Buddhism. Did not the Buddha prove the futility of this long ago? The body must be kept in health, that the soul may not be hampered. And so the monks live a very healthy, very temperate life, eating and drinking just enough to keep the body in good health; that is the first thing, that is the very beginning of the pure life.

And as he trains his body by careful treatment, so does he his soul. He must read the sacred books, he must meditate on the teachings of the great teacher, he must try by every means in his power to bring these truths home to himself, not as empty sayings, but as beliefs that are to be to him the very essence of all truth. He is not cut off from society. There are other monks, and there are visitors, men and women. He may talk to them—he is no recluse; but he must not talk too much about worldly matters. He must be careful of his thoughts, that they do not lead him into wrong paths. His life is a life of self-culture.

Being no priest, he has few duties to others to perform; he is not called upon to interfere in the business of others. He does not visit the sick; he has no concern with births and marriages and deaths. On Sunday, and on certain other occasions, he may read the laws to the people, that is all. Of this I will speak in another chapter. It does not amount to a great demand upon his time. He is also the schoolmaster of the village, but this is aside entirely from his sacred profession. Certain duties he has, however. Every morning as the earliest sunlight comes upon the monastery spires, when the birds are still calling to the day, and the cool freshness of the morning still lies along the highways, you will see from every monastery the little procession come forth. First, perhaps, there will be two schoolboys with a gong slung on a bamboo between them, which they strike now and then. And behind them, in their yellow robes, their faces cast upon the ground, and the begging-bowls in their hands, follow the monks. Very slowly they pass along the streets, amid the girls hurrying to their stalls in the bazaar with baskets of fruit upon their heads, the housewives out to buy their day's requirements, the workman going to his work, the children running and laughing and falling in the dust. Everyone makes room for them as they go in slow and solemn procession, and from this house and that come forth women and children with a little rice that they have risen before daylight to cook, a little curry, a little fruit, to put into the bowls. Never is there any money given: a monk may not touch money, and his wants are very few. Presents of books, and so on, are made at other times; but in the morning only food is given.

The gifts are never acknowledged. The cover of the bowl is removed, and when the offering has been put in, it is replaced, and the monk moves on. And when they have made their accustomed round, they return, as they went, slowly to the monastery, their bowls full of food. I do not know that this food is always eaten by the monks. Frequently in large towns they are fed by rich men, who send daily a hot, fresh, well-cooked meal for each monk, and the collected alms are given to the poor, or to schoolboys, or to animals. But the begging round is never neglected, nor is it a form. It is a very real thing, as anyone who has seen them go knows. They must beg their food, and they do; it is part of the self-discipline that the law says is necessary to help the soul to humility. And the people give because it is a good thing to give alms. Even if they know the monks are fed besides, they will fill the bowls as the monks pass along. If the monks do not want it, there are the poor, there are the schoolboys, sons of the poorest of the people, who may often be in need of a meal; and if a little be left, then there are the birds and the beasts. It is a good thing to give alms—good for yourself, I mean. So that this daily procession does good in two ways: it is good for the monk because he learns humility; it is good for the people because they have thereby offered them a chance of giving a little alms. Even the poorest may be able to give his spoonful of rice. All is accepted. Think not a great gift is more acceptable than a little one. You must judge by the giver's heart.

At every feast, every rejoicing, the central feature is presents to the monks. If a man put his son into a monastery, if he make merry at a stroke of good fortune, if he wish to celebrate a mark of favour from government, the principal ceremony of the feast will be presents to monks. They must be presents such as the monks can accept; that is understood.

Therefore, a man enters a monastery simply for this: to keep his body in health by perfect moderation and careful conduct, and to prepare his soul for heaven by meditation. That is the meaning of it all.

If you see a grove of trees before you on your ride, mangoes and tamarinds in clusters, with palms nodding overhead, and great broad-leaved plantains and flowering shrubs below, you may be sure that there is a monastery, for it is one of the commands to the monks of the Buddha to live under the shade of lofty trees, and this command they always keep. They are most beautiful, many of these monasteries—great buildings of dark-brown teak, weather-stained, with two or three roofs one above the other, and at one end a spire tapering up until it ends in a gilded 'tee.' Many of the monasteries are covered with carving along the façades and up the spires, scroll upon scroll of daintiest design, quaint groups of figures here and there, and on the gateways moulded dragons. All the carvings tell a story taken from the treasure-house of the nation's infancy, quaint tales of genii and fairy and wonderful adventure. Never, I think, do the carvings tell anything of the sacred life or teaching. The Burmese are not fond, as we are, of carving and painting scenes from sacred books. Perhaps they think the subject too holy for craftsman, and so, with, as far as I know, but one exception in all Bur by Indian architects long ago—you will look in vain for any sacred te carvings. But they are very beautiful, and their colour is so good, the (teak against the light green of the tamarinds, and the great leaves of th about. Within the monastery it will be all bare. However beautiful the building is without, no relaxation of his rules is allowed to the monk within. All is bare: only a few mats, perhaps, here and there on the plank floor, a hard wooden bed, a box or two of books.

At one end there will be sure to be the image of the teacher, wrought in alabaster. These are always one of three stereotyped designs; they are not works of art at all. The wealth of imagination and desire of beauty that finds its expression in the carved stories in the façades has no place here at all. It would be thought a sacrilege to attempt in any way to alter the time-honoured figures that have come down to us from long ago.

Over the head of the image there will be a white or golden umbrella, whence we have derived our haloes, and perhaps a lotus-blossom in an earthen pot in front. That will be all. There is this very remarkable fact: of all the great names associated with the life of the Buddha, you never see any presentment at all.

The Buddha stands alone. Of Maya his mother, of Yathodaya his wife, of Rahoula his son, of his great disciple Thariputra, of his dearest disciple and brother Ananda, you see nothing. There are no saints in Buddhism at all, only the great teacher, he who saw the light. Surely this is a curious thing, that from the time of the prince to now, two thousand four hundred years, no one has arisen to be worthy of mention of record beside him. There is only one man holy to Buddhism—Gaudama the Buddha.

On one side of the monasteries there will be many pagodas, tombs of the Buddha. They are usually solid cones, topped with a gilded 'tee,' and there are many of them. Each man will build one in his lifetime if he can. They are always white or gold.

So there is much colour about a monastery—the brown of the wood and the white of the pagoda, and tender green of the trees. The ground is always kept clean-swept and beaten and neat. And there is plenty of sound, too—the fairy music of little bells upon the pagoda-tops when the breeze moves, the cooing of the pigeons in the eaves, the voices of the schoolboys. Monastery land is sacred. No life may be taken there, no loud sounds, no noisy merriment, no abuse is permitted anywhere within the fence. Monasteries are places of meditation and peace.

Of course, all monasteries are not great and beautiful buildings; many are but huts of bamboo and straw, but little better than the villager's hut. Some villages are so poor that they can afford but little for their holy men. But always there will be trees, always the ground will be swept, always the place will be respected just the same. And as soon as a good crop gives the village a little money, it will build a teak monastery, be sure of that.

Monasteries are free to all. Any stranger may walk into a monastery and receive shelter. The monks are always hospitable. I have myself lived, perhaps, a quarter of my life in Burma in monasteries, or in the rest-houses attached to them. We break all their laws: we ride and wear boots within the sacred enclosure; our servants kill fowls for our dinners there, where all life is protected; we treat these monks, these who are the honoured of the nation, much in the offhand, unceremonious way that we treat all Orientals; we often openly laugh at their religion. And yet they always receive us; they are often even glad to see us and talk to us. Very, very seldom do you meet with any return in kind for your contempt of their faith and habits. I have heard it said sometimes that some monks stand aloof, that they like to keep to themselves. If they should do so, can you wonder? Would any people, not firmly bound by their religion, put up with it all for a moment? If you went into a Mahommedan mosque in Delhi with your boots on, you ld probably be killed. Yet we clump round the Shwe Dagon pagoda at our ease, and no one interferes. Do not suppose that it is because the Burman believes less than the Hindu or Mahommedan. It is because he believes more, because he is taught that submission and patience are strong Buddhist virtues, and that a man's conduct is an affair of his own soul. He is willing to believe that the Englishman's breaches of decorum are due to foreign manners, to the necessities of our life, to ignorance. But even if he supposed that we did these things out of sheer wantonness it would make no difference. If the foreigner is dead to every feeling of respect, of courtesy, of sympathy, that is an affair of the foreigner's own heart. It is not for the monk to enforce upon strangers the respect and reverence due to purity, to courage, to the better things. Each man is responsible for himself, the foreigner no less than the Burman. If a foreigner have no respect for what is good, that is his own business. It can hurt no one but himself if he is blatant, ignorant, contemptuous. No one is insulted by it, or requires revenge for it. You might as well try and insult gravity by jeering at Newton and his pupils, as injure the laws of righteousness by jeering at the Buddha or his monks. And so you will see foreigners take all sorts of liberties in monasteries and pagodas, break every rule wantonly, and disregard everything the Buddhist holds holy, and yet very little notice will be taken openly. Burmans will have their own opinion of you, do have their own opinion of you, without a doubt; but because you are lost to all sense of decency, that is no reason why the Buddhist monk or layman should also lower himself by getting angry and resent it; and so you may walk into any monastery or rest-house and act as you think fit, and no one will interfere with you. Nay, if you even show a little courtesy to the monks, your hosts, they will be glad to talk to you and tell you of their lives and their desires. It is very seldom that a pleasant word or a jest will not bring the monks into forgetting all your offences, and talking to you freely and openly. I have had, I have still, many friends among the monkhood; I have been beholden to them for many kindnesses; I have found them always, peasants as they are, courteous and well-mannered. Nay, there are greater things than these.

When my dear friend was murdered at the outbreak of the war, wantonly murdered by the soldiers of a brutal official, and his body drifted down the river, everyone afraid to bury it, for fear of the wrath of government, was it not at last tenderly and lovingly buried by the monks near whose monastery it floated ashore? Would all people have done this? Remember, he was one of those whose army was engaged in subduing the kingdom; whose army imprisoned the king, and had killed, and were killing, many, many hundreds of Burmans. 'We do not remember such things. All men are brothers to the dead.' They are brothers to the living, too. Is there not a monastery near Kindat, built by an Englishman as a memorial to the monk who saved his life at peril of his own at that same time, who preserved him till help came?

Can anyone ever tell when the influence of a monk has been other than for pity or mercy? Surely they believe their religion? I did not know how people could believe till I saw them.

Martyrdom—what is martyrdom, what is death, for your religion, compared to living within its commands? Death is easy; life it is that is difficult. Men have died for many things: love and hate, and religion and science, for patriotism and avarice, for self-conceit and sheer vanity, for all sorts of things, of value and of no value. Death proves nothing. Even a coward can die well. But a pure life is the outcome only of the purest religion, of the greatest belief, of the most magnificent courage. Those who can live like this can die, too, if need be—have done so often and often; that is but a little matter indeed. No Buddhist would consider that as a very great thing beside a holy life.

There is another difference between us. We think a good death hallows an evil life; no Buddhist would hear of this for a moment.

The reverence in which a monk—ay, even the monk to-day who was but an ordinary man yesterday—is held by the people is very great. All those who address him do so kneeling. Even the king himself was lower than a monk, took a lower seat than a monk in the palace. He is addressed as 'Lord,' and those who address him are his disciples. Poor as he is, living on daily charity, without any power or authority of any kind, the greatest in the land would dismount and yield the road that he should pass. Such is the people's reverence for a holy life. Never was such voluntary homage yielded to any as to these monks. There is a special language for them, the ordinary language of life being too common to be applied to their actions. They do not sleep or eat or walk as do other men.

It seems strange to us, coming from our land where poverty is an offence, where the receipt of alms is a degradation, where the ideal is power, to see here all this reversed. The monks are the poorest of the poor, they are dependent on the people for their daily bread; for although lands may be given to a monastery as a matter of fact, very few have any at all, and those only a few palm-trees. They have no power at all, either temporal or eternal; they are not very learned, and yet they are the most honoured of all people. Without any of the attributes which in our experience gather the love and honour of mankind, they are honoured above all men.

The Burman demands from the monk no assistance in heavenly affairs, no interference in worldly, only this, that he should live as becomes a follower of the great teacher. And because he does so live the Burman reverences him beyond all others. The king is feared, the wise man admired, perhaps envied, the rich man is respected, but the monk is honoured and loved. There is no one beside him in the heart of the people. If you would know what a Burman would be, see what a monk is: that is his ideal. But it is a very difficult ideal. The Burman is very fond of life, very full of life, delighting in the joy of existence, brimming over with vitality, with humour, with merriment. They are a young people, in the full flush of early nationhood. To them of all people the restraints of a monk's life must be terrible and hard to maintain. And because it is so, because they all know how hard it is to do right, and because the monks do right, they honour them, and they know they deserve honour. Remember that all these people have been monks themselves at one time or other; they know how hard the rules are, they know how well they are observed. They are reverencing what they thoroughly understand; they have seen their monkhood from the inside; their reverence is the outcome of a very real knowledge.

Of the internal management of the monkhood I have but little to say. There is the Thathanabaing, who is the head of the community; there are under him Gaing-oks, who each have charge of a district; each Gaing-ok has an assistant, 'a prop,' called Gaing-dauk; and there are the heads of monasteries. The Thathanabaing is chosen by the heads of the monasteries, and appoints his Gaing-oks and Gaing-dauks. There is no complication about it. Usually any serious dispute is decided by a court of three or four heads of monasteries, presided over by the Gaing-ok. But note this: no monk can be tried by any ecclesiastical court without his consent. Each monastery is self-governing; no monk can be called to account by any Gaing-ok or Gaing-dauk unless he consents. The discipline is voluntary entirely. There are no punishments by law for disobedience of an ecclesiastical court. A monk cannot be unfrocked by his fellows.

Therefore, it would seem that there would be no check over abuses, that monks could do as they liked, that irregularities could creep in, and that, in fact, there is nothing to prevent a monastery becoming a disgrace. This would be a great mistake. It must never be forgotten that monks are dependent on their village for everything—food and clothes, and even the monastery itself. Do not imagine that the villagers would allow their monks, their 'great glories,' to become a scandal to them. The supervision exercised by the people over their monks is most stringent. As long as the monks act as monks should, they are held in great honour, they are addressed by titles of great respect, they are supplied with all they want within the rules of the Wini, they are the glory of the village. But do you think a Burman would render this homage to a monk whom he could not respect, who did actions he should not? A monk is one who acts as a monk. Directly he breaks his laws, his holiness is gone. The villagers will have none such as he. They will hunt him out of the village, they will refuse him food, they will make him a byword, a scorn. I have known this to happen. If a monk's holiness be suspected, he must clear himself before a court, or leave that place quickly, lest worse befall him. It is impossible to conceive any supervision more close than this of the people over their monks, and so the breaches of any law by the monks are very rare—very rare indeed. You see, for one thing, that a monk never takes the vows for life. He takes them for six months, a year, two years, very often for five years; then, if he finds the life suit him, he continues. If he finds that he cannot live up to the standard required, he is free to go. There is no compulsion to stay, no stigma on going. As a matter of fact, very few monks there are but have left the monastery at one time or another. It is impossible to over-estimate the value of this safety-valve. What with the certainty of detection and punishment from his people, and the knowledge that he can leave the monastery if he will at the end of his time without any reproach, a monk is almost always able to keep within his rules.

I have had for ten years a considerable experience of criminal law. I have tried hundreds of men for all sorts of offences; I have known of many hundreds more being tried, and the only cases where a monk was concerned that I can remember are these: three times a monk has been connected in a rebellion, once in a divorce case, once in another offence. This last case happened just as we annexed the country, and when our courts were not established. He was detected by the villagers, stripped of his robes, beaten, and hunted out of the place with every ignominy possible. There is only one opinion amongst all those who have tried to study the Buddhist monkhood—that their conduct is admirable. Do you suppose the people would reverence it as they do if it were corrupt? They know: they have seen it from the inside. It is not outside knowledge they have. And when it is understood that anyone can enter a monastery—thieves and robbers, murderers and sinners of every description, can enter, are even urged to enter monasteries, and try to live the holy life; and many of them do, either as a refuge against pursuit, or because they really repent—it will be conceded that the discipline of the monks, if obtained in a different way to elsewhere, is very effective.

The more you study the monkhood, the more you see that this community is the outcome of the very heart of the people. It is a part of the people, not cut off from them, but of them; it is recruited in great numbers from all sorts and conditions of men. In every village and town—nearly every man has been a monk at one time or another—it is honoured alike by all; it is kept in the straight way, not only from the inherent righteousness of its teaching, but from the determination of the people to allow no stain to rest upon what they consider as their 'great glory.' This whole monkhood is founded on freedom. It is held together not by a strong organization, but by general consent. There is no mystery about it, there are no dark places here where the sunlight of inquiry may not come. The whole business is so simple that the very children can and do understand it. I shall have expressed myself very badly if I have not made it understood how absolutely voluntary this monkhood is, held together by no everlasting vows, restrained by no rigid discipline. It is simply the free outcome of the free beliefs of the people, as much a part of them as the fruit is of the tree. You could no more imagine grapes without a vine than a Buddhist monkhood that did not spring directly from, and depend entirely on, the people. It is the higher expression of their life.

In writing this account of the Burmese and their religion, I have tried always to see with my own eyes, to write my own thoughts without any reference to what anyone else may have thought or written. I have believed that whatever value may attach to any man's opinions consists in the fact that they are his opinions, and not a *rechauffé* of the thoughts of others, and therefore I have not even referred to, or quoted from, any other writer, preferring to write only what I have myself seen and thought. But I cannot end this chapter on the monks of the Buddha without a reference to what Bishop Bigandet has said on the same subject, for he is no observer prejudiced in favour of Buddhism, but the reverse. He was a bishop of the Church of Rome, believing always that his faith contained all truth, and that the Buddha was but a 'pretended saviour,' his teachings based on 'capital and revolting errors,' and marked with an 'inexplicable and deplorable eccentricity.' Bishop Bigandet was in no sympathy with Buddhism, but its avowed foe, desirous of undermining and destroying its influence over the hearts of men, and yet this is the way he ends his chapter:

'There is in that religious body—the monks—a latent principle of vitality that keeps it up and communicates to it an amount of strength and energy that has hitherto maintained it in the midst of wars, revolutionary and political, convulsions of all descriptions. Whether supported or not by the ruling power, it has remained always firm and unchanged. It is impossible to account satisfactorily for such a phenomenon, unless we find a clear and evident cause of such extraordinary vitality, a cause independent of ordinary occurrences of time and circumstances, a cause deeply rooted in the very soul of the populations that exhibit before the observer this great and striking religious feature.

'That cause appears to be the strong religious sentiment, the firm faith, that pervades the mass of Buddhists. The laity admire and venerate the religious, and voluntarily and cheerfully contribute to their maintenance and welfare. From its ranks the religious body is constantly recruited. There is hardly a man that has not been a member of the fraternity for a certain period of time.

'Surely such a general and continued impulse could not last long unless it were maintained by a powerful religious connection.

'The members of the order preserve, at least exteriorly, the decorum of their profession. The rules and regulations are tolerably well observed; the grades of hierarchy are maintained with scrupulous exactitude. The life of the religious is one of restraint and perpetual control. He is denied all sorts of pleasures and diversions. How could such a system of self-denial ever be maintained, were it not for the belief which the Rahans have in the merits that they amass by following a course of life which, after all, is repugnant to Nature? It cannot be denied that human motives often influence both the laity and the religious, but, divested of faith and the sentiments supplied by even a false belief, their action could not produce in a lasting and persevering manner the extraordinary and striking fact that we witness in Buddhist countries.'

This monkhood is the proof of how the people believe. Has any religion ever had for twenty-four centuries such a proof as this?

CHAPTER XI

THE MONKHOOD—II

'The restrained in hand, restrained in foot, restrained in speech, of the greatest self-control. He whose delight is inward, who is tranquil and happy when alone—him they call "mendicant."'—*Acceptance into the Monkhood.*

Besides being the ideal of the Buddhists, the monk is more: he is the schoolmaster of all the boys. It must be remembered that this is a thing aside from his monkhood. A monk need not necessarily teach; the aim and object of the monkhood is, as I have written in the last chapter, purity and abstraction from the world. If the monk acts as schoolmaster, that is a thing apart. And yet all monasteries are schools. The word in Burmese is the same; they are identified in popular speech and in popular opinion. All the monasteries are full of scholars, all the monks teach. I suppose much the same reasons have had influence here as in other nations; the desire of the parents that their children should learn religion in their childhood, the fact that the wisest and most honoured men entered the monkhood, the leisure of the monks giving them opportunity for such occupation.

Every man all through Burma has gone to a monastery school as a lad, has lived there with the monks, has learnt from them the elements of education and a knowledge of his faith. It is an exception to find a Burman who cannot read and write. Sometimes from lack of practice the art is lost in later manhood, but it has always been acquired. The education is not very deep—reading Burmese and writing; simple, very simple, arithmetic; a knowledge of the days and months, and a little geography, perhaps, and history—that is all that is secular. But of their religion they learn a great deal. They have to get by heart great portions of the sacred books, stories and teachings, and they have to learn many precepts. They have to recite them, too, as those who have lived much near monasteries know. Several times a day, at about nine o'clock at night, and again before dawn, you will hear the lads intoning clearly and loudly some of the sacred teachings. I have been awakened many a time in the early morning, before the dawn, before even the promise of the dawn in the eastern sky, by the children's voices intoning. And I have put aside my curtain and looked out from my rest-house and seen them in the dim starlight kneeling before the pagoda, the tomb of the great teacher, saying his laws. The light comes rapidly in this country: the sky reddens, the stars die quickly overhead, the first long beams of sunrise are trembling on the dewy bamboo feathers ere they have finished. It is one of the most beautiful sights imaginable to see monks and children kneeling on the bare ground, singing while the dawn comes.

The education in their religion is very good, very thorough, not only in precept, but in practice; for in the monastery you must live a holy life, as the monks live, even if you are but a schoolboy.

But the secular education is limited. It is up to the standard of education amongst the people at large, but that is saying little. Beyond reading and writing and arithmetic it generally does not go. I have seen the little boys do arithmetic. They were adding sums, and they began, not as we would, on the right, but on the left. They added, say, the hundreds first; then they wrote on the slate the number of hundreds, and added up the tens. If it happened that the tens mounted up so as to add one or more to the hundreds, a grimy little finger would wipe out the hundreds already written and write in the correct numbers. It follows that if the units on being added up came to over ten, the tens must be corrected with the grimy little finger, first put in the mouth. Perhaps both tens and hundreds had to be written again. It will be seen that when you come to thousands and tens of thousands, a good deal of wiping out and re-writing may be required. A Burman is very bad at arithmetic; a villager will often write 133 as 100,303; he would almost as soon write 43 as 34; both figures are in each number, you see.

I never met a Burman who had any idea of cubic measurement, though land measurement they pick up very quickly.

I have said that the education in the monasteries is up to the average education of the people. That is so. Whether when civilization progresses and more education is required the monasteries will be able to provide it is another thing.

The education given now is mostly a means to an end: to learning the precepts of religion. Whether the monks will provide an education beyond such a want, I doubt. A monk is by his vows, by the whole tenour of his life, apart from the world; too keen a search after knowledge, any kind of secular knowledge, would be a return to the things of this life, would, perhaps, re-kindle in him the desires that the whole meaning of his life is to annihilate. 'And after thou hast run over all things, what will it profit thee if thou hast neglected thyself?'

Besides, no knowledge, except mere theoretical knowledge, can be acquired without going about in the world. You cannot cut yourself off from the world and get knowledge of it. Yet the monk is apart from the world. It is true that Buddhism has no antagonism to science—nay, has every sympathy with, every attraction to, science. Buddhism will never try and block the progress of the truth, of light, secular or religious; but whether the monks will find it within their vows to provide that science, only time can prove. However it may be, it will not make any difference to the estimation in which the monks are held. They are not honoured for their wisdom—they often have but little; nor for their learning—they often have none at all; nor for their industry—they are never industrious; but because they are men trying to live—nay, succeeding in living—a life void of sin. Up till now the education given by the monks has met the wants of the people; in future it will do so less and less. But a community that has lived through twenty-four centuries of change, and is now of the strength and vitality that the Buddhist monkhood is, can have nothing to fear from any such change. Schoolmasters, except religious and elementary, they may cease to be, perhaps; the pattern and ensample of purity and righteousness they will always remain.

CHAPTER XII

PRAYER

'What is there that can justify tears and lamentations?'

Saying of the Buddha.

Down below my house, in a grove of palms near the river, was a little rest-house. It was but a roof and a floor of teak boarding without any walls, and it was plainly built. It might have held, perhaps, twenty people; and here, as I strolled past in the evening when the sun was setting, I would see two or three old men sitting with beads in their hands. They were making their devotions, saying to themselves that the world was all trouble, all weariness, and that there was no rest anywhere except in observing the laws of righteousness. It was very pathetic, I thought, to see them there, saying this over and over again, as they told their beads through their withered fingers, for surely there was no necessity for them to learn it. Has not everyone learnt it, this, the first truth of Buddhism, long before his hair is gray, before his hands are shaking, before his teeth are gone? But there they would sit, evening after evening, thinking of the change about to come upon them soon, realizing the emptiness of life, wishing for the Great Peace.

On Sundays the rest-house, like many others round the village, was crowded. Old men there would be, and one or two young men, a few children, and many women. Early in the morning they would come, and a monk would come down from the monastery near by, and each one would vow, with the monk as witness, that he or she would spend the day in meditation and in holy thought, would banish all thought of evil, and be for the day at least holy. And then, the vow made, the devotee would go and sit in the rest-house and meditate. The village is not very near; the sounds come very softly through the trees, not enough to disturb the mind; only there is the sigh of the wind wandering amid the leaves, and the occasional cry of birds. Once before noon a meal will be eaten, either food brought with them cold, or a simple pot of rice boiled beside the rest-house, and there they will stay till the sun sets and darkness is gathering about the foot of the trees. There is no service at all. The monk may come and read part of the sacred books—some of the Abidama, or a sermon from the Thoots—and perhaps sometimes he may expound a little; that is all. There is nothing akin to our ideas of worship. For consider what our service consists of: there is thanksgiving and praise, there is prayer, there is reading of the Bible, there is a sermon. Our thanksgiving and praise is rendered to God for things He has done, the pleasure that He has allowed us to enjoy, the punishment that He might have inflicted upon us and has not. Our prayer is to Him to preserve us in future, to assist us in our troubles, to give us our daily food, not to be too severe upon us, not to punish us as we deserve, but to be merciful and kind. We ask Him to protect us from our enemies, not to allow them to triumph over us, but to give us triumph over them.

But the Buddhist has far other thoughts than these. He believes that the world is ruled by everlasting, unchangeable laws of righteousness. The great God lives far behind His laws, and they are for ever and ever. You cannot change the laws of righteousness by praising them, or by crying against them, any more than you can change the revolution of the earth. Sin begets sorrow, sorrow is the only purifier from sin; these are eternal sequences; they cannot be altered; it would not be good that they should be altered. The Buddhist believes that the sequences are founded on righteousness, are the path to righteousness, and he does not believe he could alter them for the better, even if he had the power by prayer to do so. He believes in the everlasting *righteousness*, that all things work for *good* in the end; he has no need for prayer or praise; he thinks that the world is governed with far greater wisdom than any of his—perfect wisdom, that is too great, too wonderful, for his petty praise.

God lives far behind His laws; think not He has made them so badly as to require continual rectification at the prayer of man. Think not that God is not bound by His own laws. The Buddhist will never believe that God can break His own laws; that He is like an earthly king who imagines one code of morality for his subjects and another for himself. Not so; the great laws are founded in righteousness, so the Buddhist believes, in everlasting righteousness; they are perfect, far beyond our comprehension; they are the eternal, unchangeable, marvellous will of God, and it is our duty not to be for ever fretfully trying to change them, but to be trying to understand them. That is the Buddhist belief in the meaning of religion, and in the laws of righteousness; that is, he believes the duty of him who would follow religion to try to understand these laws, to bring them home to the heart, so to order life as to bring it into harmony with righteousness.

Now see the difference. We believe that the world is governed not by eternal laws, but by a changeable and continually changing God, and that it is our duty to try and persuade Him to make it better.

We believe, really, that we know a great deal better than God what is good, not only for us, but for others; we do not believe His will is always righteous—not at all: God has wrath to be deprecated; He has mercy to be aroused; He has partiality to be turned towards us, and hence our prayers.

But to the Buddhist the whole world is ruled by righteousness, the same for all, the same for ever, and the only sin is ignorance of these laws.

The Buddha is he who has found for us the light to see these laws, and to order our life in accordance with them.

Now it will be understood, I think, why there is no prayer, no gathering together for any ceremonial, in Buddhism; why there is no praise, no thanksgiving of any kind; why it is so very different in this way from our faith. Buddhism is a wisdom, a seeking of the light, a following of the light, each man as best he can, and it has very little to correspond with our prayer, our services of praise, our meetings together in the name of Christ.

Therefore, when you see a man kneeling before a pagoda, moving silent lips of prayer, when you see the people sitting quietly in the rest-houses on a Sunday, when you see the old men telling their beads to themselves slowly and sadly, when you hear the resonant chant of monks and children, lending a soul to the silence of the gloaming, you will know what they are doing. They are trying to understand and bring home to themselves the eternal laws of righteousness; they are honouring their great teacher.

This is all that there is; this is the meaning of all that you see and hear. The Buddhist praises and honours the Buddha, the Indian prince who so long ago went out into the wilderness to search for truth, and after many years found it in his own heart; he reverences the Buddha for seeing the light; he thanks the Buddha for his toil and exertion in making this light known to all men. It can do the Buddha no good, all this praise, for he has come to his eternal peace; but it can arouse the enthusiasm of the follower, can bring into his heart love for the memory of the great teacher, and a firm resolve to follow his teaching.

The service of his religion is to try and follow these laws, to take them home into the heart, that the follower, too, may come soon into the Great Peace.

This has been called pessimism. Surely it is the greatest optimism the world has known—this certainty that the world is ruled by righteousness, that the world has been, that the world will always be, ruled by perfect righteousness.

To the Buddhist this is a certainty. The laws are laws of righteousness, if man would but see, would but understand. Do not complain and cry and pray, but open your eyes and see. The light is all about you, if you would only cast the bandage from your eyes and look. It is so wonderful, so beautiful, far beyond what any man has dreamt of, has prayed for, and it is for ever and for ever.

This is the attitude of Buddhism towards prayer, towards thanksgiving. It considers them an impertinence and a foolishness, born of ignorance, akin to the action of him who would daily desire Atlas not to allow the heavens to drop upon the earth.

And yet, and yet.

I remember standing once on the platform of a famous pagoda, the golden spire rising before us, and carved shrines around us, and seeing a woman lying there, her face to the pagoda. She was praying fervently, so fervently that her words could be heard, for she had no care for anyone about, in such trouble was she; and what she was asking was this, that her child, her baby, might not die. She held the little thing in her arms, and as she looked upon it her eyes were full of tears. For it was very sick; its little limbs were but thin bones, with big knees and elbows, and its face was very wan. It could not even take any interest in the wonderful sights around, but hardly opened its careworn eyes now and then to blink upon the world.

'Let him recover, let him be well once more!' the woman cried, again and again.

Whom was she beseeching? I do not know.

'Thakin, there will be Someone, Someone. A Spirit may hear. Who can tell? Surely someone will help me? Men would help me if they could, but they cannot; surely there will be someone?'

So she did not remember the story of Ma Pa Da.

Women often pray, I think—they pray that their husbands and those they love may be well. It is a frequent ending to a girl's letter to her lover: 'And I pray always that you may be well.' I never heard of their praying for anything but this: that they may be loved, and those they love may be well. Nothing else is worth praying for besides this. The queen would pray at the pagoda in the palace morning and evening. 'What did she pray for?' 'What should she pray for, thakin? Surely she prayed that her husband might be true to her, and that her children might live and be strong. That is what women pray for. Do you think a queen would pray differently to any other woman?'

'Women,' say the Buddhist monks, 'never understand. They *will* not understand; they cannot learn. And so we say that most women must be born again, as men, before they can see the light and understand the laws of righteousness.'

What do women care for laws of righteousness? What do they care for justice? What for the everlasting sequences that govern the world? Would not they involve all other men, all earth and heaven, in bottomless chaos, to save one heart they loved? That is woman's religion.

CHAPTER XIII

FESTIVALS

'The law is sweet, filling the soul with joy.'

Saying of the Buddha.

The three months of the rains, from the full moon of July to the full moon of October, is the Buddhist Lent. It was during these months that the Buddha would retire to some monastery and cease from travelling and teaching for a time. The custom was far older even than that—so old that we do not know how it arose. Its origin is lost in the mists of far-away time. But whatever the beginning may have been, it fits in very well with the habits of the people; for in the rains travelling is not easy. The roads are very bad, covered even with water, often deep in mud; and the rest-houses, with open sides, are not very comfortable with the rain drifting in. Even if there were no custom of Lent, there would be but little travelling then. People would stay at home, both because of the discomfort of moving, and because there is much work then at the village. For this is the time to plough, this is the time to sow; on the villagers' exertions in these months depends all their maintenance for the rest of the year. Every man, every woman, every child, has hard work of some kind or another.

What with the difficulties of travelling, what with the work there is to do, and what with the custom of Lent, everyone stays at home. It is the time for prayer, for fasting, for improving the soul. Many men during these months will live even as the monks live, will eat but before mid-day, will abstain from tobacco. There are no plays during Lent, and there are no marriages. It is the time for preparing the land for the crop; it is the time for preparing the soul for eternity. The congregations on the Sundays will be far greater at this time than at any other; there will be more thought of the serious things of life.

It is a very long Lent—three months; but with the full moon of October comes the end. The rains then are over; the great black bank of clouds that walled up all the south so long is gone. The south wind has died away, and the light, fresh north wind is coming down the river. The roads are drying up, the work in the fields is over for a time, awaiting the ripening of the grain. The damp has gone out of the air, and it is very clear. You can see once more the purple mountains that you have missed so long; there is a new feeling in the wind, a laughter in the sunshine, a flush of blossom along the fields like the awakening of a new joy. The rains are gone and the cool weather is coming; Lent is over and gladness is returned; the crop has been sown, and soon will come the reaping. And so at this full moon of October is the great feast of the year. There are other festivals: of the New Year, in March, with its water-throwing; of each great pagoda at its appointed time; but of all, the festival at the end of Lent is the greatest.

Wherever there are great pagodas the people will come in from far and near for the feast. There are many great pagodas in Burma; there is the Arakan pagoda in Mandalay, and there was the Incomparable pagoda, which has been burnt; there are great pagodas at Pegu, at Prome, at many other places; but perhaps the greatest of all is the Shwe Dagon at Rangoon.

You see it from far away as you come up the river, steaming in from the open sea, a great tongue of flame before you. It stands on a small conical hill just behind the city of Rangoon, about two miles away from the wharves and shipping in the busy river. The hill has been levelled on the top and paved into a wide platform, to which you ascend by a flight of many steps from the gate below, where stand the dragons. This entrance-way is all roofed over, and the pillars and the ceiling are red and painted. Here it was that much fighting took place in the early wars, in 1852 especially, and many men, English and Burmese, were killed in storming and defending this strong place. For it had been made a very strong place, this holy place of him who taught that peace was the only good, and the defences round about it are standing still. Upon the top of this hill, the flat paved top, stands the pagoda, a great solid tapering cone over three hundred feet high, ending in an iron fretwork spire that glitters with gold and jewels; and the whole pagoda is covered with gold—pure leaf-gold. Down below it is being always renewed by the pious offerings of those who come to pray and spread a little gold-leaf on it; but every now and then it is all regilt, from the top, far away above you, to the golden lions that guard its base. It is a most wonderful sight, this great golden cone, in that marvellous sunlight that bathes its sides like a golden sea. It seems to shake and tremble in the light like a fire. And all about the platform, edging it ere it falls away below, are little shrines, marvels of carven woodwork and red lacquer. They have tapering roofs, one above another, till they, too, end in a golden spire full of little bells with tongues. As the wind blows the tongues move to and fro, and the air is full of music, so faint, so clear, like 'silver stir of strings in hollow shells.'

In most of these shrines there are statues of the great teacher, cut in white alabaster, glimmering whitely in the lustrous shadows there within; and in one shrine is the great bell. Long ago we tried to take this great bell; we tried to send it home as a war trophy, this bell stolen from their sacred place, but we failed. As it was being put on board a ship, it slipped and fell into the river into the mud, where the fierce tides are ever coming and going. And when all the efforts of our engineers to raise it had failed, the Burmese asked: 'The bell, our bell, is there in the water. You cannot get it up. You have tried and you have failed. If we can get it up, may we have it back to hang in our pagoda as our own again?' And they were told, with a laugh, perhaps, that they might; and so they raised it up again, the river giving back to them what it had refused to us, and they took and hung it where it used to be. There it is now, and you may hear it when you go, giving out a long, deep note, the beat of the pagoda's heart.

There are many trees, too, about the pagoda platform—so many, that seen far off you can only see the trees and the pagoda towering above them. Have not trees been always sacred things? Have not all religions been glad to give their fanes the glory and majesty of great trees?

You may look from the pagoda platform over the whole country, over the city and the river and the straight streets; and on the other side you may see the long white lakes and little hills covered with trees. It is a very beautiful place, this pagoda, and it is steeped in an odour of holiness, the perfume of the thousand thousand prayers that have been prayed there, of the thousand thousand holy thoughts that have been thought there.

The pagoda platform is always full of people kneeling, saying over and over the great precepts of their faith, trying to bring into their hearts the meaning of the teaching of him of whom this wonderful pagoda represents the tomb. There are always monks there passing to and fro, or standing leaning on the pillars of the shrines; there are always a crowd of people climbing up and down the long steps that lead from the road below. It is a place I always go to when I am in Rangoon; for, besides its beauty, there are the people; and if you go and stand near where the stairway reaches the platform you will see the people come up. They come up singly, in twos, in groups. First a nun, perhaps, walking very softly, clad in her white dress with her beads about her neck, and there in a corner by a little shrine she will spread a cloth upon the hard stones and kneel and bow her face to the great pagoda. Then she will repeat, 'Sorrow, misery, trouble,' over and over again, running her beads through her fingers, repeating the words in the hope that in the end she may understand whither they should lead her. 'Sorrow, misery, trouble'—ah! surely she must know what they mean, or she would not be a nun. And then comes a young man, and after a reverence to the pagoda he goes wandering round, looking for someone, maybe; and then comes an old man with his son. They stop at the little stalls on the stairs, and they have bought there each a candle. The old man has a plain taper, but the little lad must have one with his emblem on it. Each day has its own sign, a tiger for Monday, and so on, and the lad buys a candle like a little rat, for his birthday is Friday, and the father and son go on to the platform. There they kneel down side by side, the old man and the little chubby lad, and they, too, say that all is misery and delusion. Presently they rise and advance to the pagoda's golden base, and put their candles thereon and light them. This side of the pagoda is in shadow now, and so you can see the lights of the candles as little stars.

And then come three girls, sisters, perhaps, all so prettily dressed, with meek eyes, and they, too, buy candles; they, too, kneel and make their devotions, for long, so long, that you wonder if anything has happened, if there has been any trouble that has brought them thus in the sunset to the remembrance of religion. But at last they rise, and they light their little candles near by where the old man and the boy have lit theirs, and then they go away. They are so sad, they keep their faces so turned upon the ground, that you fear there has been something, some trouble come upon them. You feel so sorry for them, you would like to ask them what it all is; you would like to help them if you could. But you can do nothing. They go away down the steps, and you hear the nun repeating always, 'Sorrow, misery, trouble.'

So they come and go.

But on the festival days at the end of Lent it is far more wonderful. Then for units there are tens, for tens there are hundreds—all come to do reverence to the great teacher at this his great holy place. There is no especial ceremony, no great service, such as we are accustomed to on our festivals. Only there will be many offerings; there will be a procession, maybe, with offerings to the pagoda, with offerings to the monks; there will be much gold-leaf spread upon the pagoda sides; there will be many people kneeling there—that is all. For, you see, Buddhism is not an affair of a community, but of each man's own heart.

To see the great pagoda on the festival days is one of the sights of the world. There are a great crowd of people coming and going, climbing up the steps. There are all sorts of people, rich and poor, old and young. Old men there are, climbing wearily up these steps that are so steep, steps that lead towards the Great Peace; and there are old women, too—many of them.

Young men will be there, walking briskly up, laughing and talking to each other, very happy, very merry, glad to see each other, to see so many people, calling pleasant greetings to their friends as they pass. They are all so gaily dressed, with beautiful silks and white jackets and gay satin head-cloths, tied with a little end sticking up as a plume.

And the girls, how shall I describe them, so sweet they are, so pretty in their fresh dresses, with downcast eyes of modesty, tempered with little side-glances. They laugh, too, as they go, and they talk, never forgetting the sacredness of the place, never forgetting the reverences due, kneeling always first as they come up to the great pagoda, but being of good courage, happy and contented. There are children, too, numbers and numbers of them, walking along, with their little hands clasping so tightly some bigger ones, very fearful lest they should be lost. They are as gay as butterflies in their dress, but their looks are very solemn. There is no solemnity like that of a little child; it takes all the world so very, very seriously, walking along with great eyes of wonder at all it sees about it.

They are all well dressed who come here; on a festival day even the poor can be dressed well. Pinks and reds are the prevailing colours, in checks, in stripes, mixed usually with white. These colours go best with their brown skins, and they are fondest of them. But there are other colours, too: there is silver and green embroidery, and there are shot-silks in purple and orange, and there is dark blue. All the jackets, or nearly all the jackets, are white with wide sleeves, showing the arm nearly up to the elbow. Each man has his turban very gay, while each girl has a bright handkerchief which she drapes as she likes upon her arm, or carries in her hand. Such a blaze of colour would not look well with us. Under our dull skies and with our sober lights it would be too bright; but here it is not so. Everything is tempered by the sun; it is so brilliant, this sunlight, such a golden flood pouring down and bathing the whole world, that these colours are only in keeping. Before them is the gold pagoda, and about them the red lacquer and dark-brown carving of the shrines.

You hear voices like the murmur of a summer sea, rising and falling, full of laughter low and sweet, and above is the music of the fairy bells.

Everything is in keeping—the shining pagoda and the gaily-dressed people, their voices and the bells, even the great bell far beyond, and all are so happy.

The feast lasts for seven days; but of these there are three that are greater, and of these, one, the day of the full moon, is the greatest of all. On that day the offerings will be most numerous, the crowd densest. Down below the pagoda are many temporary stalls built, where you can buy all sorts of fairings, from a baby's jointed doll to a new silk dress; and there are restaurants where you may obtain refreshments; for the pagoda is some way from the streets of the city, and on festival days refreshments are much wanted.

These stalls are always crowded with people buying and selling, or looking anxiously at the many pretty wares, unable, perhaps, to buy. The refreshments are usually very simple—rice and curry for supper, and for little refreshments between whiles there are sugar-cakes and vermicelli, and other little cates.

The crowd going up and down the steps is like a gorgeous-coloured flood, crested with white foam, flowing between the dragons of the gate; and on the platform the crowd is thicker than ever. All day the festival goes on—the praying, the offering of gifts, the burning of little candles before the shrines—until the sun sets across the open country far beyond in gold and crimson glory. But even then there is no pause, no darkness, for hardly has the sun's last bright shaft faded from the pagoda spire far above, while his streamers are still bright across the west, than there comes in the east a new radiance, so soft, so wonderful, it seems more beautiful than the dying day. Across the misty fields the moon is rising; first a crimson globe hung low among the trees, but rising fast, and as it rises growing whiter. Its light comes flooding down upon the earth, pure silver with very black shadows. Then the night breeze begins to blow, very softly, very gently, and the trees give out their odour to the night, which woos them so much more sweetly than the day, till the air is heavy with incense.

Behold, the pagoda has started into a new glory, for it is all hung about with little lamps, myriads of tiny cressets, and the façades of the shrines are lit up, too. The lamps are put in long rows or in circles, to fit the places they adorn. They are little earthenware jars full of cocoanut-oil, with a lip where is the wick. They burn very redly, and throw a red light about the platform, breaking the shadows that the moonlight throws and staining its whiteness.

In the streets, too, there are lamps—the houses are lined with them—and there are little pagodas and ships curiously designed in flame.

All the people come out to see the illuminations, just as they do with us at Christmas to see the shop-windows, and the streets are crowded with people going to and fro, laughing and talking. And there are dramatic entertainments going on, dances and marionette shows, all in the open air. The people are all so happy, they take their pleasure so pleasantly, that it is a delight to see them. You cannot help but be happy, too. The men joke and laugh, and you laugh, too; the children smile at you as they pass, and you must smile, too; can you help it? And to see the girls makes the heart glad within you. There is an infection from the good temper and the gaiety about you that is irresistible, even if you should want to resist it.

The festival goes on till very late. The moon is so bright that you forget how late it is, and only remember how beautiful it is all around. You are very loath to leave it, and so it is not till the moon itself is falling low down in the same path whither the sun went before her, it is not till the lamps are dying one by one and the children are yawning very sleepily, that the crowd disperses and the pagoda is at rest.

Such is a great feast at a great pagoda.

But whenever I think of a great feast, whenever the growing autumn moon tells me that the end of Lent is drawing nigh, it is not the great feast of the Shwe Dagon, nor of any other famous pagoda that comes into my mind, but something far different.

It was on a frontier long ago that there was the festival that I remember so well. The country there was very far away from all the big towns; the people were not civilized as those of Mandalay or of Rangoon; the pagoda was a very small one. There was no gilding upon it at all, and no shrines were about it; it stood alone, just a little white plastered pagoda, with a few trees near it, on a bare rice-field. There were a few villages about, dotted here and there in the swamp, and the people of these were all that came to our festival.

For long before the villages were preparing for it, saving a little money here, doing a little extra work there, so that they might be able to have presents ready for the monks, so that they might be able to subscribe to the lights, so that they would have a good dress in which they might appear.

The men did a little more work at the fields, bamboo-cutting in the forest, making baskets in the evening, and the women wove. All had to work very hard to have even a little margin; for there, although food—plain rice—was very cheap, all other things were very expensive. It was so far to bring them, and the roads were so bad. I remember that the only European things to be bought there then were matches and tinned milk, and copper money was not known. You paid a rupee, and took the change in rice or other commodities.

The excitement of the great day of the full moon began in the morning, about ten o'clock, with the offerings to the monks. Outside the village gate there was a piece of straight road, dry and open, and on each side of this, in rows, were the people with their gifts; mostly they were eatables. You see that it is very difficult to find any variety of things to give a monk; he is very strictly limited in the things he is allowed to receive. Garments, yellow garments, curtains to partition off corners of the monasteries and keep away the draughts, sacred books and eatables—that is nearly all. But eatables allow a very wide range. A monk may accept and eat any food—not drink, of course—provided he eat but the one big meal a day before noon; and so most of the offerings were eatables. Each donor knelt there upon the road with his or her offerings in a tray in front. There was rice cooked in all sorts of shapes, ordinary rice for eating with curry, and the sweet purple rice, cooked in bamboos and coming out in sticks. There were vegetables, too, of very many kinds, and sugar and cakes and oil and honey, and many other such things. There were a few, very few, books, for they are very hard to get, being all in manuscript; and there were one or two tapestry curtains; but there were heaps of flowers. I remember there was one girl whose whole offering was a few orchid sprays, and a little, very little, heap of common rice. She was so poor; her father and mother were dead, and she was not married. It was all she could give. She sat behind her little offering, as did all the donors. And my gift? Well, although an English official, I was not then very much richer than the people about me, so my gift must be small, too—a tin of biscuits, a tin or two of jam, a new pair of scissors. I did not sit behind them myself, but gave them to the headman to put with his offerings; for the monks were old friends of mine. Did I not live in one of their monasteries for over two months when we first came and camped there with a cavalry squadron? And if there is any merit in such little charity, as the Burmese say there is, why should I not gain it, too? The monks said my present was best of all, because it was so uncommon; and the biscuits, they said, though they did not taste of much while you were eating them, had a very pleasant after-taste that lasted a long time. They were like charity, maybe: that has a pleasant after-taste, too, they tell me.

When all the presents, with the donors behind them, dressed all in their best, were ready, the monks came. There were four monasteries near by, and the monks, perhaps in all thirty, old and young, monks and novices, came in one long procession, walking very slowly, with downcast eyes, between the rows of gifts and givers. They did not look at them at all. It is not proper for a monk to notice the gifts he receives; but schoolboys who came along behind attending on them, they saw and made remarks. Perhaps they saw the chance of some overflow of these good things coming their way. 'See,' one nudged the other; 'honey—what a lot! I can smell it, can't you?' And, '*My mother!* what a lot of sweet rice. Who gave that? Oh, I see, old U Hman.' 'I wonder what's in that tin box?' remarked one as he passed my biscuits. 'I hope it's coming to our monastery, any way.'

Thus the monks passed, paying no sort of attention, while the people knelt to them; and when the procession reached the end of the line of offerings, it went on without stopping, across the fields, the monks of each monastery going to their own place; and the givers of presents rose up and followed them, each carrying his or her gifts. And so they went across the fields till each little procession was lost to sight.

That was all the ceremony for the day, but at dusk the illuminations began. The little pagoda in the fields was lighted up nearly to its top with concentric rings of lamps till it blazed like a pyramid of flame, seen far across the night. All the people came there, and placed little offerings of flowers at the foot of the pagoda, or added each his candle to the big illumination.

The house of the headman of the village was lit up with a few rows of lamps, and all the monasteries, too, were lit. There were no restaurants—everyone was at home, you see—but there were one or two little stalls, at which you could buy a cheroot, or even perhaps a cup of vermicelli; and there was a dance. It was only the village girls who had been taught, partly by their own mothers, partly by an old man, who knew something of the business. They did not dance very well, perhaps; they were none of them very beautiful; but what matter? We knew them all; they were our neighbours, the kinswomen of half the village; everyone liked to see them dance, to hear them sing; they were all young, and are not all young girls pretty? And amongst the audience were there not the girls' relations, their sisters, their lovers? would not that alone make the girls dance well, make the audience enthusiastic? And so, what with the illuminations, and the chat and laughter of friends, and the dance, we kept it up till very late; and we all went to bed happy and well pleased with each other, well pleased with ourselves. Can you imagine a more successful end than that?

To write about these festivals is so pleasant, it brings back so many delightful memories, that I could go on writing for long and long. But there is no use in doing so, as they are all very much alike, with little local differences depending on the enterprise of the inhabitants and the situation of the place. There might be boat-races, perhaps, on a festival day, or pony-races, or boxing. I have seen all these, if not at the festival at the end of Lent, at other festivals. I remember once I was going up the river on a festival night by the full moon, and we saw point after point crowned with lights upon the pagodas; and as we came near the great city we saw a new glory; for there was a boat anchored in mid-stream, and from this boat there dropped a stream of fire; myriads of little lamps burned on tiny rafts that drifted down the river in a golden band. There were every now and then bigger rafts, with figures made in light—boats and pagodas and monasteries. The lights heaved with the long swell of the great river, and bent to and fro like a great snake following the tides, until at length they died far away into the night.

I do not know what is the meaning of all these lights; I do not know that they have any inner meaning, only that the people are very glad, only that they greatly honour the great teacher who died so long ago, only that they are very fond of light and colour and laughter and all beautiful things.

But although these festivals often become also fairs, although they are the great centres for amusement, although the people look to them as their great pleasure of the year, it must not be forgotten that they are essentially religious feasts, holy days. Though there be no great ceremony of prayer, or of thanksgiving, no public joining in any religious ceremony, save, perhaps, the giving of alms to the monks, yet religion is the heart and soul of them. Their centre is the pagoda, their meaning is a religious meaning.

What if the people make merry, too, if they make their holy days into holidays, is that any harm? For their pleasures are very simple, very innocent; there is nothing that the moon, even the cold and distant moon, would blush to look upon. The people make merry because they are merry, because their religion is to them a very beautiful thing, not to be shunned or feared, but to be exalted to the eye of day, to be rejoiced in.

CHAPTER XIV

WOMEN—I

'Her cheek is more beautiful than the dawn, her eyes are deeper than the river pools; when she loosens her hair upon her shoulders, it is as night coming over the hills.'— *Burmese Love-Song.*

If you were to ask a Burman 'What is the position of women in Burma?' he would reply that he did not know what you meant. Women have no position, no fixed relation towards men beyond that fixed by the fact that women are women and men are men. They differ a great deal in many ways, so a Burman would say; men are better in some things, women are better in others; if they have a position, their relative superiority in certain things determines it. How else should it be determined?

If you say by religion, he laughs, and asks what religion has to do with such things? Religion is a culture of the soul; it is not concerned with the relationship of men and women. If you say by law, he says that law has no more to do with it than religion. In the eye of the law both are alike. 'You wouldn't have one law for a man and another for a woman?' he asks.

In the life of the Buddha nothing is said upon the subject. The great teacher never committed himself to an opinion as to whether men or women were the highest. He had men disciples, he had women disciples; he honoured both. Nowhere in any of his sayings can anything be found to show that he made any difference between them. That monks should be careful and avoid intercourse with women is merely the counterpart of the order that nuns should be careful in their intercourse with men. That man's greatest attraction is woman does not infer wickedness in woman; that woman's greatest attraction is man does not show that man is a devil. Wickedness is a thing of your own heart. If he could be sure that his desire towards women was dead, a monk might see them as much as he liked. The desire is the enemy, not the woman; therefore a woman is not damned because by her man is often tempted to evil; therefore a woman is not praised because by her a man may be led to better thoughts. She is but the outer and unconscious influence.

If, for instance, you cannot see a precipice without wishing to throw yourself down, you blame not the precipice, but your giddiness; and if you are wise you avoid precipices in future. You do not rail against steep places because you have a bad circulation. So it is with women: you should not contemn women because they rouse a devil in man.

And it is the same with man. Men and women are alike subject to the eternal laws. And they are alike subject to the laws of man; in no material points, hardly even in minor points, does the law discriminate against women.

The law as regards marriage and inheritance and divorce will come each in its own place. It is curiously the same both for the man and the woman.

The criminal law was the same for both; I have tried to find any difference, and this is all I have found: A woman's life was less valuable than a man's. The price of the body, as it is called, of a woman was less than that of a man. If a woman were accidentally killed, less compensation had to be paid than for a man. I asked a Burman about this once.

'Why is this difference?' I said. 'Why does the law discriminate?'

'It isn't the law,' he said, 'it is a fact. A woman is worth less than a man in that way. A maidservant can be hired for less than a manservant, a daughter can claim less than a son. They cannot do so much work; they are not so strong. If they had been worth more, the law would have been the other way; of course they are worth less.'

And so this sole discrimination is a fact, not dogma. It is a fact, no doubt, everywhere. No one would deny it. The pecuniary value of a woman is less than that of a man. As to the soul's value, that is not a question of law, which confines itself to material affairs. But I suppose all laws have been framed out of the necessities of mankind. It was the incessant fighting during the times when our laws grew slowly into shape, the necessity of not allowing the possession of land, and the armed wealth that land gave, to fall into the weaker hands of women, that led to our laws of inheritance.

Laws then were governed by the necessity of war, of subjecting everything else to the ability to fight. Consequently, as women were not such good fighters as men, they went to the wall. But feudalism never obtained at all in Burma. What fighting they did was far less severe than that of our ancestors, was not the dominant factor in the position, and consequently woman did not suffer.

She has thus been given the inestimable boon of freedom. Freedom from sacerdotal dogma, from secular law, she has always had.

And so, in order to preserve the life of the people, it has never been necessary to pass laws treating woman unfairly as regards inheritance; and as religion has left her free to find her own position, so has the law of the land.

And yet the Burman man has a confirmed opinion that he is better than a woman, that men are on the whole superior as a sex to women. 'We may be inferior in some ways,' he will tell you. 'A woman may steal a march on us here and there, but in the long-run the man will always win. Women have no patience.'

I have heard this said over and over again, even by women, that they have less patience than a man. We have often supposed differently. Some Burmans have even supposed that a woman must be reincarnated as a man to gain a step in holiness. I do not mean that they think men are always better than women, but that the best men are far better than the best women, and there are many more of them. However all this may be, it is only an opinion. Neither in their law, nor in their religion, nor—what is far more important—in their daily life, do they acknowledge any inferiority in women beyond those patent weaknesses of body that are, perhaps, more differences than inferiorities.

And so she has always had fair-play, from religion, from law, and from her fellow man and woman.

She has been bound by no ties, she has had perfect freedom to make for herself just such a life as she thinks best fitted for her. She has had no frozen ideals of a long dead past held up to her as eternal copies. She has been allowed to change as her world changed, and she has lived in a very real world—a world of stern facts, not fancies. You see, she has had to fight her own way; for the same laws that made woman lower than man in Europe compensated her to a certain extent by protection and guidance. In Burma she has been neither confined nor guided. In Europe and India for very long the idea was to make woman a hot-house plant, to see that no rough winds struck her, that no injuries overtook her. In Burma she has had to look out for herself: she has had freedom to come to grief as well as to come to strength. You see, all such laws cut both ways. Freedom to do ill must accompany freedom to do well. You cannot have one without the other. The Burmese woman has had both. Ideals act for good as well as for evil; if they cramp all progress, they nevertheless tend to the sustentation of a certain level of thought. She has had none. Whatever she is, she has made herself, finding under the varying circumstances of life what is the best for her; and as her surroundings change, so will she. What she was a thousand years ago I do not care, what she may be a thousand years hence I do not know; it is of what she is to-day that I have tried to know and write.

Children in Burma have, I think, a very good time when they are young. Parentage in Burma has never degenerated into a sort of slavery. It has never been supposed that gaiety and goodness are opposed. And so they grow up little merry naked things, sprawling in the dust of the gardens, sleeping in the sun with their arms round the village dogs, very sedate, very humorous, very rarely crying. Boys and girls when they are babies grow up together, but with the schooldays comes a division. All the boys go to school at the monastery without the walls, and there learn in noisy fashion their arithmetic, letters, and other useful knowledge. But little girls have nowhere to go. They cannot go to the monasteries, these are for boys alone, and the nunneries are very scarce. For twenty monasteries there is not one nunnery. Women do not seem to care to learn to become nuns as men do to become monks. Why this is so I cannot tell, but there is no doubt of the fact. And so there are no schools for girls as there are for boys, and consequently the girls are not well educated as a rule. In great towns there are, of course, regular schools for girls, generally for girls and boys together; but in the villages these very seldom exist. The girls may learn from their mothers how to read and write, but most of them cannot do so. It is an exception in country places to find a girl who can read, as it is to find a boy who cannot. If there were more nunneries, there would be more education among the women; here is cause and effect. But there are not, so the little girls work instead. While their brothers are in the monasteries, the girls are learning to weave and herd cattle, drawing water, and collecting firewood. They begin very young at this work, but it is very light; they are never overworked, and so it does them no harm usually, but good.

The daughters of better-class people, such as merchants, and clerks, and advocates, do not, of course, work at field labour. They usually learn to read and write at home, and they weave, and many will draw water. For to draw water is to go to the well, and the well is the great meeting-place of the village. As they fill their jars they lean over the curb and talk, and it is here that is told the latest news, the latest flirtation, the little scandal of the place. Very few men or boys come for water; carrying is not their duty, and there is a proper place for flirtation. So the girls have the well almost to themselves.

Almost every girl can weave. In many houses there are looms where the girls weave their dresses and those of their parents; and many girls have stalls in the bazaar. Of this I will speak later. Other duties are the husking of rice and the making of cheroots. Of course, in richer households there will be servants to do all this; but even in them the daughter will frequently weave either for herself or her parents. Almost every girl will do something, if only to pass the time.

You see, they have no accomplishments. They do not sing, nor play, nor paint. It must never be forgotten that their civilization is relatively a thousand years behind ours. Accomplishments are part of the polish that a civilization gives, and this they have not yet reached. Accomplishments are also the means to fill up time otherwise unoccupied; but very few Burmese girls have any time on their hands. There is no leisured class, and there are very few girls who have not to help, in one way or another, at the upkeep of the household.

Mr. Rudyard Kipling tells of an astonishing young lady who played the banjo. He has been more fortunate than myself, for I have never had such good luck. They have no accomplishments at all. Housekeeping they have not very much of. You see, houses are small, and households also are small; there is very little furniture; and as the cooking is all the same, there is not much to learn in that way. I fear, too, that their houses could not compete as models of neatness with any other nation. Tidiness is one of the last gifts of civilization. We now pride ourselves on our order; we forget how very recent an accomplishment it is. To them it will come with the other gifts of age, for it must never be forgotten that they are a very young people—only children, big children—learning very slowly the lessons of experience and knowledge.

When they are between eight and fourteen years of age the boys become monks for a time, as every boy must, and they have a great festival at their entrance into the monastery. Girls do not enter nunneries, but they, too, have a great feast in their honour. They have their ears bored. It is a festival for a girl of great importance, this ear-boring, and, according to the wealth of the parents, it is accompanied by pwès and other rejoicings.

A little girl, the daughter of a shopkeeper here in this town, had her ears bored the other day, and there were great rejoicings. There was a pwè open to all for three nights, and there were great quantities of food, and sweets, and many presents given away, and on the last night the river was illuminated. There was a boat anchored in mid-stream, and from this were launched myriads of tiny rafts, each with a little lamp on board. The lamps gleamed bright with golden light as they drifted on the bosom of the great water, a moving line of living fire. There were little boats, too, with the outlines marked with lamps, and there were pagodas and miniature houses all floating, floating down the river, till, in far distance by the promontory, the lamps flickered out one by one, and the river fell asleep again.

'There is only one great festival in a girl's life,' a woman told me. 'We try to make it as good as we can. Boys have many festivals, girls have but one. It is only just that it should be good.'

And so they grow up very quiet, very sedate, looking on the world about them with very clear eyes. It is strange, talking to Burmese girls, to see how much they know and understand of the world about them. It is to them no great mystery, full of unimaginable good and evil, but a world that they are learning to understand, and where good and evil are never unmixed. Men are to them neither angels nor devils, but just men, and so the world does not hold for them the disappointments, the disillusionings, that await those who do not know. They have their dreams—who shall doubt it?—dreams of him who shall love them, whom they shall love, who shall make life one great glory to them; but their dreams are dreams that can come true. They do not frame to themselves ideals out of their own ignorance and imagine these to be good, but they keep their eyes wide open to the far more beautiful realities that are around them every day. They know that a living lover is greater, and truer, and better than any ideal of a girl's dream. They live in a real world, and they know that it is good.

In time the lover comes. There is a delightful custom all through Burma, an institution, in fact, called 'courting-time.' It is from nine till ten o'clock, more especially on moonlight nights, those wonderful tropic nights, when the whole world lies in a silver dream, when the little wandering airs that touch your cheek like a caress are heavy with the scent of flowers, and your heart comes into your throat for the very beauty of life.

There is in front of every house a veranda, raised perhaps three feet from the ground, and there the girl will sit in the shadow of the eaves, sometimes with a friend, but usually alone; and her suitors will come and stand by the veranda, and talk softly in little broken sentences, as lovers do. There maybe be many young men come, one by one, if they mean business, with a friend if it be merely a visit of courtesy. And the girl will receive them all, and will talk to them all; will laugh with a little humorous knowledge of each man's peculiarities; and she may give them cheroots, of her own making; and, for one perhaps, for one, she will light the cheroot herself first, and thus kiss him by proxy.

And is the girl alone? Well, yes. To all intents and purposes she is alone; but there is always someone near, someone within call, for the veranda is free to all. She cannot tell who may come, and some men, as we know, are but wolves in sheep's clothing. Usually marriages are arranged by the parents. Girls are not very different here to elsewhere; they are very biddable, and ready to do what their mothers tell them, ready to believe that it is the best. And so if a lad comes wooing, and can gain the mother's ear, he can usually win the girl's affection, too; but I think there are more exceptions here than elsewhere. Girls are freer; they fall in love of their own accord oftener than elsewhere; they are very impulsive, full of passion. Love is a very serious matter, and they are not trained in self-restraint.

There are very many romances played out every day in the dusk beside the well, in the deep shadows of the palm-groves, in the luminous nights by the river shore—romances that end sometimes well, sometimes in terrible tragedies. For they are a very passionate people; the language is full of little love-songs, songs of a man to a girl, of a girl to a man. 'No girl,' a woman once told me, 'no good, quiet girl would tell a man she loved him first.' It may be so; if this be true, I fear there are many girls here who are not good and quiet. How many romances have I not seen in which the wooing began with the girl, with a little note perhaps, with a flower, with a message sent by someone whom she could trust! Of course many of these turned out well. Parents are good to their children, and if they can, they will give their daughter the husband of her choice. They remember what youth is—nay, they themselves never grow old, I think; they never forget what once was to them now is to their children. So if it be possible all may yet go well. Social differences are not so great as with us, and the barrier is easily overcome. I have often known servants in a house marry the daughters, and be taken into the family; but, of course, sometimes things do not go so smoothly. And then? Well, then there is usually an elopement, and a ten days' scandal; and sometimes, too, there is an elopement for no reason at all save that hot youth cannot abide the necessary delay.

For life is short, and though to-day be to us, who can tell for the morrow? During the full moon there is no night, only a change to silver light from golden; and the forest is full of delight. There are wood-cutters' huts in the ravines where the water falls, soft beds of torn bracken and fragrant grasses where great trees make a shelter from the heat; and for food, that is easily arranged. A basket of rice with a little salt-fish and spices is easily hidden in a favourable place. You only want a jar to cook it, and there is enough for two for a week; or it is brought day by day by some trusted friend to a place previously agreed upon.

All up and down the forest there are flowers for her hair, scarlet dak blossoms and orchid sprays and jasmine stars; and for occupation through the hours each has a new world to explore full of wonderful undreamt-of discoveries, lit with new light and mysterious with roseate shadows, a world of 'beautiful things made new' for those forest children. So that when the confidante, an aunt maybe or a sister, meets them by the sacred fig-tree on the hill, and tells them that all difficulties are removed, and their friends called together for the marriage, can you wonder that it is not without regret that they fare forth from that enchanted land to ordinary life again?

It is, as I have said, not always the man who is the proposer of the flight. Nay, I think indeed that it is usually the girl. 'Men have more patience.'

I had a Burmese servant, a boy, who may have been twenty, and he had been with me a year, and was beginning to be really useful. He had at last grasped the idea that electro-plate should not be cleaned with monkey-brand soap, and he could be trusted not to put up rifle cartridges for use with a double-barrelled gun; and he chose this time to fall in love with the daughter of the headman of a certain village where I was in camp.

He had good excuse, for she was a delicious little maiden with great coils of hair, and the voice of a wood-pigeon cooing in the forest, and she was very fond of him, without a doubt.

So one evening he came to me and said that he must leave me—that he wanted to get married, and could not possibly delay. Then I spoke to him with all that depth of wisdom we are so ready to display for the benefit of others. I pointed out to him that he was much too young, that she was much too young also—she was not eighteen—and that there was absolutely nothing for them to marry on. I further pointed out how ungrateful it would be of him to leave me; that he had been paid regularly for a year, and that it was not right that now, when he was at last able to do something besides destroy my property, he should go away.

The boy listened to all I had to say, and agreed with it all, and made the most fervent and sincere promise to be wise; and he went away after dinner to see the girl and tell her, and when I awoke in the morning my other servants told me the boy had not returned.

Shortly afterwards the headman came to say that his daughter had also disappeared. They had fled, those two, into the forest, and for a week we heard nothing. At last one evening, as I sat under the great fig-tree by my tent, there came to me the mother of the girl, and she sat down before me, and said she had something of great importance to impart: and this was that all had been arranged between the families, who had found work for the boy whereby he might maintain himself and his wife, and the marriage was arranged. But the boy would not return as long as I was in camp there, for he was bitterly ashamed of his broken vows and afraid to meet my anger. And so the mother begged me to go away as soon as I could, that the young couple might return. I explained that I was not angry at all, that the boy could return without any fear; on the contrary, that I should be pleased to see him and his wife. And, at the old lady's request, I wrote a Burmese letter to that effect, and she went away delighted.

They must have been in hiding close by, for it was early next morning that the boy came into my tent alone and very much abashed, and it was some little time before he could recover himself and talk freely as he would before, for he was greatly ashamed of himself.

But, after all, could he help it?

If you can imagine the tropic night, and the boy, full of high resolve, passing up the village street, now half asleep, and the girl, with shining eyes, coming to him out of the hibiscus shadows, and whispering in his ear words—words that I need not say—if you imagine all that, you will understand how it was that I lost my servant.

They both came to see me later on in the day after the marriage, and there was no bashfulness about either of them then. They came hand-in-hand, with the girl's father and mother and some friends, and she told me it was all her fault: she could not wait.

'Perhaps,' she said, with a little laugh and a side-glance at her husband—'perhaps, if he had gone with the thakin to Rangoon, he might have fallen in love with someone there and forgotten me; for I know they are very pretty, those Rangoon ladies, and of better manners than I, who am but a jungle girl.'

And when I asked her what it was like in the forest, she said it was the most beautiful place in all the world.

Things do not always go so well. Parents may be obdurate, and flight be impossible; or even her love may not be returned, and then terrible things happen. I have held, not once nor twice alone, inquests over the bodies, the fair, innocent bodies, of quite young girls who died for love. Only that, because their love was unreturned; and so the sore little heart turned in her trouble to the great river, and gave herself and her hot despair to the cold forgetfulness of its waters.

They love so greatly that they cannot face a world where love is not. All the country is full of the romance of love—of love passionate and great as woman has ever felt. It seems to me here that woman has something of the passions of man, not only the enduring affection of a woman, but the hot love and daring of a man. It is part of their heritage, perhaps, as a people in their youth. One sees so much of it, hears so much of it, here. I have seen a girl in man's attire killed in a surprise attack upon an insurgent camp. She had followed her outlawed lover there, and in the mêlée she caught up sword and gun to fight by his side, and was cut down through neck and shoulder; for no one could tell in the early dawn that it was a girl.

She died about an hour afterwards, and though I have seen many sorrowful things in many lands, in war and out of it, the memory of that dying girl, held up by one of the mounted police, sobbing out her life beneath the wild forest shadow, with no one of her sex, no one of her kin to help her, comes back to me as one of the saddest and strangest.

Her lover was killed in action some time later fighting against us, and he died as a brave man should, his face to his enemy. He played his game, he lost, and paid; but the girl?

I have seen and heard so much of this love of women and of its tragedies. Perhaps it is that to us it is usually the tragedies that are best remembered. Happiness is void of interest. And this love may be, after all, a good thing. But I do not know. Sometimes I think they would be happier if they could love less, if they could take love more quietly, more as a matter of course, as something that has to be gone through, as part of a life's training; not as a thing that swallows up all life and death and eternity in one passion.

In Burmese the love-songs are in a short, sweet rhythm, full of quaint conceits and word-music. I cannot put them into English verse, or give the flow of the originals in a translation. It always seems to me that Don Quixote was right when he said that a translation was like the wrong side of an embroidered cloth, giving the design without the beauty. But even in the plain, rough outline of a translation there is beauty here, I think:

From a Man to a Girl.

The moon wooed the lotus in the night, the lotus was wooed by the moon, and my sweetheart is their child. The blossom opened in the night, and she came forth; the petals moved, and she was born.

She is more beautiful than any blossom; her face is as delicate as the dusk; her hair is as night falling over the hills; her skin is as bright as the diamond. She is very full of health, no sickness can come near her.

When the wind blows I am afraid, when the breezes move I fear. I fear lest the south wind take her, I tremble lest the breath of evening woo her from me—so light is she, so graceful.

Her dress is of gold, even of silk and gold, and her bracelets are of fine gold. She hath precious stones in her ears, but her eyes, what jewels can compare unto them?

She is proud, my mistress; she is very proud, and all men are afraid of her. She is so beautiful and so proud that all men fear her.

In the whole world there is none anywhere that can compare unto her.

CHAPTER XV

WOMEN—II

'The husband is lord of the wife.'

Laws of Manu.

Marriage is not a religious ceremony among the Burmese. Religion has no part in it at all; as religion has refrained from interfering with Government, so does it in the relations of man and wife. Marriage is purely a worldly business, like entering into partnership; and religion, the Buddhist religion, has nothing to do with such things. Those who accept the teachings of the great teacher in all their fulness do not marry.

Indeed, marriage is not a ceremony at all. It is strange to find that the Burmese have actually no necessary ceremonial. The Laws of Manu, which are the laws governing all such matters, make no mention of any marriage ceremony; it is, in fact, a status. Just as two men may go into partnership in business without executing any deed, so a man and a woman may enter into the marriage state without undergoing any form. Amongst the richer Burmese there is, however, sometimes a ceremony.

Friends are called to the wedding, and a ribbon is stretched round the couple, and then their hands are clasped; they also eat out of the same dish. All this is very pretty, but not at all necessary.

It is, indeed, not a settled point in law what constitutes a marriage, but there are certain things that will render it void. For instance, no marriage can be a marriage without the consent of the girl's parents if she be under age, and there are certain other conditions which must be fulfilled.

But although there be this doubt about the actual ceremony of marriage, there is none at all about the status. There is no confusion between a woman who is married and a woman who is not. The condition of marriage is well known, and it brings the parties under the laws that pertain to husband and wife. A woman not married does not, of course, obtain these privileges; there is a very strict line between the two.

Amongst the poorer people a marriage is frequently kept secret for several days. The great pomp and ceremony which with us, and occasionally with a few rich Burmese, consecrate a man and a woman to each other for life, are absent at the greater number of Burmese marriages; and the reason they tell me is that the girl is shy. She does not like to be stared at, and wondered at, as a maiden about to be a wife; it troubles her that the affairs of her heart, her love, her marriage, should be so public. The young men come at night and throw stones upon the house roof, and demand presents from the bridegroom. He does not mind giving the presents; but he, too, does not like the publicity. And so marriage, which is with most people a ceremony performed in full daylight with all accessories of display, is with the Burmese generally a secret. Two or three friends, perhaps, will be called quietly to the house, and the man and woman will eat together, and thus become husband and wife. Then they will separate again, and not for several days, or even weeks perhaps, will it be known that they are married; for it is seldom that they can set up house for themselves just at once. Often they will marry and live apart for a time with their parents. Sometimes they will go and live together with the man's parents, but more usually with the girl's mother. Then after a time, when they have by their exertions made a little money, they build a house and go to live there; but sometimes they will live on with the girl's parents for years.

A girl does not change her name when she marries, nor does she wear any sign of marriage, such as a ring. Her name is always the same, and there is nothing to a stranger to denote whether she be married or not, or whose wife she is; and she keeps her property as her own. Marriage does not confer upon the husband any power over his wife's property, either what she brings with her, what she earns, or what she inherits subsequently; it all remains her own, as does his remain his own. But usually property acquired after marriage is held jointly. You will inquire, for instance, who is the owner of this garden, and be told Maung Han, Ma Shwè, the former being the husband's name and the latter the wife's. Both names are used very frequently in business and in legal proceedings, and indeed it is usual for both husband and wife to sign all deeds they may have occasion to execute. Nothing more free than a woman's position in the marriage state can be imagined. By law she is absolutely the mistress of her own property and her own self; and if it usually happens that the husband is the head of the house, that is because his nature gives him that position, not any law.

With us marriage means to a girl an utter breaking of her old ties, the beginning of a new life, of new duties, of new responsibilities. She goes out into a new and unknown world, full of strange facts, leaving one dependence for another, the shelter of a father for the shelter of a husband. She has even lost her own name, and becomes known but as the mistress of her husband; her soul is merged in his. But in Burma it is not so at all. She is still herself, still mistress of herself, an equal partner for life.

I have said that the Burmese have no ideals, and this is true; but in the Laws of Manu there are laid down some of the requisite qualities for a perfect wife. There are seven kinds of wife, say the Laws of Manu: a wife like a thief, like an enemy, like a master, like a friend, like a sister, like a mother, like a slave. The last four of these are good, but the last is the best, and these are some of her qualities:

'She should fan and soothe her master to sleep, and sit by him near the bed on which he lies. She will fear and watch lest anything should disturb him. Every noise will be a terror to her; the hum of a mosquito as the blast of a trumpet; the fall of a leaf without will sound as loud as thunder. Even she will guard her breath as it passes her lips to and fro, lest she awaken him whom she fears.

'And she will remember that when he awakens he will have certain wants. She will be anxious that the bath be to his custom, that his clothes are as he wishes, that his food is tasteful to him. Always she will have before her the fear of his anger.'

It must be remembered that the Laws of Manu are of Indian origin, and are not totally accepted by the Burmese. I fear a Burmese girl would laugh at this ideal of a wife. She would say that if a wife were always afraid of her husband's wrath, she and he, too, must be poor things. A household is ruled by love and reverence, not by fear. A girl has no idea when she marries that she is going to be her husband's slave, but a free woman, yielding to him in those things in which he has most strength, and taking her own way in those things that pertain to a woman. She has a very keen idea of what things she can do best, and what things she should leave to her husband. Long experience has taught her that there are many things she should not interfere with; and she knows it is experience that has proved it, and not any command. She knows that the reason women are not supposed to interfere in public affairs is because their minds and bodies are not fitted for them. Therefore she accepts this, in the same way as she accepts physical inferiority, as a fact against which it is useless and silly to declaim, knowing that it is not men who keep her out, but her own unfitness. Moreover, she knows that it is made good to her in other ways, and thus the balance is redressed. You see, she knows her own strength and her own weakness. Can there be a more valuable knowledge for anyone than this?

In many ways she will act for her husband with vigour and address, and she is not afraid of appearing in his name or her own in law courts, for instance, or in transacting certain kinds of business. She knows that she can do certain business as well as or better than her husband, and she does it. There is nothing more remarkable than the way in which she makes a division of these matters in which she can act for herself, and those in which, if she act at all, it is for her husband.

Thus, as I have said, she will, as regards her own property or her own business, act freely in her own name, and will also frequently act for her husband too. They will both sign deeds, borrow money on joint security, lend money repayable to them jointly. But in public affairs she will never allow her name to appear at all. Not that she does not take a keen interest in such things. She lives in no world apart; all that affects her husband interests her as keenly as it does him. She lives in a world of men and women, and her knowledge of public affairs, and her desire and powers of influencing them, is great. But she learnt long ago that her best way is to act through and by her husband, and that his strength and his name are her bucklers in the fight. Thus women are never openly concerned in any political matters. How strong their feeling is can better be illustrated by a story than in any other way.

In 1889 I was stationed far away on the north-west frontier of Burma, in charge of some four thousand square miles of territory which had been newly incorporated. I went up there with the first column that ever penetrated that country, and I remained there when, after the partial pacification of the district, the main body of the troops were withdrawn. It was a fairly exciting place to live in. To say nothing of the fever which swept down men in batches, and the trans-frontier people who were always peeping over to watch a good opportunity for a raid, my own charge simply swarmed with armed men, who seemed to rise out of the very ground—so hard was it to follow their movements—attack anywhere they saw fit, and disappear as suddenly. There was, of course, a considerable force of troops and police to suppress these insurgents, but the whole country was so roadless, so unexplored, such a tangled labyrinth of hill and forest, dotted with sparse villages, that it was often quite impossible to trace the bands who committed these attacks; and to the sick and weary pursuers it sometimes seemed as if we should never restore peace to the country.

The villages were arranged in groups, and over each group there was a headman with certain powers and certain duties, the principal of the latter being to keep his people quiet, and, if possible, protect them from insurgents.

Now, it happened that among these headmen was one named Saw Ka, who had been a free-lance in his day, but whose services were now enlisted on the side of order—or, at least, we hoped so. He was a fighting-man, and rather fond of that sort of exercise; so that I was not much surprised one day when I got a letter from him to say that his villagers had pursued and arrested, after a fight, a number of armed robbers, who had tried to lift some of the village cattle. The letter came to me when I was in my court-house, a tent ten feet by eight, trying a case. So, saying I would see Saw Ka's people later, and giving orders for the prisoners to be put in the lock-up, I went on with my work. When my case was finished, I happened to notice that among those sitting and waiting without my tent-door was Saw Ka himself, so I sent to call him in, and I complimented him upon his success. 'It shall be reported,' I said, 'to the Commissioner, who will, no doubt, reward you for your care and diligence in the public service.'

As I talked I noticed that the man seemed rather bewildered, and when I had finished he said that he really did not understand. He was aware, he added modestly, that he was a diligent headman, always active in good deeds, and a terror to dacoits and other evil-doers; but as to these particular robbers and this fighting he was a little puzzled.

I was considerably surprised, naturally, and I took from the table the Burmese letter describing the affair. It began, 'Your honour, I, Maung Saw Ka, headman,' etc., and was in the usual style. I handed it to Saw Ka, and told him to read it. As he read, his wicked black eyes twinkled, and when he had finished he said he had not been home for a week.

'I came in from a visit to the river,' he said, 'where I have gathered for your honour some private information. I had not been here five minutes before I was called in. All this the letter speaks of is news to me, and must have happened while I was away.'

'Then, who wrote the letter?' I asked.

'Ah!' he said, 'I think I know; but I will go and make sure.'

Then Saw Ka went to find the guard who had come in with the prisoners, and I dissolved court and went out shooting. After dinner, as we sat round a great bonfire before the mess, for the nights were cold, Saw Ka and his brother came to me, and they sat down beside the fire and told me all about it.

It appeared that three days after Saw Ka left his village, some robbers came suddenly one evening to a small hamlet some two miles away and looted from there all the cattle, thirty or forty head, and went off with them. The frightened owners came in to tell the headman about it, and in his absence they told his wife. And she, by virtue of the order of appointment as headman, which was in her hands, ordered the villagers to turn out and follow the dacoits. She issued such government arms as she had in the house, and the villagers went and pursued the dacoits by the cattle tracks, and next day they overtook them, and there was a fight. When the villagers returned with the cattle and the thieves, she had the letter written to me, and the prisoners were sent in, under her husband's brother, with an escort. Everything was done as well, as successfully, as if Saw Ka himself had been present. But if it had not been for the accident of Saw Ka's sudden appearance, I should probably never have known that this exploit was due to his wife; for she was acting for her husband, and she would not have been pleased that her name should appear.

'A good wife,' I said to Saw Ka.

'Like many,' he answered.

But in her own line she has no objection to publicity. I have said that nearly all women work, and that is so. Married or unmarried, from the age of sixteen or seventeen, almost every woman has some occupation besides her own duties. In the higher classes she will have property of her own to manage; in the lower classes she will have some trade. I cannot find that in Burma there have ever been certain occupations told off for women in which they may work, and others tabooed to them. As there is no caste for the men, so there is none for the women. They have been free to try their hands at anything they thought they could excel in, without any fear of public opinion. But nevertheless, as is inevitable, it has been found that there are certain trades in which women can compete successfully with men, and certain others in which they cannot. And these are not quite the same as in the West. We usually consider sewing to be a feminine occupation. In Burma, there being no elaborately cut and trimmed garments, the amount of sewing done is small, but that is usually done by men. Women often own and use small hand-machines, but the treadles are always used by men only. As I am writing, my Burmese orderly is sitting in the garden sewing his jacket. He is usually sewing when not sent on messages. He seems to sew very well.

Weaving is usually done by women. Under nearly every house there will be a loom, where the wife or daughter weaves for herself or for sale. But many men weave also, and the finest silks are all woven by men. I once asked a woman why they did not weave the best silks, instead of leaving them all to the men.

'Men do them better,' she said, with a laugh. 'I tried once, but I cannot manage that embroidery.'

They also work in the fields—light work, such as weeding and planting. The heavy work, such as ploughing, is done by men. They also work on the roads carrying things, as all Oriental women do. It is curious that women carry always on their heads, men always on their shoulders. I do not know why.

But the great occupation of women is petty trading. I have already said that there are few large merchants among the Burmese. Nearly all the retail trade is small, most of it is very small indeed, and practically the whole of it is in the hands of the women.

Women do not often succeed in any wholesale trade. They have not, I think, a wide enough grasp of affairs for that. Their views are always somewhat limited; they are too pennywise and pound-foolish for big businesses. The small retail trade, gaining a penny here and a penny there, just suits them, and they have almost made it a close profession.

This trade is almost exclusively done in bazaars. In every town there is a bazaar, from six till ten each morning. When there is no town near, the bazaar will be held on one day at one village and on another at a neighbouring one. It depends on the density of population, the means of communication, and other matters. But a bazaar within reach there must always be, for it is only there that most articles can be bought. The bazaar is usually held in a public building erected for the purpose, and this may vary from a great market built of brick and iron to a small thatched shed. Sometimes, indeed, there is no building at all, merely a space of beaten ground.

The great bazaar in Mandalay is one of the sights of the city. The building in which it is held is the property of the municipality, but is leased out. It is a series of enormous sheds, with iron roofs and beaten earth floor. Each trade has a shed or sheds to itself. There is a place for rice-sellers, for butchers, for vegetable-sellers, for the vendors of silks, of cottons, of sugars and spices, of firewood, of jars, of fish. The butchers are all natives of India. I have explained elsewhere why this should be. The firewood-sellers will mostly be men, as will also the large rice-merchants, but nearly all the rest are women.

You will find the sellers of spices, fruit, vegetables, and other such matters seated in long rows, on mats placed upon the ground. Each will have a square of space allotted, perhaps six feet square, and there she will sit with her merchandise in a basket or baskets before her. For each square they will pay the lessee a halfpenny for the day, which is only three hours or so. The time to go is in the morning from six till eight, for that is the busy time. Later on all the stalls will be closed, but in the early morning the market is thronged. Every householder is then buying his or her provisions for the day, and the people crowd in thousands round the sellers. Everyone is bargaining and chaffing and laughing, both buyers and sellers; but both are very keen, too, on business.

The cloth and silk sellers, the large rice-merchants, and a few other traders, cannot carry on business sitting on a mat, nor can they carry their wares to and fro every day in a basket. For such there are separate buildings or separate aisles, with wooden stalls, on either side of a gangway. The wooden floor of the stalls is raised two to three feet, so that the buyer, standing on the ground, is about on a level with the seller sitting in the stall. The stall will be about eight feet by ten, and each has at the back a strong lock-up cupboard or wardrobe, where the wares are shut at night; but in the day they will be taken out and arranged daintily about the girl-seller. Home-made silks are the staple—silks in checks of pink and white, of yellow and orange, of indigo and dark red. Some are embroidered in silk, in silver, or in gold; some are plain. All are thick and rich, none are glazed, and none are gaudy. There will also be silks from Bangkok, which are of two colours—purple shot with red, and orange shot with red, both very beautiful. All the silks are woven the size of the dress: for men, about twenty-eight feet long and twenty inches broad; and for women, about five feet long and much broader. Thus, there is no cutting off the piece. The *anas*, too, which are the bottom pieces for a woman's dress, are woven the proper size. There will probably, too, be piles of showy cambric jackets and gauzy silk handkerchiefs; but often these are sold at separate stalls.

But prettier than the silks are the sellers, for these are nearly all girls and women, sweet and fresh in their white jackets, with flowers in their hair. And they are all delighted to talk to you and show you their goods, even if you do not buy; and they will take a compliment sedately, as a girl should, and they will probably charge you an extra rupee for it when you come to pay for your purchases. So it is never wise for a man, unless he have a heart of stone, to go marketing for silks. He should always ask a lady friend to go with him and do the bargaining, and he will lose no courtesy thereby, for these women know how to be courteous to fellow-women as well as to fellow-men.

In the provincial bazaars it is much the same. There may be a few travelling merchants from Rangoon or Mandalay, most of whom are men; but nearly all the retailers are women. Indeed, speaking broadly, it may be said that the retail trade of the country is in the hands of the women, and they nearly all trade on their own account. Just as the men farm their own land, the women own their businesses. They are not saleswomen for others, but traders on their own account; and with the exception of the silk and cloth branches of the trade, it does not interfere with home-life. The bazaar lasts but three hours, and a woman has ample time for her home duties when her daily visit to the bazaar is over; she is never kept away all day in shops and factories.

Her home-life is always the centre of her life; she could not neglect it for any other: it would seem to her a losing of the greater in the less. But the effect of this custom of nearly every woman having a little business of her own has a great influence on her life. It broadens her views; it teaches her things she could not learn in the narrow circle of home duties; it gives her that tolerance and understanding which so forcibly strikes everyone who knows her. It teaches her to know her own strength and weakness, and how to make the best of each. Above all, by showing her the real life about her, and how much beauty there is everywhere, to those whose eyes are not shut by conventions, it saves her from that dreary, weary pessimism that seeks its relief in fancied idealism, in a smattering of art, of literature, or of religion, and which is the curse of so many of her sisters in other lands.

And yet, with all their freedom, Burmese women are very particular in their conduct. Do not imagine that young girls are allowed, or allow themselves, to go about alone except on very frequented roads. I suppose there are certain limits in all countries to the freedom a woman allows herself, that is to say, if she is wise. For she knows that she cannot always trust herself; she knows that she is weak sometimes, and she protects herself accordingly. She is timid, with a delightful timidity that fears, because it half understands; she is brave, with the bravery of a girl who knows that as long as she keeps within certain limits she is safe. Do not suppose that they ever do, or ever can, allow themselves that freedom of action that men have; it is an impossibility. Girls are very carefully looked after by their mothers, and wives by their husbands; and they delight in observing the limits which experience has indicated to them. There is a funny story which will illustrate what I mean. A great friend of mine, an officer in Government service, went home not very long ago and married, and came out again to Burma with his wife. They settled down in a little up-country station. His duties were such as obliged him to go very frequently on tour far away from his home, and he would be absent ten days at a time or more. So when it came for the first time that he was obliged to go out and leave his wife behind him alone in the house, he gave his head-servant very careful directions. This servant was a Burman who had been with him for many years, who knew all his ways, and who was a very good servant. He did not speak English; and my friend gave him strict orders.

'The mistress,' he said, 'has only just come here to Burma, and she does not know the ways of the country, nor what to do. So you must see that no harm comes to her in any way while I am in the jungle.'

Then he gave directions as to what was to be done in any eventuality, and he went out.

He was away for about a fortnight, and when he returned he found all well. The house had not caught fire, nor had thieves stolen anything, nor had there been any difficulty at all. The servant had looked after the other servants well, and my friend was well pleased. But his wife complained.

'It has been very dull,' she said, 'while you were away. No one came to see me; of all the officers here, not one ever called. I saw only two or three ladies, but not a man at all.'

And my friend, surprised, asked his servant how it was.

'Didn't anyone come to call?' he asked.

'Oh yes,' the servant answered; 'many gentlemen came to call—the officers of the regiment and others. But I told them the thakin was out, and that the thakinma could not see anyone. I sent them all away.'

At the club that evening my friend was questioned as to why in his absence no one was allowed to see his wife. The whole station laughed at him, but I think he and his wife laughed most of all at the careful observances of Burmese etiquette by the servant; for it is the Burmese custom for a wife not to receive in her husband's absence. Anyone who wants to see her must stay outside or in the veranda, and she will come out and speak to him. It would be a grave breach of decorum to receive visitors while her husband is out.

So even a Burmese woman is not free from restrictions—restrictions which are merely rules founded upon experience. No woman, no man, can ever free herself or himself from the bonds that even a young civilization demands. A freedom from all restraint would be a return, not only to savagery, but to the condition of animals—nay, even animals are bound by certain conventions.

The higher a civilization, the more conventions are required; and freedom does not mean an absence of all rules, but that all rules should be founded on experience and common-sense.

There are certain restrictions on a woman's actions which must be observed as long as men are men and women women. That the Burmese woman never recognises them unless they are necessary, and then accepts the necessity as a necessity, is the fact wherein her freedom lies. If at any time she should recognise that a restriction was unnecessary, she would reject it. If experience told her further restrictions were required, she would accept them without a doubt.

CHAPTER XVI

WOMEN—III

'For women are very tender-hearted.'

Wethandaya.

'You know, thakin,' said a man to me, 'that we say sometimes that women cannot attain unto the great deliverance, that only men will come there. We think that a woman must be born again as a man before she can enter upon the way that leads to heaven.'

'Why should that be so?' I asked. 'I have looked at the life of the Buddha, I have read the sacred books, and I can find nothing about it. What makes you think that?'

He explained it in this way: 'Before a soul can attain deliverance it must renounce the world, it must have purified itself by wisdom and meditation from all the lust of the flesh. Only those who have done this can enter into the Great Peace. Many men do this. The country is full of monks, men who have left the world, and are trying to follow in the path of the great teacher. Not all these will immediately attain to heaven, for purification is a very long process; but they have entered into the path, they have seen the light, if it be even a long way off yet. They know whither they would go. But women, see how few become nuns! Only those who have suffered such shipwreck in life that this world holds nothing more for them worth having become nuns. And they are very few. For a hundred monks there is not one nun. Women are too attached to their home, to their fathers, their husbands, their children, to enter into the holy life; and, therefore, how shall they come to heaven except they return as men? Our teacher says nothing about it, but we have eyes, and we can see.'

All this is true. Women have no desire for the holy life. They cannot tear themselves away from their home-life. If their passions are less than those of men, they have even less command over them than men have. Only the profoundest despair will drive a woman to a renunciation of the world. If on an average their lives are purer than those of men, they cannot rise to the heights to which men can. How many monks there are—how few nuns! Not one to a hundred.

Yet in some ways women are far more religious than men. If you go to the golden pagoda on the hilltop and count the people kneeling there doing honour to the teacher, you will find they are nearly all women. If you go to the rest-houses by the monastery, where the monks recite the law on Sundays, you will find that the congregations are nearly all women. If you visit the monastery without the gate, you will see many visitors bringing little presents, and they will be women.

'Thakin, many men do not care for religion at all, but when a man does do so, he takes it very seriously. He follows it out to the end. He becomes a monk, and surrenders the whole world. But with women it is different. Many women, nearly all women, will like religion, and none will take it seriously. We mix it up with our home-life, and our affections, and our worldly doings; for we like a little of everything.' So said a woman to me.

Is this always true? I do not know, but it is very true in Burma. Nearly all the women are religious, they like to go to the monastery and hear the law, they like to give presents to the monks, they like to visit the pagoda and adore Gaudama the Buddha. I am sure that if it were not for their influence the laws against taking life and against intoxicants would not be observed as stringently as they are. So far they will go. As far as they can use the precepts of religion and retain their home-life they will do so; as it was with Yathodaya so long ago, so it is now. But when religion calls them and says, 'Come away from the world, leave all that you love, all that your heart holds good, for it is naught; see the light, and prepare your soul for peace,' they hold back. This they cannot do; it is far beyond them. 'Thakin, we *cannot do so*. It would seem to us terrible,' that is what they say.

A man who renounces the world is called 'the great glory,' but not so a woman.

I have said that the Buddhist religion holds men and women as equal. If women can observe its laws as men do, it is surely their own fault if they be held the less worthy.

Women themselves admit this. They honour a man greatly who becomes a monk, not so a nun. Nuns have but little consideration. And why? Because what is good for a man is not good for a woman; and if, indeed, renunciation of the world be the only path to the Great Peace, then surely it must be true that women must be born again.

CHAPTER XVII

DIVORCE

'They are to each other as a burning poison falling into a man's eye.'—*Burmese saying.*

I remember a night not so long ago; it was in the hot weather, and I was out in camp with my friend the police-officer. It was past sunset, and the air beneath the trees was full of luminous gloom, though overhead a flush still lingered on the cheek of the night. We were sitting in the veranda of a Government rest-house, enjoying the first coolness of the coming night, and talking in disjointed sentences of many things; and there came up the steps of the house into the veranda a woman. She came forward slowly, and then sat down on the floor beside my friend, and began to speak. There was a lamp burning in an inner room, and a long bar of light came through the door and lit her face. I could see she was not good-looking, but that her eyes were full of tears, and her face drawn with trouble. I recognised who she was, the wife of the head-constable in charge of the guard near by, a woman I had noticed once or twice in the guard.

She spoke so fast, so fast; the words fell over each other as they came from her lips, for her heart was very full.

I sat quite still and said nothing; I think she hardly noticed I was there. It was all about her husband. Everything was wrong; all had gone crooked in their lives, and she did not know what she could do. At first she could hardly tell what it was all about, but at last she explained. For some years, three or four years, matters had not been very smooth between them. They had quarrelled often, she said, about this thing and the other, little things mostly; and gradually the rift had widened till it became very broad indeed.

'Perhaps,' she said, 'if I had been able to have a child it would have been different.' But fate was unkind and no baby came, and her husband became more and more angry with her. 'And yet I did all for the best, thakin; I always tried to act for the best. My husband has sisters at Henzada, and they write to him now and then, and say, "Send ten rupees," or "Send five rupees," or even twenty rupees. And I always say, "Send, send." Other wives would say, "No, we cannot afford it;" but I said always, "Send, send." I have always done for the best, always for the best.'

It was very pitiable to hear her opening her whole heart, such a sore troubled heart, like this. Her words were full of pathos; her uncomely face was not beautified by the sorrow in it. And at last her husband took a second wife.

'She is a girl from a village near; the thakin knows, Taungywa. He did not tell me, but I soon heard of it; and although I thought my heart would break, I did not say anything. I told my husband, "Bring her here, let us live all together; it will be best so." I always did for the best, thakin. So he brought her, and she came to live with us a week ago. Ah, thakin, I did not know! She tramples on me. My head is under her feet. My husband does not care for me, only for her. And to-day, this evening, they went out together for a walk, and my husband took with him the concertina. As they went I could hear him play upon it, and they walked down through the trees, he playing and she leaning upon him. I heard the music.'

Then she began to cry bitterly, sobbing as if her heart would break. The sunset died out of the sky, and the shadows took all the world and made it gray and dark. No one said anything, only the woman cried.

'Thakin,' she said at last, 'what am I to do? Tell me.'

Then my friend spoke.

'You can divorce him,' he said; 'you can go to the elders and get a divorce. Won't that be best?'

'But, thakin, you do not know. We are both Christians; we are married for ever. We were both at the mission-school in Rangoon, and we were married there, "for ever and for ever," so the padre said. We are not married according to Burmese customs, but according to your religion; we are husband and wife for ever.'

My friend said nothing. It seemed to him useless to speak to her of the High Court, five hundred miles away, and a decree nisi; it would have been a mockery of her trouble.

'Your husband had no right to take a second wife, if you are Christians and married,' he said.

'Ah,' she answered, 'we are Burmans; it is allowed by Burmese law. Other officials do it. What does my husband care that we were married by your law? Here we are alone with no other Christians near. But I would not mind so much,' she went on, 'only she treads me under her feet. And he takes her out and not me, who am the elder wife, and he plays music to her; and I did all for the best. This trouble has come upon me, though all my life I have acted for the best.'

There came another footstep up the stair, and a man entered. It was her husband. On his return he had missed his wife, and guessed whither she had gone, and had followed her. He came alone.

Then there was a sad scene, only restrained by respect for my friend. I need not tell it. There was a man's side to the question, a strong one. The wife had a terrible temper, a peevish, nagging, maddening fashion of talking. She was a woman very hard for a man to live with.

Does it matter much which was right or wrong, now that the mischief was done? They went away at last, not reconciled. Could they be reconciled? I cannot tell. I left there next day, and have never returned.

There they had lived for many years among their own people, far away from the influence that had come upon their childhood, and led them into strange ways. And now all that was left of that influence was the chain that bound them together. Had it not been for that they would have been divorced long ago; for they had never agreed very well, and both sides had bitter grounds for complaint. They would have been divorced, and both could have gone their own way. But now, what was to be done?

That is one of my memories: this is another.

There was a girl I knew, the daughter of a man who had made some money by trading, and when the father died the property was divided according to law between the girl and her brother. She was a little heiress in her way, owning a garden, where grew many fruit-trees, and a piece of rice land. She had also a share in a little shop which she managed, and she had many gold bracelets and fine diamond earrings. She was much wooed by the young men about there, and at last she married. He was a young man, good-looking, a sergeant of police, and for a time they were very happy. And then trouble came. The husband took to bad ways. The knowledge that he could get money for nothing was too much for him. He drank and he wasted her money, and he neglected his work, and at last he was dismissed from Government employ. And his wife got angry with him, and complained of him to the neighbours; and made him worse, though she was at heart a good girl. Quickly he went from bad to worse, until in a very short time, six months, I think, he had spent half her little fortune. Then she began to limit supplies—the husband did no work at all—and in consequence he began to neglect her; they had many quarrels, and her tongue was sharp, and matters got worse and worse until they were the talk of the village. All attempts of the headman and elders to restrain him were useless. He became quarrelsome, and went on from one thing to another, until at last he was suspected of being concerned in a crime. So then when all means had failed to restore her husband to her, when they had drifted far apart and there was nothing before them but trouble, she went to the elders of the village and demanded a divorce. And the elders granted it to her. Her husband objected; he did not want to be divorced. He claimed this, and he claimed that, but it was all of no use. So the tie that had united them was dissolved, as the love had been dissolved long before, and they parted. The man went away to Lower Burma.

They tell me he has become a cultivator and has reformed, and is doing well; and the girl is ready to marry again. Half her property is gone, but half remains, and she has still her little business. I think they will both do well. But if they had been chained together, what then?

In Burma divorce is free. Anyone can obtain it by appearing before the elders of the village and demanding it. A writing of divorcement is made out, and the parties are free. Each retains his or her own property, and that earned during marriage is divided; only that the party claiming the divorce has to leave the house to the other—that is the only penalty, and it is not always enforced, unless the house be joint property.

As religion has nothing to do with marriage, neither has it with divorce. Marriage is a status, a partnership, nothing more. But it is all that. Divorce is a dissolution of that partnership. A Burman would not ask, 'Were they married?' but, 'Are they man and wife?' And so with divorce, it is a cessation of the state of marriage.

Elders tell me that women ask for divorce far more than men do. 'Men have patience, and women have not,' that is what they say. For every little quarrel a woman will want a divorce. 'Thakin, if we were to grant divorces every time a woman came and demanded it, we should be doing nothing else all day long. If a husband comes home to find dinner not cooked, and speaks angrily, his wife will rush to us in tears for a divorce. If he speaks to another woman and smiles, if he does not give his wife a new dress, if he be fond of going out in the evenings, all these are reasons for a breathless demand for a divorce. The wives get cross and run to us and cry, "My husband has been angry with me. Never will I live with him again. Give me a divorce." Or, "See my clothes, how old they are. I cannot buy any new dress. I will have a divorce." And we say, "Yes, yes; it is very sad. Of course, you must have a divorce; but we cannot give you one to-night. Go away, and come again in three days or in four days, when we have more time." They go away, thakin, and they do not return. Next day it is all forgotten. You see, they don't know what they want; they turn with the wind—they have no patience.'

Yet sometimes they repent too late. Here is another of my memories about divorce:

There was a man and his wife, cultivators, living in a small village. The land that he cultivated belonged to his wife, for she had inherited it from her father, together with a house and a little money. The man had nothing when he married her, but he was hardworking and honest and good-tempered, and they kept themselves going comfortably enough. But he had one fault: every now and then he would drink too much. This was in Lower Burma, where liquor shops are free to Burmans. In Upper Burma no liquor can be sold to them. He did not drink often. He was a teetotaler generally; but once a month, or once in two months, he would meet some friends, and they would drink in good fellowship, and he would return home drunk. His wife felt this very bitterly, and when he would come into the house, his eyes red and his face swollen, she would attack him with bitter words, as women do. She would upbraid him for his conduct, she would point at him the finger of scorn, she would tell him in biting words that he was drinking the produce of her fields, of her inheritance; she would even impute to him, in her passion, worse things than these, things that were not true. And the husband was usually good-natured, and admitted his wrong, and put up with all her abuse, and they lived more or less happily till the next time.

And after this had been going on for a few years, instead of getting accustomed to her husband, instead of seeing that if he had this fault he had many virtues, and that he was just as good a husband as she was a wife, or perhaps better, her anger against him increased every time, till now she would declare that she would abide it no longer, that he was past endurance, and she would have a divorce; and several times she even ran to the elders to demand it. But the elders would put it by. 'Let it wait,' they said, 'for a few days, and then we will see;' and by that time all was soothed down again. But at last the end came. One night she passed all bounds in her anger, using words that could never be forgiven; and when she declared as usual that she must have a divorce, her husband said: 'Yes, we will divorce. Let there be an end of it.' And so next day they went to the elders both of them, and as both demanded the divorce, the elders could not delay very long. A few days' delay they made, but the man was firm, and at last it was done. They were divorced. I think the woman would have drawn back at the last moment, but she could not, for very shame, and the man never wavered. He was offended past forgiveness.

So the divorce was given, and the man left the house and went to live elsewhere.

In a few days—a very few days—the wife sent for him again. 'Would he return?' And he refused. Then she went to the headman and asked him to make it up, and the headman sent for the husband, who came.

The woman asked her husband to return.

'Come back,' she said, 'come back. I have been wrong. Let us forgive. It shall never happen again.'

But the man shook his head.

'No,' he said; 'a divorce is a divorce. I do not care to marry and divorce once a week. You were always saying "I will divorce you, I will divorce you." Now it is done. Let it remain.'

The woman was struck with grief.

'But I did not know,' she said; 'I was hot-tempered. I was foolish. But now I know. Ah! the house is so lonely! I have but two ears, I have but two eyes, and the house is so large.'

But the husband refused again.

'What is done, is done. Marriage is not to be taken off and put on like a jacket. I have made up my mind.'

Then he went away, and after a little the woman went away too. She went straight to the big, lonely house, and there she hanged herself.

You see, she loved him all the time, but did not know till too late.

Men do not often apply for divorce except for very good cause, and with their minds fully made up to obtain it. They do obtain it, of course.

With this facility for divorce, it is remarkable how uncommon it is. In the villages and amongst respectable Burmans in all classes of life it is a great exception to divorce or to be divorced. The only class amongst whom it is at all common is the class of hangers-on to our Administration, the clerks and policemen, and so on. I fear there is little that is good to be said of many of them. It is terrible to see how demoralizing our contact is to all sorts and conditions of men. To be attached to our Administration is almost a stigma of disreputableness. I remember remarking once to a headman that a certain official seemed to be quite regardless of public opinion in his life, and asked him if the villagers did not condemn him. And the headman answered with surprise: 'But he is an official;' as if officials were quite *super grammaticam* of morals.

And yet this is the class from whom we most of us obtain our knowledge of Burmese life, whom we see most of, whose opinions we accept as reflecting the truth of Burmese thought. No wonder we are so often astray.

Amongst these, the taking of second, and even third, wives is not at all uncommon, and naturally divorce often follows. Among the great mass of the people it is very uncommon. I cannot give any figures. There are no records kept of marriage or of divorce. What the proportion is it is impossible to even guess. I have heard all sorts of estimates, none founded on more than imagination. I have even tried to find out in small villages what the number of divorces were in a year, and tried to estimate from this the percentage. I made it from 2 to 5 per cent. of the marriages. But I cannot offer these figures as correct for any large area. Probably they vary from place to place and from year to year. In the old time the queen was very strict upon the point. As she would allow no other wife to her king, so she would allow no taking of other wives, no abuse of divorce among her subjects. Whatever her influence may have been in other ways, here it was all for good. But the queen has gone, and there is no one left at all. No one but the hangers-on of whom I have spoken, examples not to be followed, but to be shunned.

But of this there is no manner of doubt, that this freedom of marriage and divorce leads to no license. There is no confusion between marriage or non-marriage, and even yet public opinion is a very great check upon divorce. It is considered not right to divorce your husband or your wife without good—very good and sufficient cause. And what is good and sufficient cause is very well understood. That a woman should have a nagging tongue, that a man should be a drunkard, what could be better cause than this? The gravity of the offence lies in whether it makes life unbearable together, not in the name you may give it.

The facility for divorce has other effects too. It makes a man and a woman very careful in their behaviour to each other. The chain that binds them is a chain of mutual forbearance, of mutual endurance, of mutual love; and if these be broken, then is the bond gone. Marriage is no fetter about a man or woman, binding both to that which they may get to hate.

In the first Burmese war in 1825 there was a man, an Englishman, taken prisoner in Ava and put in prison, and there he found certain Europeans and Americans. After a time, for fear of attempts at escape, these prisoners were chained together two and two. He tells you, this Englishman, how terrible this was, and of the hate and repulsion that arose in your heart to your co-bondsman. Before they were chained together they lived in close neighbourhood, in peace and amity; but when the chains came it was far otherwise, though they were no nearer than before. They got to hate each other.

And this is the Burmese idea of marriage, that it is a partnership of love and affection, and that when these die, all should be over. An unbreakable marriage appears to them as a fetter, a bond, something hateful and hate inspiring. They are a people who love to be free: they hate bonds and dogmas of every description. It is always religion that has made a bond of marriage, and here religion has not interfered. Theirs is a religion of free men and free women.

CHAPTER XVIII

DRINK

'The ignorant commit sins in consequence of drunkenness, and also make others drunk.'—*Acceptance into the Monkhood.*

The Buddhist religion forbids the use of all stimulants, including opium and other drugs; and in the times of the Burmese rule this law was stringently kept. No one was allowed to make, to sell, or to consume, liquors of any description. That this law was kept as firmly as it was was due, not to the vigilance of the officials, but to the general feeling of the people. It was a law springing from within, and therefore effectual; not imposed from without, and useless. That there were breaches and evasions of the law is only natural. The craving for some stimulant amongst all people is very great—so great as to have forced itself to be acknowledged and regulated by most states, and made a great source of revenue. Amongst the Burmans the craving is, I should say, as strong as amongst other people; and no mere legal prohibition would have had much effect in a country like this, full of jungle, where palms grow in profusion, and where little stills might be set up anywhere to distil their juice. But the feelings of the respectable people and the influence of the monks is very great, very strong; and the Burmans were, and in Upper Burma, where the old laws remain in force, are still, an absolutely teetotal people. No one who was in Upper Burma before and just after the war but knows how strictly the prohibition against liquor was enforced. The principal offenders against the law were the high officials, because they were above popular reach. No bribe was so gratefully accepted as some whisky. It was a sure step to safety in trouble.

A gentleman—not an Englishman—in the employ of a company who traded in Upper Burma in the king's time told me lately a story about this.

He lived in a town on the Irrawaddy, where was a local governor, and this governor had a head clerk. This head clerk had a wife, and she was, I am told, very beautiful. I cannot write scandal, and so will not repeat here what I have heard about this lady and the merchant; but one day his Burman servant rushed into his presence and told him breathlessly that the bailiff of the governor's court was just entering the garden with a warrant for his arrest, for, let us say, undue flirtation. The merchant, horrified at the prospect of being lodged in gaol and put in stocks, fled precipitately out of the back-gate and gained the governor's court. The governor was in session, seated on a little daïs, and the merchant ran in and knelt down, as is the custom, in front of the daïs. He began to hurriedly address the governor:

'My lord, my lord, an unjust complaint has been made against me. Someone has abused your justice and caused a warrant to be taken out against me. I have just escaped the bailiff, and came to your honour for protection. It is all a mistake. I will explain. I——'

But here the governor interposed. He bent forward till his head was close to the merchant's head, and whispered:

'Friend, have you any whisky?'

The merchant gave a sigh of relief.

'A case newly arrived is at your honour's disposal,' he answered quickly. 'I will give orders for it to be sent over at once. No, two cases—I have two. And this charge is all a mistake.'

The governor waved his hand as if all explanation were superfluous. Then he drew himself up, and, addressing the officials and crowd before him, said:

'This is my good friend. Let no one touch him.' And in an undertone to the merchant: 'Send it soon.'

So the merchant went home rejoicing, and sent the whisky. And the lady? Well, my story ends there with the governor and the whisky. No doubt it was all a mistake about the lady, as the merchant said. All officials were not so bad as this, and many officials were as strongly against the use of liquor, as urgent in the maintenance of the rules of the religion, as the lowest peasant.

It was the same with opium: its use was absolutely prohibited. Of course, Chinese merchants managed to smuggle enough in for their own use, but they had to bribe heavily to be able to do so, and the people remained uncontaminated. 'Opium-eater,' 'gambler,' are the two great terms of reproach and contempt.

It used to be a custom in the war-time—it has died out now, I think—for officers of all kinds to offer to Burmans who came to see them—officials, I mean—a drink of whisky or beer on parting, just as you would to an Englishman. It was often accepted. Burmans are, as I have said, very fond of liquor, and an opportunity like this to indulge in a little forbidden drink, under the encouragement of the great English soldier or official, was too much for them. Besides, it would have been a discourtesy to refuse. And so it was generally accepted. I do not think it did much harm to anyone, or to anything, except, perhaps, to our reputation.

I remember in 1887 that I went up into a semi-independent state to see the prince. I travelled up with two of his officials, men whom I had seen a good deal of for some months before, as his messengers and spokesmen, about affairs on the border. We travelled for three days, and came at last to where he had pitched his camp in the forest. He had built me a house, too, next to his camp, where I put up. I had a long interview with him about official matters—I need not tell of that here—and after our business was over we talked of many things, and at last I got up to take my leave. I had seen towards the end that the prince had something on his mind, something he wanted to say, but was afraid, or too shy, to mention; and when I got up, instead of moving away, I laughed and said:

'Well, what is it? I think there is something the prince wants to say before I go.'

And the prince smiled back awkwardly, still desirous to have his say, still clearly afraid to do so, and at last it was his wife who spoke.

'It is about the whisky,' she said. 'We know that you drink it. That is your own business. We hear, too, that it is the custom in the part of the country you have taken for English officers to give whisky and beer to officials who come to see you—to *our* officials,' and she looked at the men who had come up with me, and they blushed. 'The prince wishes to ask you not to do it here. Of course, in your own country you do what you like, but in the prince's country no one is allowed to drink or to smoke opium. It is against our faith. That is what the prince wanted to say. The thakin will not be offended if he is asked that here in our country he will not tempt any of us to break our religion.'

I almost wished I had not encouraged the prince to speak. I am afraid that the embarrassment passed over to my side. What could I say but that I would remember, that I was not offended, but would be careful? I had been lecturing the prince about his shortcomings; I had been warning him of trouble to come, unless he mended his ways; I had been telling him wonderful things of Europe and our power. I thought that I had produced an impression of superiority—I was young then—but when I left I had my doubts who it was that scored most in that interview. However, I have remembered ever since. I was not a frequent offender before—I have never offered a Burman liquor since.

CHAPTER XIX

MANNERS

'Not where others fail, or do, or leave undone—the wise should notice what himself has done, or left undone.'—*Dammapada.*

A remarkable trait of the Burmese character is their unwillingness to interfere in other people's affairs. Whether it arises from their religion of self-culture or no, I cannot say, but it is in full keeping with it. Every man's acts and thoughts are his own affair, think the Burmans; each man is free to go his own way, to think his own thoughts, to act his own acts, as long as he does not too much annoy his neighbours. Each man is responsible for himself and for himself alone, and there is no need for him to try and be guardian also to his fellows. And so the Burman likes to go his own way, to be a free man within certain limits; and the freedom that he demands for himself, he will extend also to his neighbours. He has a very great and wide tolerance towards all his neighbours, not thinking it necessary to disapprove of his neighbours' acts because they may not be the same as his own, never thinking it necessary to interfere with his neighbours as long as the laws are not broken. Our ideas that what habits are different to our habits must be wrong, and being wrong, require correction at our hands, is very far from his thoughts. He never desires to interfere with anyone. Certain as he is that his own ideas are best, he is contented with that knowledge, and is not ceaselessly desirous of proving it upon other people. And so a foreigner may go and live in a Burman village, may settle down there and live his own life and follow his own customs in perfect freedom, may dress and eat and drink and pray and die as he likes. No one will interfere. No one will try and correct him; no one will be for ever insisting to him that he is an outcast, either from civilization or from religion. The people will accept him for what he is, and leave the matter there. If he likes to change his ways and conform to Burmese habits and Buddhist forms, so much the better; but if not, never mind.

It is, I think, a great deal owing to this habit of mind that the manners of the Burmese are usually so good, children in civilization as they are. There is amongst them no rude inquisitiveness and no desire to in any way circumscribe your freedom, by either remark or act. Surely of all things that cause trouble, nothing is so common amongst us as the interference with each other's ways, as the needless giving of advice. It seems to each of us that we are responsible, not only for ourselves, but also for everyone else near us; and so if we disapprove of any act, we are always in a hurry to express our disapproval and to try and persuade the actor to our way of thinking. We are for ever thinking of others and trying to improve them; as a nation we try to coerce weaker nations and to convert stronger ones, and as individuals we do the same. We are sure that other people cannot but be better and happier for being brought into our ways of thinking, by force even, if necessary. We call it philanthropy.

But the Buddhist does not believe this at all. Each man, each nation, has, he thinks, enough to do managing his or its own affairs. Interference, any sort of interference, he is sure can do nothing but harm. *You* cannot save a man. He can save himself; you can do nothing for him. You may force or persuade him into an outer agreement with you, but what is the value of that? All dispositions that are good, that are of any value at all, must come spontaneously from the heart of man. First, he must desire them, and then struggle to obtain them; by this means alone can any virtue be reached. This, which is the key of his religion, is the key also of his private life. Each man is a free man to do what he likes, in a way that we have never understood.

Even under the rule of the Burmese kings there was the very widest tolerance. You never heard of a foreigner being molested in any way, being forbidden to live as he liked, being forbidden to erect his own places of worship. He had the widest freedom, as long as he infringed no law. The Burmese rule may not have been a good one in many ways, but it was never guilty of persecution, of any attempt at forcible conversion, of any desire to make such an attempt.

This tolerance, this inclination to let each man go his own way, is conspicuous even down to the little events of life. It is very marked, even in conversation, how little criticism is indulged in towards each other, how there is an absolute absence of desire to proselytize each other in any way. 'It is his way,' they will say, with a laugh, of any peculiar act of any person; 'it is his way. What does it matter to us?' Of all the lovable qualities of the Burmese, and they are many, there are none greater than these—their light-heartedness and their tolerance.

A Burman will always assume that you know your own business, and will leave you alone to do it. How great a boon this is I think we hardly can understand, for we have none of it. And he carries it to an extent that sometimes surprises us.

Suppose you are walking along a road and there is a broken bridge on the way, a bridge that you might fall through. No one will try and prevent you going. Any Burman who saw you go will, if he think at all about it, give you the credit for knowing what you are about. It will not enter into his head to go out of his way to give you advice about that bridge. If you ask him he will help you all he can, but he will not volunteer; and so if you depend on volunteered advice, you may fall through the bridge and break your neck, perhaps.

At first this sort of thing seems to us to spring from laziness or from discourtesy. It is just the reverse of this latter; it is excess of courtesy that assumes you to be aware of what you are about, and capable of judging properly.

You may get yourself into all sorts of trouble, and unless you call out no one will assist you. They will suppose that if you require help you will soon ask for it. You could drift all the way from Bhamo to Rangoon on a log, and I am sure no one would try to pick you up unless you shouted for help. Let anyone try to drift down from Oxford to Richmond, and he will be forcibly saved every mile of his journey, I am sure. The Burman boatmen you passed would only laugh and ask how you were getting on. The English boatman would have you out of that in a jiffy, saving you despite yourself. You might commit suicide in Burma, and no one would stop you. 'It is your own look-out,' they would say; 'if you want to die why should we prevent you? What business is it of ours?'

Never believe for a moment that this is cold-heartedness. Nowhere is there any man so kind-hearted as a Burman, so ready to help you, so hospitable, so charitable both in act and thought.

It is only that he has another way of seeing these things to what we have. He would resent as the worst discourtesy that which we call having a friendly interest in each other's doings. Volunteered advice comes, so he thinks, from pure self-conceit, and is intolerable; help that he has not asked for conveys the assumption that he is a fool, and the helper ever so much wiser than he. It is in his eyes simply a form of self-assertion, an attempt at governing other people, an infringement of good manners not to be borne.

Each man is responsible for himself, each man is the maker of himself. Only he can do himself good by good thought, by good acts; only he can hurt himself by evil intentions and deeds. Therefore in your intercourse with others remember always yourself, remember that no one can injure you but yourself; be careful, therefore, of your acts for your own sake. For if you lose your temper, who is the sufferer? Yourself; no one but yourself. If you are guilty of disgraceful acts, of discourteous words, who suffers? Yourself. Remember that; remember that courtesy and good temper are due from you to everyone. What does it matter who the other person be? you should be courteous to him, not because he deserves it, but because you deserve it. Courtesy is measured by the giver, not by the receiver. We are apt sometimes to think that this continual care of self is selfishness; it is the very reverse. Self-reverence is the antipode of self-conceit, of selfishness. If you honour yourself, you will be careful that nothing dishonourable shall come from you. 'Self-reverence, self-knowledge, self-control;' we, too, have had a poet who taught this.

And so dignity of manner is very marked amongst this people. It is cultivated as a gift, as the outward sign of a good heart.

'A rough diamond;' no Burman would understand this saying. The value of a diamond is that it can be polished. As long as it remains in the rough, it has no more beauty than a lump of mud. If your heart be good, so, too, will be your manners. A good tree will bring forth good fruit. If the fruit be rotten, can the tree be good? Not so. If your manners are bad, so, too, is your heart. To be courteous, even tempered, to be tolerant and full of sympathy, these are the proofs of an inward goodness. You cannot have one without the other. Outward appearances are not deceptive, but are true.

Therefore they strive after even temper. Hot-tempered as they are, easily aroused to wrath, easily awakened to pleasure, men with the passions of a child, they have very great command over themselves. They are ashamed of losing their temper; they look upon it as a disgrace. We are often proud of it; we think sometimes we do well to be angry.

So they are very patient, very long-suffering, accepting with resignation the troubles of this world, the kicks and spurns of fortune, secure in this, that each man's self is in his own keeping. If there be trouble for to-day, what can it matter if you do but command yourself? If others be discourteous to you, that cannot hurt you, if you do not allow yourself to be discourteous in return. Take care of your own soul, sure that in the end you will win, either in this life or in some other, that which you deserve. What you have made your soul fit for, that you will obtain, sooner or later, whether it be evil or whether it be good. The law of righteousness is for ever this, that what a man deserves that he will obtain. And in the end, if you cultivate your soul with unwearying patience, striving always after what is good, purifying yourself from the lust of life, you will come unto that lake where all desire shall be washed away.

CHAPTER XX

'NOBLESSE OBLIGE'

'Sooner shall the cleft rock reunite so as to make a whole, than may he who kills any living being be admitted into our society.'—*Acceptance into the Monkhood.*

It is very noticeable throughout the bazaars of Burma that all the beef butchers are natives of India. No Burman will kill a cow or a bullock, and no Burman will sell its meat. It is otherwise with pork and fowls. Burmans may sometimes be found selling these; and fish are almost invariably sold by the wives of the fishermen. During the king's time, any man who was even found in possession of beef was liable to very severe punishment. The only exception, as I have explained elsewhere, was in the case of the queen when expecting an addition to her family, and it was necessary that she should be strengthened in all ways. None, not even foreigners, were allowed to kill beef, and this law was very stringently observed. Other flesh and fish might, as far as the law of the country went, be sold with impunity. You could not be fined for killing and eating goats, or fowls, or pigs, and these were sold occasionally. It is now ten years since King Thibaw was overthrown, and there is now no law against the sale of beef. And yet, as I have said, no respectable Burman will even now kill or sell beef. The law was founded on the beliefs of the people, and though the law is dead, the beliefs remain.

It is true that the taking of life is against Buddhist commands. No life at all may be taken by him who adheres to Buddhistic teaching. Neither for sport, nor for revenge, nor for food, may any animal be deprived of the breath that is in it. And this is a command wonderfully well kept. There are a few exceptions, but they are known and accepted as breaches of the law, for the law itself knows no exceptions. Fish, as I have said, can be obtained almost everywhere. They are caught in great quantities in the river, and are sold in most bazaars, either fresh or salted. It is one of the staple foods of the Burmese. But although they will eat fish, they despise the fisherman. Not so much, perhaps, as if he killed other living things, but still, the fisherman is an outcast from decent society. He will have to suffer great and terrible punishment before he can be cleansed from the sins that he daily commits. Notwithstanding this, there are many fishermen in Burma.

A fish is a very cold-blooded beast. One must be very hard up for something to love to have any affection to spare upon fishes. They cannot be, or at all events they never are, domesticated, and most of them are not beautiful. I am not aware that they have ever been known to display any attachment to anyone, which accounts, perhaps, for the comparatively lenient eye with which their destruction is contemplated.

For with warm-blooded animals it is very different. Cattle, as I have said, can never be killed nor their meat sold by a Burman, and with other animals the difficulty is not much less.

I was in Upper Burma for some months before the war, and many a time I could get no meat at all. Living in a large town among prosperous people, I could get no flesh at all, only fish and rice and vegetables. When, after much trouble, my Indian cook would get me a few fowls, he would often be waylaid and forced to release them. An old woman, say, anxious to do some deed of merit, would come to him as he returned triumphantly home with his fowls and tender him money, and beg him to release the fowls. She would give the full price or double the price of the fowls; she had no desire to gain merit at another person's expense, and the unwilling cook would be obliged to give up the fowls. Public opinion was so strong he dare not refuse. The money was paid, the fowls set free, and I dined on tinned beef.

And yet the villages are full of fowls. Why they are kept I do not know. Certainly not for food. I do not mean to say that an accidental meeting between a rock and a fowl may not occasionally furnish forth a dinner, but this is not the object with which they are kept—of this I am sure.

You would not suppose that fowls were capable of exciting much affection, yet I suppose they are. Certainly in one case ducks were. There is a Burman lady I know who is married to an Englishman. He kept ducks. He bought a number of ducklings, and had them fed up so that they might be fat and succulent when the time came for them to be served at table. They became very fine ducks, and my friend had promised me one. I took an interest in them, and always noticed their increasing fatness when I rode that way. Imagine, then, my disappointment when one day I saw that all the ducks had disappeared.

I stopped to inquire. Yes, truly they were all gone, my friend told me. In his absence his wife had gone up the river to visit some friends, and had taken the ducks with her. She could not bear, she said, that they should be killed, so she took them away and distributed them among her friends, one here and one there, where she was sure they would be well treated and not killed. When she returned she was quite pleased at her success, and laughed at her husband and me.

This same lady was always terribly distressed when she had to order a fowl to be killed for her husband's breakfast, even if she had never seen it before. I have seen her, after telling the cook to kill a fowl for breakfast, run away and sit down in the veranda with her hands over her ears, and her face the very picture of misery, fearing lest she should hear its shrieks. I think that this was the one great trouble to her in her marriage, that her husband would insist on eating fowls and ducks, and that she had to order them to be killed.

As she is, so are most Burmans. If there is all this trouble about fowls, it can be imagined how the trouble increases when it comes to goats or any larger beasts. In the jungle villages meat of any kind at all is never seen: no animals of any kind are allowed to be killed. An officer travelling in the district would be reduced to what he could carry with him, if it were not for an Act of Government obliging villages to furnish—on payment, of course—supplies for officers and troops passing through. The mere fact of such a law being necessary is sufficient proof of the strength of the feeling against taking life.

Of course, all shooting, either for sport or for food, is looked upon as disgraceful. In many jungle villages where deer abound there are one or two hunters who make a living by hunting. But they are disgraced men. They are worse than fishermen, and they will have a terrible penalty to pay for it all. It will take much suffering to wash from their souls the cruelty, the blood-thirstiness, the carelessness to suffering, the absence of compassion, that hunting must produce. 'Is there no food in the bazaar, that you must go and take the lives of animals?' has been said to me many a time. And when my house-roof was infested by sparrows, who dropped grass and eggs all over my rooms, so that I was obliged to shoot them with a little rifle, this was no excuse. 'You should have built a sparrow-cote,' they told me. 'If you had built a sparrow-cote, they would have gone away and left you in peace. They only wanted to make nests and lay eggs and have little ones, and you went and shot them.' There are many sparrow-cotes to be seen in the villages.

I might give example after example of this sort, for they happen every day. We who are meat-eaters, who delight in shooting, who have a horror of insects and reptiles, are continually coming into collision with the principles of our neighbours; for even harmful reptiles they do not care to kill. Truly I believe it is a myth, the story of the Burmese mother courteously escorting out of the house the scorpion which had just bitten her baby. A Burmese mother worships her baby as much as the woman of any other nation does, and I believe there is no crime she would not commit in its behalf. But if she saw a scorpion walking about in the fields, she would not kill it as we should. She would step aside and pass on. 'Poor beast!' she would say, 'why should I hurt it? It never hurt me.'

The Burman never kills insects out of sheer brutality. If a beetle drone annoyingly, he will catch it in a handkerchief and put it outside, and so with a bee. It is a great trouble often to get your Burmese servants to keep your house free of ants and other annoying creatures. If you tell them to kill the insects they will, for in that case the sin falls on you. Without special orders they would rather leave the ants alone.

In the district in which I am now living snakes are very plentiful. There are cobras and keraits, but the most dreaded is the Russell's viper. He is a snake that averages from three to four feet long, and is very thick, with a big head and a stumpy tail. His body is marked very prettily with spots and blurs of light on a dark, grayish green, and he is so like the shadows of the grass and weeds in a dusty road, that you can walk on him quite unsuspectingly. Then he will bite you, and you die. He comes out usually in the evening before dark, and lies about on footpaths to catch the home-coming ploughman or reaper, and, contrary to the custom of other snakes, he will not flee on hearing a footstep. When anyone approaches he lies more still than ever, not even a movement of his head betraying him. He is so like the colour of the ground, he hopes he will be passed unseen; and he is slow and lethargic in his movements, and so is easy to kill when once detected. As a Burman said, 'If he sees you first, he kills you; if you see him first, you kill him.'

In this district no Burman hesitates a moment in killing a viper when he has the chance. Usually he has to do it in self-defence. This viper is terribly feared, as over a hundred persons a year die here by his bite. He is so hated and feared that he has become an outcast from the law that protects all life.

But with other snakes it is not so. There is the hamadryad, for instance. He is a great snake about ten to fourteen feet long, and he is the only snake that will attack you first. He is said always to do so, certainly he often does. One attacked me once when out quail-shooting. He put up his great neck and head suddenly at a distance of only five or six feet, and was just preparing to strike, when I literally blew his head off with two charges of shot.

You would suppose he was vicious enough to be included with the Russell's viper in the category of the exceptions, but no. Perhaps he is too rare to excite such fierce and deadly hate as makes the Burman forget his law and kill the viper. However it may be, the Burman is not ready to kill the hamadryad. A few weeks ago a friend of mine and myself came across two little Burman boys carrying a jar with a piece of broken tile over it. The lads kept lifting up the tile and peeping in, and then putting the tile on again in a great hurry, and their actions excited our curiosity. So we called them to come to us, and we looked into the jar. It was full of baby hamadryads. The lads had found a nest of them in the absence of the mother, who would have killed them if she had been there, and had secured all the little snakes. There were seven of them.

We asked the boys what they intended to do with the snakes, and they answered that they would show them to their friends in the village. 'And then?' we asked. And then they would let them go in the water. My friend killed all the hamadryads on the spot, and gave the boys some coppers, and we went on. Can you imagine this happening anywhere else? Can you think of any other schoolboys sparing any animal they caught, much less poisonous snakes? The extraordinary hold that this tenet of their religion has upon the Burmese must be seen to be understood. What I write will sound like some fairy story, I fear, to my people at home. It is far beneath the truth. The belief that it is wrong to take life is a belief with them as strong as any belief could be. I do not know anywhere any command, earthly or heavenly, that is acted up to with such earnestness as this command is amongst the Burmese. It is an abiding principle of their daily life.

Where the command came from I do not know. I cannot find any allusion to it in the life of the great teacher. We know that he ate meat. It seems to me that it is older even than he. It has been derived both by the Burmese Buddhists and the Hindus from a faith whose origin is hidden in the mists of long ago. It is part of that far older faith on which Buddhism was built, as was Christianity on Judaism.

But if not part of his teaching—and though it is included in the sacred books, we do not know how much of them are derived from the Buddha himself—it is in strict accordance with all his teaching. That is one of the most wonderful points of Buddhism, it is all in accordance; there are no exceptions.

I have heard amongst Europeans a very curious explanation of this refusal of Buddhists to take life. 'Buddhists,' they say, 'believe in the transmigration of souls. They believe that when a man dies his soul may go into a beast. You could not expect him to kill a bull, when perchance his grandfather's soul might inhabit there.' This is their explanation, this is the way they put two and two together to make five. They know that Buddhists believe in transmigration, they know that Buddhists do not like to take life, and therefore one is the cause of the other.

I have mentioned this explanation to Burmans while talking of the subject, and they have always laughed at it. They had never heard of it before. It is true that it is part of their great theory of life that the souls of men have risen from being souls of beasts, and that we may so relapse if we are not careful. Many stories are told of cases that have occurred where a man has been reincarnated as an animal, and where what is now the soul of a man used to live in a beast. But that makes no difference. Whatever a man may have been, or may be, he is a man now; whatever a beast may have been, he is a beast now. Never suppose that a Burman has any other idea than this. To him men are men, and animals are animals, and men are far the higher. But he does not deduce from this that man's superiority gives him permission to illtreat or to kill animals. It is just the reverse. It is because man is so much higher than the animal that he can and must observe towards animals the very greatest care, feel for them the very greatest compassion, be good to them in every way he can. The Burman's motto should be *Noblesse oblige*; he knows the meaning, if he knows not the words.

For the Burman's compassion towards animals goes very much farther than a mere reluctance to kill them. Although he has no command on the subject, it seems to him quite as important to treat animals well during their lives as to refrain from taking those lives. His refusal to take life he shares with the Hindu; his perpetual care and tenderness to all living creatures is all his own. And here I may mention a very curious contrast, that whereas in India the Hindu will not take life and the Mussulman will, yet the Mussulman is by reputation far kinder to his beasts than the Hindu. Here the Burman combines both qualities. He has all the kindness to animals that the Mahommedan has, and more, and he has the same horror of taking life that the Hindu has.

Coming from half-starved, over-driven India, it is a revelation to see the animals in Burma. The village ponies and cattle and dogs in India are enough to make the heart bleed for their sordid misery, but in Burma they are a delight to the eye. They are all fat, every one of them—fat and comfortable and impertinent; even the ownerless dogs are well fed. I suppose the indifference of the ordinary native of India to animal suffering comes from the evil of his own lot. He is so very poor, he has such hard work to find enough for himself and his children, that his sympathy is all used up. He has none to spare. He is driven into a dumb heartlessness, for I do not think he is actually cruel.

The Burman is full of the greatest sympathy towards animals of all kinds, of the greatest understanding of their ways, of the most humorously good-natured attitude towards them. Looking at them from his manhood, he has no contempt for them; but the gentle toleration of a father to very little children who are stupid and troublesome often, but are very lovable. He feels himself so far above them that he can condescend towards them, and forbear with them.

His ponies are pictures of fatness and impertinence and go. They never have any vice because the Burman is never cruel to them; they are never well trained, partly because he does not know how to train them, partly because they are so near the aboriginal wild pony as to be incapable of very much training. But they are willing; they will go for ever, and are very strong, and they have admirable constitutions and tempers. You could not make a Burman ill-use his pony if you tried, and I fancy that to break these little half-wild ponies to go in cabs in crowded streets requires severe treatment. At least, I never knew but one hackney-carriage driver either in Rangoon or Mandalay who was a Burman, and he very soon gave it up. He said that the work was too heavy either for a pony or a man. I think, perhaps, it was for the safety of the public that he resigned, for his ponies were the very reverse of meek—which a native of India says a hackney-carriage pony should be—and he drove entirely by the light of Nature.

So all the drivers of gharries, as we call them, are natives of India or half-breeds, and it is amongst them that the work of the Society for the Prevention of Cruelty to Animals principally lies. While I was in Rangoon I tried a number of cases of over-driving, of using ponies with sore withers and the like. I never tried a Burman. Even in Rangoon, which has become almost Indianized, his natural humanity never left the Burman. As far as Burmans are concerned, the Society for the Prevention of Cruelty to Animals need not exist. They are kinder to their animals than even the members of the Society could be. Instances occur every day; here is one of the most striking that I remember.

There is a town in Burma where there are some troops stationed, and which is the headquarters of the civil administration of the district. It is, or was then, some distance from a railway-station, and it was necessary to make some arrangement for the carriage of the mails to and from the town and station. The Post-Office called for tenders, and at length it was arranged through the civil authorities that a coach should run once a day each way to carry the mails and passengers. A native of India agreed to take the contract—for Burmans seldom or never care to take them—and he was to comply with certain conditions and receive a certain subsidy.

There was a great deal of traffic between the town and station, and it was supposed that the passenger traffic would pay the contractor well, apart from his mail subsidy. For Burmans are always free with their money, and the road was long and hot and dusty. I often passed that coach as I rode. I noticed that the ponies were poor, very poor, and were driven a little hard, but I saw no reason for interference. It did not seem to me that any cruelty was committed, nor that the ponies were actually unfit to be driven. I noticed that the driver used his whip a good deal, but then some ponies require the whip. I never thought much about it, as I always rode my own ponies, and they always shied at the coach, but I should have noticed if there had been anything remarkable. Towards the end of the year it became necessary to renew the contract, and the contractor was approached on the subject. He said he was willing to continue the contract for another year if the mail subsidy was largely increased. He said he had lost money on that year's working. When asked how he could possibly have lost considering the large number of people who were always passing up and down, he said that they did not ride in his coach. Only the European soldiers and a few natives of India came with him. Officers had their own ponies and rode, and the Burmans either hired a bullock-cart or walked. They hardly ever came in his coach, but he could not say what the reason might be.

So an inquiry was made, and the Burmese were asked why they did not ride on the coach. Were the fares too high?—was it uncomfortable? But no, it was for neither of these reasons that they left the coach to the soldiers and natives of India. It was because of the ponies. No Burman would care to ride behind ponies who were treated as these ponies were—half fed, overdriven, whipped. It was a misery to see them; it was twice a misery to drive behind them. 'Poor beasts!' they said; 'you can see their ribs, and when they come to the end of a stage they are fit to fall down and die. They should be turned out to graze.'

The opinion was universal. The Burmans preferred to spend twice or thrice the money and hire a bullock-cart and go slowly, while the coach flashed past them in a whirl of dust, or they preferred to walk. Many and many times have I seen the roadside rest-houses full of travellers halting for a few minutes' rest. They walked while the coach came by empty; and nearly all of them could have afforded the fare. It was a very striking instance of what pure kind-heartedness will do, for there would have been no religious command broken by going in the coach. It was the pure influence of compassion towards the beasts and refusal to be a party to such hard-heartedness. And yet, as I have said, I do not think the law could have interfered with success. Surely a people who could act like this have the very soul of religion in their hearts, although the act was not done in the name of religion.

All the animals—the cattle, the ponies, and the buffaloes—are so tame that it is almost an unknown thing for anyone to get hurt.

The cattle are sometimes afraid of the white face and strange attire of a European, but you can walk through the herds as they come home in the evening with perfect confidence that they will not hurt you. Even a cow with a young calf will only eye you suspiciously; and with the Burmans even the huge water buffaloes are absolutely tame. You can see a herd of these great beasts, with horns six feet across, come along under the command of a very small boy or girl perched on one of their broad backs. He flourishes a little stick, and issues his commands like a general. It is one of the quaintest imaginable sights to see this little fellow get off his steed, run after a straggler, and beat him with his stick. The buffalo eyes his master, whom he could abolish with one shake of his head, submissively, and takes the beating, which he probably feels about as much as if a straw fell on him, good-humouredly. The children never seem to come to grief. Buffaloes occasionally charge Europeans, but the only place where I have known of Burmans being killed by buffaloes is in the Kalè Valley. There the buffaloes are turned out into the jungle for eight months in the year, and are only caught for ploughing and carting. Naturally they are quite wild; in fact, many of them are the offspring of wild bulls.

The Burmans, too, are very fond of dogs. Their villages are full of dogs; but, as far as I know, they never use them for anything, and they are never trained to do anything. They are supposed to be useful as watch-dogs, but I do not think they are very good even at that. I have surrounded a village before dawn, and never a dog barked, and I have heard them bark all night at nothing.

But when a Burman sees a fox-terrier or any English dog his delight is unfeigned. When we first took Upper Burma, and such sights were rare, half a village would turn out to see the little 'tail-less' dog trotting along after its master. And if the terrier would 'beg,' then he would win all hearts. I am not only referring to children, but to grown men and women; and then there is always something peculiarly childlike and frank in these children of the great river.

Only to-day, as I was walking up the bank of the river in the early dawn, I heard some Burman boatmen discussing my fox-terrier. They were about fifteen yards from the shore, poling their boat up against the current, which is arduous work; and as I passed them my little dog ran down the bank and looked at them across the water, and they saw her.

'See now,' said one man to another, pausing for a moment with his pole in his hand—'see the little white dog with the brown face, how wise she looks!'

'And how pretty!' said a man steering in the stern. 'Come!' he cried, holding out his hand to it.

But the dog only made a splash in the water with her paws, and then turned and ran after me. The boatmen laughed and resumed their poling, and I passed on. In the still morning across the still water I could hear every word, but I hardly took any note; I have heard it so often. Only now when I come to write on this subject do I remember.

It has been inculcated in us from childhood that it is a manly thing to be indifferent to pain—not to our own pain only, but to that of all others. To be sorry for a hunted hare, to compassionate the wounded deer, to shrink from torturing the brute creation, has been accounted by us as namby-pamby sentimentalism, not fit for man, fit only for a squeamish woman. To the Burman it is one of the highest of all virtues. He believes that all that is beautiful in life is founded on compassion and kindness and sympathy—that nothing of great value can exist without them. Do you think that a Burmese boy would be allowed to birds'-nest, or worry rats with a terrier, or go ferreting? Not so. These would be crimes.

That this kindness and compassion for animals has very far-reaching results no one can doubt. If you are kind to animals, you will be kind, too, to your fellow-man. It is really the same thing, the same feeling in both cases. If to be superior in position to an animal justifies you in torturing it, so it would do with men. If you are in a better position than another man, richer, stronger, higher in rank, that would—that does often in our minds—justify ill-treatment and contempt. Our innate feeling towards all that we consider inferior to ourselves is scorn; the Burman's is compassion. You can see this spirit coming out in every action of their daily life, in their dealings with each other, in their thoughts, in their speech. 'You are so strong, have you no compassion for him who is weak, who is tempted, who has fallen?' How often have I heard this from a Burman's lips! How often have I seen him act up to it! It seems to them the necessary corollary of strength that the strong man should be sympathetic and kind. It seems to them an unconscious confession of weakness to be scornful, revengeful, inconsiderate. Courtesy, they say, is the mark of a great man, discourtesy of a little one. No one who feels his position secure will lose his temper, will persecute, will be disdainful. Their word for a fool and for a hasty-tempered man is the same. To them it is the same thing, one infers the other. And so their attitude towards animals is but an example of their attitude to each other. That an animal or a man should be lower and weaker than you is the strongest claim he can have on your humanity, and your courtesy and consideration for him is the clearest proof of your own superiority. And so in his dealings with animals the Buddhist considers himself, consults his own dignity, his own strength, and is kind and compassionate to them out of the greatness of his own heart. Nothing is more beautiful than the Burman in his ways with his children, and his beasts, with all who are lesser than himself.

Even to us, who think so very differently from him on many points, there is a great and abiding charm in all this, to which we can find only one exception; for to our ideas there is one exception, and it is this: No Burman will take any life if he can help it, and therefore, if any animal injure itself, he will not kill it—not even to put it out of its pain, as we say. I have seen bullocks split on slippery roads, I have seen ponies with broken legs, I have seen goats with terrible wounds caused by accidental falls, and no one would kill them. If, when you are out shooting, your beaters pick up a wounded hare or partridge, do not suppose that they wring its neck; you must yourself do that, or it will linger on till you get home. Under no circumstances will they take the life even of a wounded beast. And if you ask them, they will say: 'If a man be sick, do you shoot him? If he injure his spine so that he will be a cripple for life, do you put him out of his pain?'

If you reply that men and beasts are different, they will answer that in this point they do not recognise the difference. 'Poor beast! let him live out his little life.' And they will give him grass and water till he dies.

This is the exception that I meant, but now, after I have written it, I am not so sure. Is it an exception?

CHAPTER XXI

ALL LIFE IS ONE

'I heard a voice that cried,

"Balder the Beautiful

Is dead, is dead,"

And through the misty air

Passed like the mournful cry

Of sunward-sailing cranes.'

Tegner's *Drapa*.

All romance has died out of our woods and hills in England, all our fairies are dead long ago. Knowledge so far has brought us only death. Later on it will bring us a new life. It is even now showing us how this may be, and is bringing us face to face again with Nature, and teaching us to know and understand the life that there is about us. Science is telling us again what we knew long ago and forgot, that our life is not apart from the life about us, but of it. Everything is akin to us, and when we are more accustomed to this knowledge, when we have ceased to regard it as a new, strange teaching, and know that we are but seeing again with clearer eyes what a half-knowledge blinded us to, then the world will be bright and beautiful to us as it was long ago.

But now all is dark. There are no dryads in our trees, nor nymphs among the reeds that fringe the river; even our peaks hold for us no guardian spirit, that may take the reckless trespasser and bind him in a rock for ever. And because we have lost our belief in fairies, because we do not now think that there are goblins in our caves, because there is no spirit in the winds nor voice in the thunder, we have come to think that the trees and the rocks, the flowers and the storm, are all dead things. They are made up, we say, of materials that we know, they are governed by laws that we have discovered, and there is no life anywhere in Nature.

And yet this cannot be true. Far truer is it to believe in fairies and in spirits than in nothing at all; for surely there is life all about us. Who that has lived out alone in the forest, that has lain upon the hillside and seen the mountains clothe themselves in lustrous shadows shot with crimson when the day dies, who that has heard the sigh come up out of the ravines where the little breezes move, that has watched the trees sway their leaves to and fro, beckoning to each other with wayward amorous gestures, but has known that these are not dead things?

Watch the stream coming down the hill with a flash and a laugh in the sunlight, look into the dark brown pools in the deep shadows beneath the rocks, or voyage a whole night upon the breast of the great river, drifting past ghostly monasteries and silent villages, and then say if there be no life in the waters, if they, too, are dead things. There is no consolation like the consolation of Nature, no sympathy like the sympathy of the hills and streams; and sympathy comes from life. There is no sympathy with the dead.

When you are alone in the forest all this life will come and talk to you, if you are quiet and understand. There is love deep down in the passionate heart of the flower, as there is in the little quivering honeysucker flitting after his mate, as there was in Romeo long ago. There is majesty in the huge brown precipice greater than ever looked from the face of a king. All life is one. The soul that moves within you when you hear the deer call to each other far above in the misty meadows of the night is the same soul that moves in everything about you. No people who have lived much with Nature have failed to descry this. They have recognised the life, they have felt the sympathy of the world about them, and to this life they have given names and forms as they would to friends whom they loved. Fairies and goblins, fauns and spirits, these are but names and personifications of a real life. But to him who has never felt this life, who has never been wooed by the trees and hills, these things are but foolishness, of course.

To the Burman, not less than to the Greek of long ago, all nature is alive. The forest and the river and the mountains are full of spirits, whom the Burmans call Nats. There are all kinds of Nats, good and bad, great and little, male and female, now living round about us. Some of them live in the trees, especially in the huge fir-tree that shades half an acre without the village; or among the fernlike fronds of the tamarind; and you will often see beneath such a tree, raised upon poles or nestled in the branches, a little house built of bamboo and thatch, perhaps two feet square. You will be told when you ask that this is the house of the Tree-Nat. Flowers will be offered sometimes, and a little water or rice maybe, to the Nat, never supposing that he is in need of such things, but as a courteous and graceful thing to do; for it is not safe to offend these Nats, and many of them are very powerful. There is a Nat of whom I know, whose home is in a great tree at the crossing of two roads, and he has a house there built for him, and he is much feared. He is such a great Nat that it is necessary when you pass his house to dismount from your pony and walk to a respectful distance. If you haughtily ride past, trouble will befall you. A friend of mine riding there one day rejected all the advice of his Burmese companions and did not dismount, and a few days later he was taken deadly sick of fever. He very nearly died, and had to go away to the Straits for a sea-trip to take the fever out of his veins. It was a very near thing for him. That was in the Burmese times, of course. After that he always dismounted. But all Nats are not so proud nor so much to be feared as this one, and it is usually safe to ride past.

Even as I write I am under the shadow of a tree where a Nat used to live, and the headman of the village has been telling me all about it. This is a Government rest-house on a main road between two stations, and is built for Government officials travelling on duty about their districts. To the west of it is a grand fig-tree of the kind called Nyaungbin by the Burmese. It is a very beautiful tree, though now a little bare, for it is just before the rains; but it is a great tree even now, and two months hence it will be glorious. It was never planted, the headman tells me, but came up of itself very many years ago, and when it was grown to full size a Nat came to live in it. The Nat lived in the tree for many years, and took great care of it. No one might injure it or any living creature near it, so jealous was the Nat of his abode. And the villagers built a little Nat-house, such as I have described, under the branches, and offered flowers and water, and all things went well with those who did well. But if anyone did ill the Nat punished him. If he cut the roots of the tree, the Nat hurt his feet; and if he injured the branches, the Nat injured his arms; and if he cut the trunk, the Nat came down out of the tree, and killed the sacrilegious man right off. There was no running away, because, as you know, the headman said, Nats can go a great deal faster than any man. Many men, careless strangers, who camped under the tree and then abused the hospitality of the Nat by hunting near his home, came to severe grief.

But the Nat has gone now, alas! The tree is still there, but the Nat has fled away these many years.

'I suppose he didn't care to stay,' said the headman. 'You see that the English Government officials came and camped here, and didn't fear the Nats. They had fowls killed here for their dinner, and they sang and shouted; and they shot the green pigeons who ate his figs, and the little doves that nested in his branches.'

All these things were an abomination to the Nat, who hated loud, rough talk and abuse, and to whom all life was sacred.

So the Nat went away. The headman did not know where he was gone, but there are plenty of trees.

'He has gone somewhere to get peace,' the headman said. 'Somewhere in the jungle, where no one ever comes save the herd-boy and the deer, he will be living in a tree, though I do not think he will easily find a tree so beautiful as this.'

The headman seemed very sorry about it, and so did several villagers who were with him; and I suggested that if the Nat-houses were rebuilt, and flowers and water offered, the Nat might know and return. I even offered to contribute myself, that it might be taken as an *amende honorable* on behalf of the English Government. But they did not think this would be any use. No Nat would come where there was so much going and coming, so little care for life, such a disregard for pity and for peace. If we were to take away our rest-house, well then, perhaps, after a time, something could be done, but not under present circumstances.

And so, besides dethroning the Burmese king, and occupying his golden palace, we are ousting from their pleasant homes the guardian spirits of the trees. They flee before the cold materialism of our belief, before the brutality of our manners. The headman did not say this; he did not mean to say this, for he is a very courteous man and a great friend of all of us; but that is what it came to, I think.

The trunk of this tree is more than ten feet through—not a round bole, but like the pillar in a Gothic cathedral, as of many smaller boles growing together; and the roots spread out into a pedestal before entering the ground. The trunk does not go up very far. At perhaps twenty-five feet above the ground it divides into a myriad of smaller trunks, not branches, till it looks more like a forest than a single tree; it is full of life still. Though the pigeons and the doves come here no longer, there are a thousand other birds flitting to and fro in their aerial city and chirping to each other. Two tiny squirrels have just run along a branch nearly over my head, in a desperate hurry apparently, their tails cocked over their backs, and a sky blue chameleon is standing on the trunk near where it parts. There is always a breeze in this great tree; the leaves are always moving, and there is a continuous rustle and murmur up there. A mango-tree and tamarind near by are quite still. Not a breath shakes their leaves; they are as still as stone, but the shadow of the fig-tree is chequered with ever-changing lights. Is the Nat really gone? Perhaps not; perhaps he is still there, still caring for his tree, only shy now and distrustful, and therefore no more seen.

Whole woods are enchanted sometimes, and no one dare enter them. Such a wood I know, far away north, near the hills, which is full of Nats. There was a great deal of game in it, for animals sought shelter there, and no one dared to disturb them; not the villagers to cut firewood, nor the girls seeking orchids, nor the hunter after his prey, dared to trespass upon that enchanted ground.

'What would happen,' I asked once, 'if anyone went into that wood? Would he be killed, or what?'

And I was told that no one could tell what would happen, only that he would never be seen again alive. 'The Nats would confiscate him,' they said, 'for intruding on their privacy.' But what they would do to him after the confiscation no one seemed to be quite sure. I asked the official who was with me, a fine handsome Burman who had been with us in many fights, whether he would go into the wood with me, but he declined at once. Enemies are one thing, Nats are quite another, and a very much more dreadful thing. You can escape from enemies, as witness my companion, who had been shot at times without number and had only once been hit, in the leg, but you cannot escape Nats. Once, he told me, there were two very sacrilegious men, hunters by profession, only more abandoned than even the majority of hunters, and they went into this wood to hunt 'They didn't care for Nats,' they said. They didn't care for anything at all apparently. 'They were absolutely without reverence, worse than any beast,' said my companion.

So they went into the wood to shoot, and they never came out again. A few days later their bare bones were found, flung out upon the road near the enchanted wood. The Nats did not care to have even the bones of such scoundrels in their wood, and so thrust them out. That was what happened to them, and that was what might happen to us if we went in there. We did not go.

Though the Nats of the forest will not allow even one of their beasts to be slain, the Nats of the rivers are not so exclusive. I do not think fish are ever regarded in quite the same light as animals. It is true that a fervent Buddhist will not kill even a fish, but a fisherman is not quite such a reprobate as a hunter in popular estimation. And the Nats think so too, for the Nat of a pool will not forbid all fishing. You must give him his share; you must be respectful to him, and not offend him; and then he will fill your nets with gleaming fish, and all will go well with you. If not, of course, you will come to grief; your nets will be torn, and your boat upset; and finally, if obstinate, you will be drowned. A great arm will seize you, and you will be pulled under and disappear for ever.

A Nat is much like a human being; if you treat him well he will treat you well, and conversely. Courtesy is never wasted on men or Nats, at least, so a Burman tells me.

The highest Nats live in the mountains. The higher the Nat the higher the mountain; and when you get to a very high peak indeed, like Mainthong Peak in Wuntho, you encounter very powerful Nats.

They tell a story of Mainthong Peak and the Nats there, how all of a sudden, one day in 1885, strange noises came from the hill. High up on his mighty side was heard the sound of great guns firing slowly and continuously; there was the thunder of falling rocks, cries as of someone bewailing a terrible calamity, and voices calling from the precipices. The people living in their little hamlets about his feet were terrified. Something they knew had happened of most dire import to them, some catastrophe which they were powerless to prevent, which they could not even guess. But when a few weeks later there came even into those remote villages the news of the fall of Mandalay, of the surrender of the king, of the 'great treachery,' they knew that this was what the Nats had been sorrowing over. All the Nats everywhere seem to have been distressed at our arrival, to hate our presence, and to earnestly desire our absence. They are the spirits of the country and of the people, and they cannot abide a foreign domination.

But the greatest place for Nats is the Popa Mountain, which is an extinct volcano standing all alone about midway between the river and the Shan Mountains. It is thus very conspicuous, having no hills near it to share its majesty; and being in sight from many of the old capitals, it is very well known in history and legend. It is covered with dense forest, and the villages close about are few. At the top there is a crater with a broken side, and a stream comes flowing out of this break down the mountain. Probably it was the denseness of its forests, the abundance of water, and its central position, more than its guardian Nats, that made it for so many years the last retreating-place of the half-robber, half-patriot bands that made life so uneasy for us. But the Nats of Popa Mountains are very famous.

When any foreigner was taken into the service of the King of Burma he had to swear an oath of fidelity. He swore upon many things, and among them were included 'all the Nats in Popa.' No Burman would have dared to break an oath sworn in such a serious way as this, and they did not imagine that anyone else would. It was and is a very dangerous thing to offend the Popa Nats; for they are still there in the mountain, and everyone who goes there must do them reverence.

A friend of mine, a police officer, who was engaged in trying to catch the last of the robber chiefs who hid near Popa, told me that when he went up the mountain shooting he, too, had to make offerings. Some way up there is a little valley dark with overhanging trees, and a stream flows slowly along it. It is an enchanted valley, and if you look closely you will see that the stream is not as other streams, for it flows uphill. It comes rushing into the valley with a great display of foam and froth, and it leaves in a similar way, tearing down the rocks, and behaving like any other boisterous hill rivulet; but in the valley itself it lies under a spell. It is slow and dark, and has a surface like a mirror, and it flows uphill. There is no doubt about it; anyone can see it. When they came here, my friend tells me, they made a halt, and the Burmese hunters with him unpacked his breakfast. He did not want to eat then, he said, but they explained that it was not for him, but for the Nats. All his food was unpacked, cold chicken and tinned meats, and jam and eggs and bread, and it was spread neatly on a cloth under a tree. Then the hunters called upon the Nats to come and take anything they desired, while my friend wondered what he should do if the Nats took all his food and left him with nothing. But no Nats came, although the Burmans called again and again. So they packed up the food, saying that now the Nats would be pleased at the courtesy shown to them, and that my friend would have good sport. Presently they went on, leaving, however, an egg or two and a little salt, in case the Nats might be hungry later, and true enough it was that they did have good luck. At other times, my friend says, when he did not observe this ceremony, he saw nothing to shoot at all, but on this day he did well.

The former history of all Nats is not known. Whether they have had a previous existence in another form, and if so, what, is a secret that they usually keep carefully to themselves, but the history of the Popa Nats is well known. Everyone who lives near the great hill can tell you that, for it all happened not so long ago. How long exactly no one can say, but not so long that the details of the story have become at all clouded by the mists of time.

They were brother and sister, these Popa Nats, and they had lived away up North. The brother was a blacksmith, and he was a very strong man. He was the strongest man in all the country; the blow of his hammer on the anvil made the earth tremble, and his forge was as the mouth of hell. No one was so much feared and so much sought after as he. And as he was strong, so his sister was beautiful beyond all the maidens of the time. Their father and mother were dead, and there was no one but those two, the brother and sister, so they loved each other dearly, and thought of no one else. The brother brought home no wife to his house by the forge. He wanted no one while he had his sister there, and when lovers came wooing to her, singing amorous songs in the amber dusk, she would have nothing to do with them. So they lived there together, he growing stronger and she more beautiful every day, till at last a change came.

The old king died, and a new king came to the throne, and orders were sent about to all the governors of provinces and other officials that the most beautiful maidens were to be sent down to the Golden City to be wives to the great king. So the governor of that country sent for the blacksmith and his sister to his palace, and told them there what orders he had received, and asked the blacksmith to give his sister that she might be sent as queen to the king. We are not told what arguments the governor used to gain his point, but only this, that when he failed, he sent the girl in unto his wife, and there she was persuaded to go. There must have been something very tempting, to one who was but a village girl, in the prospect of being even one of the lesser queens, of living in the palace, the centre of the world. So she consented at last, and her brother consented, and the girl was sent down under fitting escort to find favour in the eyes of her king. But the blacksmith refused to go. It was no good the governor saying such a great man as he must come to high honour in the Golden City, it was useless for the girl to beg and pray him to come with her—he always refused. So she sailed away down the great river, and the blacksmith returned to his forge.

As the governor had said, the girl was acceptable in the king's sight, and she was made at last one of the principal queens, and of all she had most power over the king. They say she was most beautiful, that her presence was as soothing as shade after heat, that her form was as graceful as a young tree, and the palms of her hands were like lotus blossoms. She had enemies, of course. Most of the other queens were her enemies, and tried to do her harm. But it was useless telling tales of her to the king, for the king never believed; and she walked so wisely and so well, that she never fell into any snare. But still the plots never ceased.

There was one day when she was sitting alone in the garden pavilion, with the trees making moving shadows all about her, that the king came to her. They talked for a time, and the king began to speak to her of her life before she came to the palace, a thing he had never done before. But he seemed to know all about it, nevertheless, and he spoke to her of her brother, and said that he, the king, had heard how no man was so strong as this blacksmith, the brother of the queen. The queen said it was true, and she talked on and on and praised her brother, and babbled of the days of her childhood, when he carried her on his great shoulder, and threw her into the air, catching her again. She was delighted to talk of all these things, and in her pleasure she forgot her discretion, and said that her brother was wise as well as strong, and that all the people loved him. Never was there such a man as he. The king did not seem very pleased with it all, but he said only that the blacksmith was a great man, and that the queen must write to him to come down to the city, that the king might see him of whom there was such great report.

Then the king got up and went away, and the queen began to doubt; and the more she thought the more she feared she had not been acting wisely in talking as she did, for it is not wise to praise anyone to a king. She went away to her own room to consider, and to try if she could hear of any reason why the king should act as he had done, and desire her brother to come to him to the city; and she found out that it was all a plot of her enemies. Herself they had failed to injure, so they were now plotting against her through her brother. They had gone to the king, and filled his ear with slanderous reports. They had said that the queen's brother was the strongest man in all the kingdom. 'He was cunning, too,' they said, 'and very popular among all the people; and he was so puffed up with pride, now that his sister was a queen, that there was nothing he did not think he could do.' They represented to the king how dangerous such a man was in a kingdom, that it would be quite easy for him to raise such rebellion as the king could hardly put down, and that he was just the man to do such a thing. Nay, it was indeed proved that he must be disloyally plotting something, or he would have come down with his sister to the city when she came. But now many months had passed, and he never came. Clearly he was not to be trusted. Any other man whose sister was a queen would have come and lived in the palace, and served the king and become a minister, instead of staying up there and pretending to be a blacksmith.

The king's mind had been much disturbed by this, for it seemed to him that it must be in part true; and he went to the queen, as I have said, and his suspicions had not been lulled by what she told him, so he had ordered her to write to her brother to come down to the palace.

The queen was terrified when she saw what a mistake she had made, and how she had fallen into the trap of her enemies; but she hoped that the king would forget, and she determined that she would send no order to her brother to come. But the next day the king came back to the subject, and asked her if she had yet sent the letter, and she said 'No!' The king was very angry at this disobedience to his orders, and he asked her how it came that she had not done as he had commanded, and sent a letter to her brother to call him to the palace.

Then the queen fell at the king's feet and told him all her fears that her brother was sent for only to be imprisoned or executed, and she begged and prayed the king to leave him in peace up there in his village. She assured the king that he was loyal and good, and would do no evil.

The king was rather abashed that his design had been discovered, but he was firm in his purpose. He assured the queen that the blacksmith should come to no harm, but rather good; and he ordered the queen to obey him, threatening her that if she refused he would be sure that she was disloyal also, and there would be no alternative but to send and arrest the blacksmith by force, and punish her, the queen, too. Then the queen said that if the king swore to her that her brother should come to no harm, she would write as ordered. *And the king swore.*

So the queen wrote to her brother, and adjured him by his love to her to come down to the Golden City. She said she had dire need of him, and she told him that the king had sworn that no harm should come to him.

The letter was sent off by a king's messenger. In due time the blacksmith arrived, and he was immediately seized and thrown into prison to await his trial.

When the queen saw that she had been deceived, she was in despair. She tried by every way, by tears and entreaties and caresses, to move the king, but all without avail. Then she tried by plotting and bribery to gain her brother's release, but it was all in vain. The day for trial came quickly, and the blacksmith was tried, and he was condemned and sentenced to be burnt alive by the river on the following day.

On the evening of the day of trial the queen sent a message to the king to come to her; and when the king came reluctantly, fearing a renewal of entreaties, expecting a woman made of tears and sobs, full of grief, he found instead that the queen had dried her eyes and dressed herself still more beautifully than ever, till she seemed to the king the very pearl among women. And she told the king that he was right, and she was wrong. She said, putting her arms about him and caressing him, that she had discovered that it was true that her brother had been plotting against the king, and therefore his death was necessary. It was terrible, she said, to find that her brother, whom she had always held as a pattern, was no better than a traitor; but it was even so, and her king was the wisest of all kings to find it out.

The king was delighted to find his queen in this mood, and he soothed her and talked to her kindly and sweetly, for he really loved her, though he had given in to bad advice about the brother. And when the king's suspicions were lulled, the queen said to him that she had now but one request to make, and that was that she might have permission to go down with her maids to the river-shore in the early morning, and see herself the execution of her traitor brother. The king, who would now have granted her anything—anything she asked, except just that one thing, the life of her brother—gave permission; and then the queen said that she was tired and wished to rest after all the trouble of the last few days, and would the king leave her. So the king left her to herself, and went away to his own chambers.

Very early in the morning, ere the crimson flush upon the mountains had faded in the light of day, a vast crowd was gathered below the city, by the shore of the great river. Very many thousands were there, of many countries and peoples, crowding down to see a man die, to see a traitor burnt to death for his sins, for there is nothing men like so much as to see another man die.

Upon a little headland jutting out into the river the pyre was raised, with brushwood and straw, to burn quickly, and an iron post in the middle to which the man was to be chained. At one side was a place reserved, and presently down from the palace in a long procession came the queen and her train of ladies to the place kept for her. Guards were put all about to prevent the people crowding; and then came the soldiers, and in the midst of them the blacksmith; and amid many cries of 'Traitor, traitor!' and shouts of derision, he was bound to the iron post within the wood and the straw, and the guards fell back.

The queen sat and watched it all, and said never a word. Fire was put to the pyre, and it crept rapidly up in long red tongues with coils of black smoke. It went very quickly, for the wood was very dry, and a light breeze came laughing up the river and helped it. The flames played about the man chained there in the midst, and he made never a sign; only he looked steadily across at the purple mountain where his home lay, and it was clear that in a few more moments he would be dead. There was a deep silence everywhere.

Then of a sudden, before anyone knew, before a hand could be held out to hinder her, the queen rose from her seat and ran to the pyre. In a moment she was there and had thrown herself into the flames, and with her arms about her brother's neck she turned and faced the myriad eyes that glared upon them—the queen, in all the glory of her beauty, glittering with gems, and the man with great shackled bare limbs, dressed in a few rags, his muscles already twisted with the agony of the fire. A great cry of horror came from the people, and there was the movement of guards and officers rushing to stop the fire; but it was all of no use. A flash of red flames came out of the logs, folding these twain like an imperial cloak, a whirl of sparks towered into the air, and when one could see again the woman and her brother were no longer there. They were dead and burnt, and the bodies mingled with the ashes of the fire. She had cost her brother his life, and she went with him into death.

Some days after this a strange report was brought to the palace. By the landing-place near the spot where the fire had been was a great fig-tree. It was so near to the landing-place, and was such a magnificent tree, that travellers coming from the boats, or waiting for a boat to arrive, would rest in numbers under its shade. But the report said that something had happened there. To travellers sleeping beneath the tree at night it was stated that two Nats had appeared, very large and very beautiful, a man Nat and a woman Nat, and had frightened them very much indeed. Noises were heard in the tree, voices and cries, and a strange terror came upon those who approached it. Nay, it was even said that men had been struck by unseen hands and severely hurt, and others, it was said, had disappeared. Children who went to play under the tree were never seen again: the Nats took them, and their parents sought for them in vain. So the landing-place was deserted, and a petition was brought to the king, and the king gave orders that the tree should be hewn down. So the tree was cut down, and its trunk was thrown into the river; it floated away out of sight, and nothing happened to the men who cut the tree, though they were deadly afraid.

The tree floated down for days, until at last it stranded near a landing-place that led to a large town, where the governor of these parts lived; and at this landing-place the portents that had frightened the people at the great city reappeared and terrified the travellers here too, and they petitioned the governor.

The governor sought out a great monk, a very holy man learned in these matters, and sent him to inquire, and the monk came down to the tree and spoke. He said that if any Nats lived in the tree, they should speak to him and tell him what they wanted. 'It is not fit,' he said, 'for great Nats to terrify the poor villagers at the landing-place. Let the Nats speak and say what they require. All that they want shall be given.' And the Nats spake and said that they wanted a place to live in where they could be at peace, and the monk answered for the governor that all his land was at their disposal. 'Let the Nats choose,' he said; 'all the country is before them.' So the Nats chose, and said that they would have Popa Mountain, and the monk agreed.

The Nats then left the tree and went away, far away inland, to the great Popa Mountain, and took up their abode there, and all the people there feared and reverenced them, and even made to their honour two statues with golden heads and set them up on the mountain.

This is the story of the Popa Nats, the greatest Nats of all the country of Burma, the guardian spirits of the mysterious mountain. The golden heads of the statues are now in one of our treasuries, put there for safe custody during the troubles, though it is doubtful if even then anyone would have dared to steal them, so greatly are the Nats feared. And the hunters and the travellers there must offer to the Nats little offerings, if they would be safe in these forests, and even the young man must obtain permission from the Nats before he marry.

I think these stories that I have told, stories selected from very many that I have heard, will show what sort of spirits these are that the Burmese have peopled their trees and rivers with; will show what sort of religion it is that underlies, without influencing, the creed of the Buddha that they follow. It is of the very poetry of superstition, free from brutality, from baseness, from anything repulsive, springing, as I have said, from their innate sympathy with Nature and recognition of the life that works in all things. It always seems to me that beliefs such as these are a great key to the nature of a people, are, apart from all interest in their beauty, and in their akinness to other beliefs, of great value in trying to understand the character of a nation.

For to beings such as Nats and fairies the people who believe in them will attribute such qualities as are predominant in themselves, as they consider admirable; and, indeed, all supernatural beings are but the magnified shadows of man cast by the light of his imagination upon the mists of his ignorance.

Therefore, when you find that a people make their spirits beautiful and fair, calm and even tempered, loving peace and the beauty of the trees and rivers, shrinkingly averse from loud words, from noises, and from the taking of life, it is because the people themselves think that these are great qualities. If no stress be laid upon their courage, their activity, their performance of great deeds, it is because the people who imagine them care not for such things. There is no truer guide, I am sure, to the heart of a young people than their superstitions; these they make entirely for themselves, apart from their religion, which is, to a certain extent, made for them. That is why I have written this chapter on Nats: not because I think it affects Buddhism very much one way or another, but because it seems to me to reveal the people themselves, because it helps us to understand them better, to see more with their eyes, to be in unison with their ideas— because it is a great key to the soul of the people.

CHAPTER XXII

DEATH, THE DELIVERER

'The end of my life is near at hand; seven days hence, like a man who rids himself of a heavy load, I shall be free from the burden of my body.'—*Death of the Buddha.*

There is a song well known to all the Burmese, the words of which are taken from the sacred writings. It is called the story of Ma Pa Da, and it was first told to me by a Burmese monk, long ago, when I was away on the frontier.

It runs like this:

In the time of the Buddha, in the city of Thawatti, there was a certain rich man, a merchant, who had many slaves. Slaves in those days, and, indeed, generally throughout the East, were held very differently to slaves in Europe. They were part of the family, and were not saleable without good reason, and there was a law applicable to them. They were not *hors de la loi*, like the slaves of which we have conception. There are many cases quoted of sisters being slaves to sisters, and of brothers to brothers, quoted not for the purpose of saying that this was an uncommon occurrence, but merely of showing points of law in such cases.

One day in the market the merchant bought another slave, a young man, handsome and well mannered, and took him to his house, and kept him there with his family and the other slaves. The young man was earnest and careful in his work, and the merchant approved of him, and his fellow-slaves liked him. But Ma Pa Da, the merchant's daughter, fell in love with him. The slave was much troubled at this, and he did his best to avoid her; but he was a slave and under orders, and what could he do? When she would come to him secretly and make love to him, and say, 'Let us flee together, for we love each other,' he would refuse, saying that he was a slave, and the merchant would be very angry. He said he could not do such a thing. And yet when the girl said, 'Let us flee, for we love each other,' he knew that it was true, and that he loved her as she loved him; and it was only his honour to his master that held him from doing as she asked.

But because his heart was not of iron, and there are few men that can resist when a woman comes and woos them, he at last gave way; and they fled away one night, the girl and the slave, taking with them her jewels and some money. They travelled rapidly and in great fear, and did not rest till they came to a city far away where the merchant would never, they thought, think of searching for them.

Here, in this city where no one knew of their history, they lived in great happiness, husband and wife, trading with the money they had with them.

And in time a little child was born to them.

About two or three years after this it became necessary for the husband to take a journey, and he started forth with his wife and child. The journey was a very long one, and they were unduly delayed; and so it happened that while still in the forest the wife fell ill, and could not go on any further. So the husband built a hut of branches and leaves, and there, in the solitude of the forest, was born to them another little son.

The mother recovered rapidly, and in a little time she was well enough to go on. They were to start next morning on their way again; and in the evening the husband went out, as was his custom, to cut firewood, for the nights were cold and damp.

Ma Pa Da waited and waited for him, but he never came back.

The sun set and the dark rose out of the ground, and the forest became full of whispers, but he never came. All night she watched and waited, caring for her little ones, fearful to leave them alone, till at last the gray light came down, down from the sky to the branches, and from the branches to the ground, and she could see her way. Then, with her new-born babe in her arms and the elder little fellow trotting by her side, she went out to search for her husband. Soon enough she found him, not far off, stiff and cold beside his half-cut bundle of firewood. A snake had bitten him on the ankle, and he was dead.

So Ma Pa Da was alone in the great forest, but a girl still, with two little children to care for.

But she was brave, despite her trouble, and she determined to go on and gain some village. She took her baby in her arms and the little one by the hand, and started on her journey.

And for a time all went well, till at last she came to a stream. It was not very deep, but it was too deep for the little boy to wade, for it came up to his neck, and his mother was not strong enough to carry both at once. So, after considering for a time, she told the elder boy to wait. She would cross and put the baby on the far side, and return for him.

'Be good,' she said; 'be good, and stay here quietly till I come back;' and the boy promised.

The stream was deeper and swifter than she thought; but she went with great care and gained the far side, and put the baby under a tree a little distance from the bank, to lie there while she went for the other boy. Then, after a few minutes' rest, she went back.

She had got to the centre of the stream, and her little boy had come down to the margin to be ready for her, when she heard a rush and a cry from the side she had just left; and, looking round, she saw with terror a great eagle sweep down upon the baby, and carry it off in its claws. She turned round and waved her arms and cried out to the eagle, 'He! he!' hoping it would be frightened and drop the baby. But it cared nothing for her cries or threats, and swept on with long curves over the forest trees, away out of sight.

Then the mother turned to gain the bank once more, and suddenly she missed her son who had been waiting for her. He had seen his mother wave her arms; he had heard her shout, and he thought she was calling him to come to her. So the brave little man walked down into the water, and the black current carried him off his feet at once. He was gone, drowned in the deep water below the ford, tossing on the waves towards the sea.

No one can write of the despair of the girl when she threw herself under a tree in the forest. The song says it was very terrible.

At last she said to herself, 'I will get up now and return to my father in Thawatti; he is all I have left. Though I have forsaken him all these years, yet now that my husband and his children are dead, my father will take me back again. Surely he will have pity on me, for I am much to be pitied.'

So she went on, and at length, after many days, she came to the gates of the great city where her father lived.

At the entering of the gates she met a large company of people, mourners, returning from a funeral, and she spoke to them and asked them:

'Who is it that you have been burying to-day so grandly with so many mourners?'

And the people answered her, and told her who it was. And when she heard, she fell down upon the road as one dead: for it was her father and mother who had died yesterday, and it was their funeral train that she saw. They were all dead now, husband and sons and father and mother; in all the world she was quite alone.

So she went mad, for her trouble was more than she could bear. She threw off all her clothes, and let down her long hair and wrapped it about her naked body, and walked about raving.

At last she came to where the Buddha was teaching, seated under a fig-tree. She came up to the Buddha, and told him of her losses, and how she had no one left; and she demanded of the Buddha that he should restore to her those that she had lost. And the Buddha had great compassion upon her, and tried to console her.

'All die,' he said; 'it comes to everyone, king and peasant, animal and man. Only through many deaths can we obtain the Great Peace. All this sorrow,' he said, 'is of the earth. All this is passion which we must get rid of, and forget before we reach heaven. Be comforted, my daughter, and turn to the holy life. All suffer as you do. It is part of our very existence here, sorrow and trouble without any end.'

But she would not be comforted, but demanded her dead of the Buddha. Then, because he saw it was no use talking to her, that her ears were deaf with grief, and her eyes blinded with tears, he said to her that he would restore to her those who were dead.

'You must go,' he said, 'my daughter, and get some mustard-seed, a pinch of mustard-seed, and I can bring back their lives. Only you must get this seed from the garden of him near whom death has never come. Get this, and all will be well.'

So the woman went forth with a light heart. It was so simple, only a pinch of mustard-seed, and mustard grew in every garden. She would get the seed and be back very quickly, and then the Lord Buddha would give her back those she loved who had died. She clothed herself again and tied up her hair, and went cheerfully and asked at the first house, 'Give me a pinch of mustard-seed,' and it was given readily. So with her treasure in her hand she was going forth back to the Buddha full of delight, when she remembered.

'Has ever anyone died in your household?' she asked, looking round wistfully.

The man answered 'Yes,' that death had been with them but recently. Who could this woman be, he thought, to ask such a question? And the woman went forth, the seed dropping from her careless fingers, for it was of no value. So she would try again and again, but it was always the same. Death had taken his tribute from all. Father or mother, son or brother, daughter or wife, there was always a gap somewhere, a vacant place beside the meal. From house to house throughout the city she went, till at last the new hope faded away, and she learned from the world, what she had not believed from the Buddha, that death and life are one.

So she returned, and she became a nun, poor soul! taking on her the two hundred and twenty-seven vows, which are so hard to keep that nowadays nuns keep but five of them.

This is the teaching of the Buddha, that death is inevitable; this is the consolation he offers, that all men must know death; no one can escape death; no one can escape the sorrow of the death of those whom he loves. Death, he says, and life are one; not antagonistic, but the same; and the only way to escape from one is to escape from the other too. Only in the Great Peace, when we have found refuge from the passion and tumult of life, shall we find the place where death cannot come. Life and death are one.

This is the teaching of the Buddha, repeated over and over again to his disciples when they sorrowed for the death of Thariputra, when they were in despair at the swift-approaching end of the great teacher himself. Hear what he says to Ananda, the beloved disciple, who is mourning over Thariputra.

'Ananda,' he said, 'often and often have I sought to bring shelter to your soul from the misery caused by such grief as this. There are two things alone that can separate us from father and mother, from brother and sister, from all those who are most cherished by us, and those two things are distance and death. Think not that I, though the Buddha, have not felt all this even as any other of you; was I not alone when I was seeking for wisdom in the wilderness?

'And yet what would I have gained by wailing and lamenting either for myself or for others? Would it have brought to me any solace from my loneliness? Would it have been any help to those whom I had left? There is nothing that can happen to us, however terrible, however miserable, that can justify tears and lamentations and make them aught but a weakness.'

And so, we are told, in this way the Buddha soothed the affliction of Ananda, and filled his soul with consolation—the consolation of resignation.

For there is no other consolation possible but this, resignation to the inevitable, the conviction of the uselessness of sorrow, the vanity and selfishness of grief.

There is no meeting again with the dead. Nowhere in the recurring centuries shall we meet again those whom we have loved, whom we love, who seem to us to be parts of our very soul. That which survives of us, the part which is incarnated again and again, until it be fit for heaven, has nothing to do with love and hate.

Even if in the whirlpool of life our paths should cross again the paths of those whom we have loved, we are never told that we shall know them again and love them.

A friend of mine has just lost his mother, and he is very much distressed. He must have been very fond of her, for although he has a wife and children, and is happy in his family, he is in great sorrow. He proposes even to build a pagoda over her remains, a testimony of respect which in strict Buddhism is reserved to saints. He has been telling me about this, and how he is trying to get a sacred relic to put in the pagoda, and I asked him if he never hoped again to meet the soul of his mother on earth or in heaven, and he answered:

'No. It is very hard, but so are many things, and they have to be borne. Far better it is to face the truth than to escape by a pleasant falsehood. There is a Burmese proverb that tells us that all the world is one vast burial-ground; there are dead men everywhere.'

'One of our great men has said the same,' I answered.

He was not surprised.

'As it is true,' he said, 'I suppose all great men would see it.'

Thus there is no escape, no loophole for a delusive hope, only the cultivation of the courage of sorrow.

There are never any exceptions to the laws of the Buddha. If a law is a law, that is the end of it. Just as we know of no exceptions to the law of gravitation, so there are no exceptions to the law of death.

But although this may seem to be a religion of despair, it is not really so. This sorrow to which there is no relief is the selfishness of sorrow, the grief for our own loneliness; for of sorrow, of fear, of pity for the dead, there is no need. We know that in time all will be well with them. We know that, though there may be before them vast periods of suffering, yet that they will all at last be in Nebhan with us. And if we shall not know them there, still we shall know that they are there, all of them—not one will be wanting. Purified from the lust of life, white souls steeped in the Great Peace, all living things will attain rest at last.

There is this remarkable fact in Buddhism, that nowhere is any fear expressed of death itself, nowhere any apprehension of what may happen to the dead. It is the sorrow of separation, the terror of death to the survivors, that is always dwelt upon with compassion, and the agony of which it is sought to soothe.

That the dying man himself should require strengthening to face the King of Terrors is hardly ever mentioned. It seems to be taken for granted that men should have courage in themselves to take leave of life becomingly, without undue fears. Buddhism is the way to show us the escape from the miseries of life, not to give us hope in the hour of death.

It is true that to all Orientals death is a less fearful thing than it is to us. I do not know what may be the cause of this, courage certainly has little to do with it; but it is certain that the purely physical fear of death, that horror and utter revulsion that seizes the majority of us at the idea of death, is absent from most Orientals. And yet this cannot explain it all. For fear of death, though less, is still there, is still a strong influence upon their lives, and it would seem that no religion which ignored this great fact could become a great living religion.

Religion is made for man, to fit his necessities, not man for religion, and yet the faith of Buddhism is not concerned with death.

Consider our faith, how much of its teaching consists of how to avoid the fear of death, how much of its consolation is for the death-bed. How we are taught all our lives that we should live so as not to fear death; how we have priests and sacraments to soothe the dying man, and give him hope and courage, and how the crown and summit of our creed is that we should die easily. And consider that in Buddhism all this is absolutely wanting. Buddhism is a creed of life, of conduct; death is the end of that life, that is all.

We have all seen death. We have all of us watched those who, near and dear to us, go away out of our ken. There is no need for me to recall the last hours of those of our faith, to bring up again the fading eye and waning breath, the messages of hope we search for in our Scriptures to give hope to him who is going, the assurances of religion, the cross held before the dying eyes.

Many men, we are told, turn to religion at the last after a life of wickedness, and a man may do so even at the eleventh hour and be saved.

That is part of our belief; that is the strongest part of our belief; and that is the hope that all fervent Christians have, that those they love may be saved even at the end.

I think it may truly be said that our Western creeds are all directed at the hour of death, as the great and final test of that creed.

And now think of Buddhism; it is a creed of life. In life you must win your way to salvation by urgent effort, by suffering, by endurance. On your death-bed you can do nothing. If you have done well, then it is well; if ill, then you must in future life try again and again till you succeed. A life is not washed, a soul is not made fit for the dwelling of eternity, in a moment.

Repentance to a Buddhist is but the opening of the eyes to see the path to righteousness; it has no virtue in itself. To have seen that we are sinners is but the first step to cleansing our sin; in itself it cannot purify.

As well ask a robber of the poor to repent, and suppose thereby that those who have suffered from his guilt are compensated for the evil done to them by his repentance, as to ask a Buddhist to believe that a sinner can at the last moment make good to his own soul all the injuries caused to that soul by the wickedness of his life.

Or suppose a man who has destroyed his constitution by excess to be by the very fact of acknowledging that excess restored to health.

The Buddhist will not have that at all. A man is what he makes himself; and that making is a matter of terrible effort, of unceasing endeavour towards the right, of constant suppression of sin, till sin be at last dead within him. If a man has lived a wicked life, he dies a wicked man, and no wicked man can obtain the perfect rest of the sinless dead. Heaven is shut to him. But if heaven is shut it is not shut for ever; if hell may perhaps open to him it is only for a time, only till he is purified and washed from the stain of his sins; and then he can begin again, and have another chance to win heaven. If there is no immediate heaven there is no eternal hell, and in due time all will reach heaven; all will have learnt, through suffering, the wisdom the Buddha has shown to us, that only by a just life can men reach the Great Peace even as he did.

So that if Buddhism has none of the consolation for the dying man that Christianity holds out, in the hope of heaven, so it has none of the threats and terrors of our faith. There is no fear of an angry Judge—of a Judge who is angry.

And yet when I came to think over the matter, it seemed to me that surely there must be something to calm him in the face of death. If Buddhism does not furnish this consolation, he must go elsewhere for it. And I was not satisfied, because I could find nothing in the sacred books about a man's death, that therefore the creed of the people had ignored it. A living creed must, I was sure, provide for this somehow.

So I went to a friend of mine, a Burman magistrate, and I asked him:

'When a man is dying, what does he try to think of? What do you say to comfort him that his last moments may be peace? The monks do not come, I know.'

'The monks!' he said, shaking his head; 'what could they do?'

I did not know.

'Can you do anything,' I asked, 'to cheer him? Do you speak to him of what may happen after death, of hopes of another life?'

'No one can tell,' said my friend, 'what will happen after death. It depends on a man's life, if he has done good or evil, what his next existence will be, whether he will go a step nearer to the Peace. When the man is dying no monks will come, truly; but an old man, an old friend, father, perhaps, or an elder of the village, and he will talk to the dying man. He will say, "Think of your good deeds; think of all that you have done well in this life. Think of your good deeds."'

'What is the use of that?' I asked. 'Suppose you think of your good deeds, what then? Will that bring peace?'

The Burman seemed to think that it would.

'Nothing,' he said, 'was so calming to a man's soul as to think of even one deed he had done well in his life.'

Think of the man dying. The little house built of bamboo and thatch, with an outer veranda, where the friends are sitting, and the inner room, behind a wall of bamboo matting, where the man is lying. A pot of flowers is standing on a shelf on one side, and a few cloths are hung here and there beneath the brown rafters. The sun comes in through little chinks in roof and wall, making curious lights in the semi-darkness of the room, and it is very hot.

From outside come the noises of the village, cries of children playing, grunts of cattle, voices of men and women clearly heard through the still clear air of the afternoon. There is a woman pounding rice near by with a steady thud, thud of the lever, and there is a clink of a loom where a girl is weaving ceaselessly. All these sounds come into the house as if there were no walls at all, but they are unheeded from long custom.

The man lies on a low bed with a fine mat spread under him for bedding. His wife, his grown-up children, his sister, his brother are about him, for the time is short, and death comes very quickly in the East. They talk to him kindly and lovingly, but they read to him no sacred books; they give him no messages from the world to which he is bound; they whisper to him no hopes of heaven. He is tortured with no fears of everlasting hell. Yet life is sweet and death is bitter, and it is hard to go; and as he tosses to and fro in his fever there comes in to him an old friend, the headman of the village perhaps, with a white muslin fillet bound about his kind old head, and he sits beside the dying man and speaks to him.

'Remember,' he says slowly and clearly, 'all those things that you have done well. Think of your good deeds.'

And as the sick man turns wearily, trying to move his thoughts as he is bidden, trying to direct the wheels of memory, the old man helps him to remember.

'Think,' he says, 'of your good deeds, of how you have given charity to the monks, of how you have fed the poor. Remember how you worked and saved to build the little rest-house in the forest where the traveller stays and finds water for his thirst. All these are pleasant things, and men will always be grateful to you. Remember your brother, how you helped him in his need, how you fed him and went security for him till he was able again to secure his own living. You did well to him, surely that is a pleasant thing.'

I do not think it difficult to see how the sick man's face will lighten, how his eyes will brighten at the thoughts that come to him at the old man's words. And he goes on:

'Remember when the squall came up the river and the boat upset when you were crossing here; how it seemed as if no man could live alone in such waves, and yet how you clung to and saved the boy who was with you, swimming through the water that splashed over your head and very nearly drowned you. The boy's father and mother have never forgotten that, and they are even now mourning without in the veranda. It is all due to you that their lives have not been full of misery and despair. Remember their faces when you brought their little son to them saved from death in the great river. Surely that is a pleasant thing. Remember your wife who is now with you; how you have loved her and cherished her, and kept faithful to her before all the world. You have been a good husband to her, and you have honoured her. She loves you, and you have loved her all your long life together. Surely that is a pleasant thing.'

Yes, surely these are pleasant things to have with one at the last. Surely a man will die easier with such memories as these before his eyes, with love in those about him, and the calm of good deeds in his dying heart. If it be a different way of soothing a man's end from those which other nations use, is it the worse for that?

Think of your good deeds. It seems a new idea to me that in doing well in our life we are making for ourselves a pleasant death, because of the memory of those things. And if we have none? or if evil so outnumbered the good deeds as to hide and overwhelm them, what then? A man's death will be terrible indeed if he cannot in all his days remember one good deed that he has done.

'All a man's life comes before him at the hour of death,' said my informant; 'all, from the earliest memory to the latest breath. Like a whole landscape called by a flash of lightning out of the dark night. It is all there, every bit of it, good and evil, pleasure and pain, sin and righteousness.'

A man cannot escape from his life even in death. In our acts of to-day we are determining what our death will be; if we have lived well, we shall die well; and if not, then not. As a man lives so shall he die, is the teaching of Buddhism as of other creeds.

So what Buddhism has to offer to the dying believer is this, that if he live according to its tenets he will die happily, and that in the life that he will next enter upon he will be less and less troubled by sin, less and less wedded to the lust of life, until sometime, far away, he shall gain the great Deliverance. He shall have perfect Peace, perfect rest, perfect happiness, he and his, in that heaven where his teacher went before him long ago.

And if we should say that this Deliverance from life, this Great Peace, is Death, what matter, if it be indeed Peace?

FOOTNOTE:

These five vows are:

1. Not to take life.
2. To be honest.
3. To tell the truth.
4. To abstain from intoxicants.
5. Chastity.

CHAPTER XXIII

THE POTTER'S WHEEL

'Life is like a great whirlpool wherein we are dashed to and fro by our passions.'—*Saying of the Buddha.*

It is a hard teaching, this of the Buddha about death. It is a teaching that may appeal to the reason, but not to the soul, that when life goes out, this thing which we call 'I' goes out with it, and that love and remembrance are dead for ever.

It is so hard a teaching that in its purity the people cannot believe it. They accept it, but they have added on to it a belief which changes the whole form of it, a belief that is the outcome of that weakness of humanity which insists that death is not and cannot be all.

Though to the strict Buddhist death is the end of all worldly passion, to the Burmese villager that is not so. He cannot grasp, he cannot endure that it should be so, and he has made for himself out of Buddhism a belief that is opposed to all Buddhism in this matter.

He believes in the transmigration of souls, in the survival of the 'I.' The teaching that what survives is not the 'I,' but only the result of its action, is too deep for him to hold. True, if a flame dies the effects that it has caused remain, and the flame is dead for ever.

A new flame is a new flame. But the 'I' of man cannot die, he thinks; it lives and loves for all time.

He has made out of the teaching a new teaching that is very far from that of the Buddha, and the teaching is this: When a man dies his soul remains, his 'I' has only changed its habitation. Still it lives and breathes on earth, not the effect, but the soul itself. It is reborn among us, and it may even be recognised very often in its new abode.

And that we should never forget this, that we should never doubt that this is true, it has been so ordered that many can remember something of these former lives of theirs. This belief is not to a Burman a mere theory, but is as true as anything he can see. For does he not daily see people who know of their former lives? Nay, does he not himself, often vaguely, have glimpses of that former life of his? No man seems to be quite without it, but of course it is clearer to some than others. Just as we tell stories in the dusk of ghosts and second sight, so do they, when the day's work is over, gossip of stories of second birth; only that they believe in them far more than we do in ghosts.

A friend of mine put up for the night once at a monastery far away in the forest near a small village. He was travelling with an escort of mounted police, and there was no place else to sleep but in the monastery. The monk was, as usual, hospitable, and put what he had, bare house-room, at the officer's disposal, and he and his men settled down for the night.

After dinner a fire was built on the ground, and the officer went and sat by it and talked to the headman of the village and the monk. First they talked of the dacoits and of crops, unfailing subjects of interest, and gradually they drifted from one subject to another till the Englishman remarked about the monastery, that it was a very large and fine one for such a small secluded village to have built. The monastery was of the best and straightest teak, and must, he thought, have taken a very long time and a great deal of labour to build, for the teak must have been brought from very far away; and in explanation he was told a curious story.

It appeared that in the old days there used to be only a bamboo and grass monastery there, such a monastery as most jungle villages have; and the then monk was distressed at the smallness of his abode and the little accommodation there was for his school—a monastery is always a school. So one rainy season he planted with great care a number of teak seedlings round about, and he watered them and cared for them. 'When they are grown up,' he would say, 'these teak-trees shall provide timber for a new and proper building; and I will myself return in another life, and with those trees will I build a monastery more worthy than this.' Teak-trees take a hundred years to reach a mature size, and while the trees were still but saplings the monk died, and another monk taught in his stead. And so it went on, and the years went by, and from time to time new monasteries of bamboo were built and rebuilt, and the teak-trees grew bigger and bigger. But the village grew smaller, for the times were troubled, and the village was far away in the forest. So it happened that at last the village found itself without a monk at all: the last monk was dead, and no one came to take his place.

It is a serious thing for a village to have no monk. To begin with, there is no one to teach the lads to read and write and do arithmetic; and there is no one to whom you can give offerings and thereby get merit, and there is no one to preach to you and tell you of the sacred teaching. So the village was in a bad way.

Then at last one evening, when the girls were all out at the well drawing water, they were surprised by the arrival of a monk walking in from the forest, weary with a long journey, footsore and hungry. The villagers received him with enthusiasm, fearing, however, that he was but passing through, and they furbished up the old monastery in a hurry for him to sleep in. But the curious thing was that the monk seemed to know it all.

He knew the monastery and the path to it, and the ways about the village, and the names of the hills and the streams. It seemed, indeed, as if he must once have lived there in the village, and yet no one knew him or recognised his face, though he was but a young man still, and there were villagers who had lived there for seventy years. Next morning, instead of going on his way, the monk came into the village with his begging-bowl, as monks do, and went round and collected his food for the day; and in the evening, when the villagers went to see him at the monastery, he told them he was going to stay. He recalled to them the monk who had planted the teak-trees, and how he had said that when the trees were grown he would return. 'I,' said the young monk, 'am he that planted these trees. Lo, they are grown up, and I am returned, and now we will build a monastery as I said.'

When the villagers, doubting, questioned him, and old men came and talked to him of traditions of long-past days, he answered as one who knew all. He told them he had been born and educated far away in the South, and had grown up not knowing who he had been; and that he had entered a monastery, and in time became a Pongyi. The remembrance came to him, he went on, in a dream of how he had planted the trees and had promised to return to that village far away in the forest.

The very next day he had started, and travelled day after day and week upon week, till at length he had arrived, as they saw. So the villagers were convinced, and they set to work and cut down the great boles, and built the monastery such as my friend saw. And the monk lived there all his life, and taught the children, and preached the marvellous teaching of the great Buddha, till at length his time came again and he returned; for of monks it is not said that they die, but that they return.

This is the common belief of the people. Into this has the mystery of Dharma turned, in the thoughts of the Burmese Buddhists, for no one can believe the incomprehensible. A man has a soul, and it passes from life to life, as a traveller from inn to inn, till at length it is ended in heaven. But not till he has attained heaven in his heart will he attain heaven in reality.

Many children, the Burmese will tell you, remember their former lives. As they grow older the memories die away and they forget, but to the young children they are very clear. I have seen many such.

About fifty years ago in a village named Okshitgon were born two children, a boy and a girl. They were born on the same day in neighbouring houses, and they grew up together, and played together, and loved each other. And in due course they married and started a family, and maintained themselves by cultivating their dry, barren fields about the village. They were always known as devoted to each other, and they died as they had lived—together. The same death took them on the same day; so they were buried without the village and were forgotten; for the times were serious.

It was the year after the English army had taken Mandalay, and all Burma was in a fury of insurrection. The country was full of armed men, the roads were unsafe, and the nights were lighted with the flames of burning villages. It was a bad time for peace-loving men, and many such, fleeing from their villages, took refuge in larger places nearer the centres of administration.

Okshitgon was in the midst of one of the worst of all the distressed districts, and many of its people fled, and one of them, a man named Maung Kan, with his young wife went to the village of Kabyu and lived there.

Now, Maung Kan's wife had born to him twin sons. They were born at Okshitgon shortly before their parents had to run away, and they were named, the eldest Maung Gyi, which is Brother Big-fellow, and the younger Maung Ngè, which means Brother Little-fellow. These lads grew up at Kabyu, and soon learned to talk; and as they grew up their parents were surprised to hear them calling to each other at play, and calling each other, not Maung Gyi and Maung Ngè, but Maung San Nyein and Ma Gywin. The latter is a woman's name, and the parents remembered that these were the names of the man and wife who had died in Okshitgon about the time the children were born.

So the parents thought that the souls of the man and wife had entered into the children, and they took them to Okshitgon to try them. The children knew everything in Okshitgon; they knew the roads and the houses and the people, and they recognised the clothes they used to wear in a former life; there was no doubt about it. One of them, the younger, remembered, too, how she had borrowed two rupees once of a woman, Ma Thet, unknown to her husband, and left the debt unpaid. Ma Thet was still living, and so they asked her, and she recollected that it was true she had lent the money long ago.

Shortly afterwards I saw these two children. They are now just over six years old. The elder, into whom the soul of the man entered, is a fat, chubby little fellow, but the younger twin is smaller, and has a curious dreamy look in his face, more like a girl than a boy. They told me much about their former lives. After they died they said they lived for some time without a body at all, wandering in the air and hiding in the trees. This was for their sins. Then, after some months, they were born again as twin boys. 'It used,' said the elder boy, 'to be so clear, I could remember everything; but it is getting duller and duller, and I cannot now remember as I used to do.'

Of children such as this you may find any number. Only you have to look for them, as they are not brought forward spontaneously. The Burmese, like other people, hate to have their beliefs and ideas ridiculed, and from experience they have learned that the object of a foreigner in inquiring into their ways is usually to be able to show by his contempt how very much cleverer a man he is than they are. Therefore they are very shy. But once they understand that you only desire to learn and to see, and that you will always treat them with courtesy and consideration, they will tell you all that they think.

A fellow officer of mine has a Burmese police orderly, a young man about twenty, who has been with him since he came to the district two years ago. Yet my friend only discovered accidentally the other day that his orderly remembers his former life. He is very unwilling to talk about it. He was a woman apparently in that former life, and lived about twenty miles away. He must have lived a good life, for it is a step of promotion to be a man in this life; but he will not talk of it. He forgets most of it, he says, though he remembered it when he was a child.

Sometimes this belief leads to lawsuits of a peculiarly difficult nature. In 1883, two years before the annexation of Upper Burma, there was a case that came into the local Court of the oil district, which depended upon this theory of transmigration.

Opposite Yenangyaung there are many large islands in the river. These islands during the low water months are joined to the mainland, and are covered with a dense high grass in which many deer live.

When the river rises, it rises rapidly, communication with the mainland is cut off, and the islands are for a time, in the higher rises, entirely submerged. During the progress of the first rise some hunters went to one of these islands where many deer were to be found and set fire to the grass to drive them out of cover, shooting them as they came out. Some deer, fleeing before the fire, swam across and escaped, others fell victims, but one fawn, barely half grown, ran right down the island, and in its blind terror it leaped into a boat at anchor there. This boat was that of a fisherman who was plying his trade at some distance, and the only occupant of the boat was his wife. Now this woman had a year or so before lost her son, very much loved by her, but who was not quite of the best character, and when she saw the deer leaping into the boat, she at once fancied that she saw the soul of her erring son looking at her out of its great terrified eyes. So she got up and took the poor panting beast in her arms and soothed it, and when the hunters came running to her to claim it she refused. 'He is my son,' she said, 'he is mine. Shall I give him up to death?' The hunters clamoured and threatened to take the deer by force, but the woman was quite firm. She would never give him up except with her life. 'You can see,' she said, 'that it is true that he is my son. He came running straight to me, as he always did in his trouble when he was a boy, and he is now quite quiet and contented, instead of being afraid of me as an ordinary deer would be.' And it was quite true that the deer took to her at once, and remained with her willingly. So the hunters went off to the court of the governor and filed a suit for the deer.

The case was tried in open court, and the deer was produced with a ribbon round its neck. Evidence there was naturally but little. The hunters claimed the deer because they had driven it out of the island by their fire. The woman resisted the claim on the ground that it was her son.

The decision of the court was this:

'The hunters are not entitled to the deer because they cannot prove that the woman's son's soul is not in the animal. The woman is not entitled to the deer because she cannot prove that it is. The deer will therefore remain with the court until some properly authenticated claim is put in.'

So the two parties were turned out, the woman in bitter tears, and the hunters angry and vexed, and the deer remained the property of the judge.

But this decision was against all Burmese ideas of justice. He should have given the deer to the woman. 'He wanted it for himself,' said a Burman, speaking to me of the affair. 'He probably killed it and ate it. Surely it is true that officials are of all the five evils the greatest.' Then my friend remembered that I was myself an official, and he looked foolish, and began to make complimentary remarks about English officials, that they would never give such an iniquitous decision. I turned it off by saying that no doubt the judge was now suffering in some other life for the evil wrought in the last, and the Burman said that probably he was now inhabiting a tiger.

It is very easy to laugh at such beliefs; nothing is, indeed, easier than to be witty at the expense of any belief. It is also very easy to say that it is all self-deception, that the children merely imagine that they remember their former lives, or are citing conversation of their elders.

How this may be I do not know. What is the explanation of this, perhaps the only belief of which we have any knowledge which is at once a living belief to-day and was so as far back as we can get, I do not pretend to say. For transmigration is no theory of Buddhism at all, but was a leading tenet in the far older faith of Brahmanism, of which Buddhism was but an offshoot, as was Christianity of Judaism.

I have not, indeed, always attempted to reach the explanation of things I have seen. When I have satisfied myself that a belief is really held by the people, that I am not the subject of conscious deception, either by myself or others, I have conceived that my work was ended.

There are those who, in investigating any foreign customs and strange beliefs, can put their finger here and say, 'This is where they are right'; and there and say, 'This belief is foolishly wrong and idiotic.' I am not, unfortunately, one of these writers. I have no such confident belief in my own infallibility of judgment as to be able to sit on high and say, 'Here is truth, and here is error.'

I will leave my readers to make their own judgment, if they desire to do so; only asking them (as they would not like their own beliefs to be scoffed and sneered at) that they will treat with respect the sincere beliefs of others, even if they cannot accept them. It is only in this way that we can come to understand a people and to sympathize with them.

It is hardly necessary to emphasize the enormous effect that a belief in transmigration such as this has upon the life and intercourse of the people. Of their kindness to animals I have spoken elsewhere, and it is possible this belief in transmigration has something to do with it, but not, I think, much. For if you wished to illtreat an animal, it would be quite easy, even more easy, to suppose that an enemy or a murderer inhabited the body of the animal, and that you were but carrying out the decrees of fate by ill-using it. But when you love an animal, it may increase that love and make it reasonable, and not a thing to be ashamed of; and it brings the animal world nearer to you in general, it bridges over the enormous void between man and beast that other religions have made. Nothing humanizes a man more than love of animals.

I do not know if this be a paradox, I know that it is a truth.

There was one point that puzzled me for a time in some of these stories of transmigration, such as the one I told about the man and wife being reborn twins. It was this: A man dies and leaves behind children, let us say, to whom he is devoutly attached. He is reborn in another family in the same village, maybe. It would be natural to suppose that he would love his former family as much as, or even more than, his new one. Complications might arise in this way which it is easy to conceive would cause great and frequent difficulties.

I explained this to a Burman one day, and asked him what happened, and this is what he said: 'The affection of mother to son, of husband to wife, of brother to sister, belongs entirely to the body in which you may happen to be living. When it dies, so do these affections. New affections arise from the new body. The flesh of the son, being of one with his father, of course loves him; but as his present flesh has no sort of connection with his former one, he does not love those to whom he was related in his other lives. These affections are as much a part of the body as the hand or the eyesight; with one you put off the other.'

Thus all love, to the learned, even the purest affection of daughter to mother, of man to his friend, is in theory a function of the body—with the one we put off the other; and this may explain, perhaps, something of what my previous chapter did not make quite clear, that in the hereafter of Buddhism there is no affection.

When we have put off all bodies, when we have attained Nirvana, love and hate, desire and repulsion, will have fallen from us for ever.

Meanwhile, in each life, we are obliged to endure the affections of the body into which we may be born. It is the first duty of a monk, of him who is trying to lead the purer life, to kill all these affections, or rather to blend them into one great compassion to all the world alike. 'Gayūna,' compassion, that is the only passion that will be left to us. So say the learned.

I met a little girl not long ago, a wee little maiden about seven years old, and she told me all about her former life when she was a man. Her name was Maung Mon, she said, and she used to work the dolls in a travelling marionette show. It was through her knowledge and partiality for marionettes that it was first suspected, her parents told me, whom she had been in her former life. She could even as a sucking-child manipulate the strings of a marionette-doll. But the actual discovery came when she was about four years old, and she recognised a certain marionette booth and dolls as her own. She knew all about them, knew the name of each doll, and even some of the words they used to say in the plays. 'I was married four times,' she told me. 'Two wives died, one I divorced; one was living when I died, and is living still. I loved her very much indeed. The one I divorced was a dreadful woman. See,' pointing to a scar on her shoulder, 'this was given me once in a quarrel. She took up a chopper and cut me like this. Then I divorced her. She had a dreadful temper.'

It was immensely quaint to hear this little thing discoursing like this. The mark was a birth-mark, and I was assured that it corresponded exactly with one that had been given to the man by his wife in just such a quarrel as the one the little girl described.

The divorced wife and the much-loved wife are still alive and not yet old. The last wife wanted the little girl to go and live with her. I asked her why she did not go.

'You loved her so much,' I said. 'She was such a good wife to you. Surely you would like to live with her again.'

'But all that,' she replied, 'was in a former life.'

Now she loved only her present father and mother. The last life was like a dream. Broken memories of it still remained, but the loves and hates, the passions and impulses, were all dead.

Another little boy told me once that the way remembrance came to him was by seeing the silk he used to wear made into curtains, which are given to the monks and used as partitions in their monasteries, and as walls to temporary erections made at festival times. He was taken when some three years old to a feast at the making of a lad, the son of a wealthy merchant, into a monk. There he recognised in the curtain walling in part of the bamboo building his old dress. He pointed it out at once.

This same little fellow told me that he passed three months between his death and his next incarnation without a body. This was because he had once accidentally killed a fowl. Had he killed it on purpose, he would have been punished very much more severely. Most of this three months he spent dwelling in the hollow shell of a palm-fruit. The nuisance was, he explained, that this shell was close to the cattle-path, and that the lads as they drove the cattle afield in the early morning would bang with a stick against the shell. This made things very uncomfortable for him inside.

It is not an uncommon thing for a woman when about to be delivered of a baby to have a dream, and to see in that dream the spirit of someone asking for permission to enter the unborn child; for, to a certain extent, it lies within a woman's power to say who is to be the life of her child.

There was a woman once who loved a young man, not of her village, very dearly. And he loved her, too, as dearly as she loved him, and he demanded her in marriage from her parents; but they refused. Why they refused I do not know, but probably because they did not consider the young man a proper person for their daughter to marry. Then he tried to run away with her, and nearly succeeded, but they were caught before they got clear of the village.

The young man had to leave the neighbourhood. The attempted abduction of a girl is an offence severely punishable by law, so he fled; and in time, under pressure from her people, the girl married another man; but she never forgot. She lived with her husband quite happily; he was good to her, as most Burmese husbands are, and they got along well enough together. But there were no children.

After some years, four or five, I believe, the former lover returned to his village. He thought that after this lapse of time he would be safe from prosecution, and he was, moreover, very ill.

He was so ill that very soon he died, without ever seeing again the girl he was so fond of; and when she heard of his death she was greatly distressed, so that the desire of life passed away from her. It so happened that at this very time she found herself enceinte with her first child, and not long before the due time came for the child to be born she had a dream.

She dreamt that her soul left her body, and went out into space and met there the soul of her lover who had died. She was rejoiced to meet him again, full of delight, so that the return of her soul to her body, her awakening to a world in which he was not, filled her with despair. So she prayed her lover, if it was now time for him again to be incarnated, that he would come to her—that his soul would enter the body of the little baby soon about to be born, so that they two might be together in life once more.

And in the dream the lover consented. He would come, he said, into the child of the woman he loved.

When the woman awoke she remembered it all, and the desire of life returned to her again, and all the world was changed because of the new life she felt within her. But she told no one then of the dream or of what was to happen.

Only she took the greatest care of herself; she ate well, and went frequently to the pagoda with flowers, praying that the body in which her lover was about to dwell might be fair and strong, worthy of him who took it, worthy of her who gave it.

In due time the baby was born. But alas and alas for all her hopes! The baby came but for a moment, to breathe a few short breaths, to cry, and to die; and a few hours later the woman died also. But before she went she told someone all about it, all about the dream and the baby, and that she was glad to go and follow her lover. She said that her baby's soul was her lover's soul, and that as he could not stay, neither would she; and with these words on her lips she followed him out into the void.

The story was kept a secret until the husband died, not long afterwards; but when I came to the village all the people knew it.

I must confess that this story is to me full of the deepest reality, full of pathos. It seems to me to be the unconscious protestation of humanity against the dogmas of religion and of the learned. However it may be stated that love is but one of the bodily passions that dies with it; however, even in some of the stories themselves, this explanation is used to clear certain difficulties; however opposed eternal love may be to one of the central doctrines of Buddhism, it seems to me that the very essence of this story is the belief that love does not die with the body, that it lives for ever and ever, through incarnation after incarnation. Such a story is the very cry of the agony of humanity.

'Love is strong as death; many waters cannot quench love;' ay, and love is stronger than death. Not any dogmas of any religion, not any philosophy, nothing in this world, nothing in the next, shall prevent him who loves from the certainty of rejoining some time the soul he loves.

FOOTNOTE:

The hereafter = the state to which we attain when we have done with earthly things.

CHAPTER XXIV

THE FOREST OF TIME

'The gate of that forest was Death.'

There was a great forest. It was full of giant trees that grew so high and were so thick overhead that the sunshine could not get down below. And there were huge creepers that ran from tree to tree climbing there, and throwing down great loops of rope. Under the trees, growing along the ground, were smaller creepers full of thorns, that tore the wayfarer and barred his progress. The forest, too, was full of snakes that crept along the ground, so like in their gray and yellow skins to the earth they travelled on that the traveller trod upon them unawares and was bitten; and some so beautiful with coral red and golden bars that men would pick them up as some dainty jewel till the snake turned upon them.

Here and there in this forest were little glades wherein there were flowers. Beautiful flowers they were, with deep white cups and broad glossy leaves hiding the purple fruit; and some had scarlet blossoms that nodded to and fro like drowsy men, and there were long festoons of white stars. The air there was heavy with their scent. But they were all full of thorns, only you could not see the thorns till after you had plucked the blossom.

This wood was pierced by roads. Many were very broad, leading through the forest in divers ways, some of them stopping now and then in the glades, others avoiding them more or less, but none of them were straight. Always, if you followed them, they bent and bent until after much travelling you were where you began; and the broader the road, the softer the turf beneath it; the sweeter the glades that lined it, the quicker did it turn.

One road there was that went straight, but it was far from the others. It led among the rocks and cliffs that bounded one side of the valley. It was very rough, very far from all the glades in the lowlands. No flowers grew beside it, there was no moss or grass upon it, only hard sharp rocks. It was very narrow, bordered with precipices.

There were many lights in this wood, lights that flamed out like sunsets and died, lights that came like lightning in the night and were gone. This wood was never quite dark, it was so full of these lights that flickered aimlessly.

There were men in this wood who wandered to and fro. The wood was full of them.

They did not know whither they went; they did not know whither they wished to go. Only this they knew, that they could never keep still; for the keeper of this wood was Time. He was armed with a keen whip, and kept driving them on and on; there was no rest.

Many of these when they first came loved the wood. The glades, they said, were very beautiful, the flowers very sweet. They wandered down the broad roads into the glades, and tried to lie upon the moss and love the flowers; but Time would not let them. Just for a few moments they could have peace, and then they must on and on. But they did not care. 'The forest is full of glades,' they said; 'if we cannot live in one, we can find another.' And so they went on finding others and others, and each one pleased them less.

Some few there were who did not go to the glades at all. 'They are very beautiful,' they said, 'but these roads that pass through them, whither do they lead? Round and round and round again. There is no peace there. Time rules in those glades, Time with his whip and goad, and there is no peace. What we want is rest. And those lights,' they said, 'they are wandering lights, like the summer lightning far down in the South, moving hither and thither. We care not for such lights. Our light is firm and clear. What we desire is peace; we do not care to wander for ever round this forest, to see for ever those shifting lights.'

And so they would not go down the winding roads, but essayed the path upon the cliffs. 'It is narrow,' they said, 'it has no flowers, it is full of rocks, but it is straight. It will lead us somewhere, not round and round and round again—it will take us somewhere. And there is a light,' they said, 'before us, the light of a star. It is very small now, but it is always steady; it never flickers or wanes. It is the star of Truth. Under that star we shall find that which we seek.'

And so they went upon their road, toiling upon the rocks, falling now and then, bleeding with wounds from the sharp points, sore-footed, but strong-hearted. And ever as they went they were farther and farther from the forest, farther and farther from the glades and the flowers with deadly scents; they heard less and less the crack of the whip of Time falling upon the wanderers' shoulders.

The star grew nearer and nearer, the light grew greater and greater, the false lights died behind them, until at last they came out of the forest, and there they found the lake that washes away all desire under the sun of Truth.

They had won their way. Time and Life and Fight and Struggle were behind them, could not follow them, as they came, weary and footsore, into the Great Peace.

And of those who were left behind, of those who stayed in the glades to gather the deadly flowers, to be driven ever forward by the whip of Time—what of them? Surely they will learn. The kindly whip of Time is behind: he will never let them rest in such a deadly forest; they must go ever forward; and as they go they grow more and more weary, the glades are more and more distasteful, the heavy-scented blossoms more and more repulsive. They will find out the thorns too. At first they forgot the thorns in the flowers. 'The blossoms are beautiful,' they said; 'what care we for the thorns? Nay, the thorns are good. It is a pleasure to fight with them. What would the forest be without its thorns? If we could gather the flowers and find no thorns, we should not care for them. The more the thorns, the more valuable the blossoms.'

So they said, and they gathered the blossoms, and they faded. But the thorns did not fade; they were ever there. The more blossoms a man had gathered, the more thorns he had to wear, and Time was ever behind him. They wanted to rest in the glades, but Time willed that ever they must go forward; no going back, no rest, ever and ever on. So they grew very weary.

'These flowers,' they said at last, 'are always the same. We are tired of them; their smell is heavy; they are dead. This forest is full of thorns only. How shall we escape from it? Ever as we go round and round we hate the flowers more, we feel the thorns more acutely. We must escape! We are sick of Time and his whip, our feet are very, very weary, our eyes are dazzled and dim. We, too, would seek the Peace. We laughed at those before who went along the rocky path; we did not want peace; but now it seems to us the most beautiful thing in the world. Will Time never cease to drive us on and on? Will these lights *never* cease to flash to and fro?'

Each man at last will turn to the straight road. He will find out. Every man will find out at last that the forest is hateful, that the flowers are deadly, that the thorns are terrible; every man will learn to fear Time.

Then, when the longing for peace has come, he will go to the straight way and find it; no man will remain in the forest for ever. He will learn. When he is very, very weary, when his feet are full of thorns, and his back scarred with the lashes of Time—great, kindly Time, the schoolmaster of the world—he will learn.

Not till he has learnt will he desire to enter into the straight road.

But in the end all men will come. We at the last shall all meet together where Time and Life shall be no more.

This is a Burman allegory of Buddhism. It was told me long ago. I trust I have not spoilt it in the retelling.

CHAPTER XXV

CONCLUSION

This is the end of my book. I have tried always as I wrote to remember the principles that I laid down for myself in the first chapter. Whether I have always done so I cannot say. It is so difficult, so very difficult, to understand a people—any people—to separate their beliefs from their assents, to discover the motives of their deeds, that I fear I must often have failed.

My book is short. It would have been easy to make a book out of each chapter, to write volumes on each great subject that I have touched on; but I have not done so—I have always been as brief as I could.

I have tried always to illustrate only the central thought, and not the innumerable divergencies, because only so can a great or strange thought be made clear. Later, when the thought is known, then it is easy to stray into the byways of thought, always remembering that they are byways, wandering from a great centre.

For the Burman's life and belief is one great whole.

I thought before I began to write, and I have become more and more certain of it as I have taken up subject after subject, that to all the great differences of thought between them and us there is one key. And this key is that they believe the world is governed by eternal laws, that have never changed, that will never change, that are founded on absolute righteousness; while we believe in a personal God, altering laws, and changing moralities according to His will.

If I were to rewrite this book, I should do so from this standpoint of eternal laws, making the book an illustration of the proposition.

Perhaps it is better as it is, in that I have discovered the key at the end of my work instead of at the beginning. I did not write the book to prove the proposition, but in writing the book this truth has become apparent to me.

The more I have written, the clearer has this teaching become to me, until now I wonder that I did not understand long ago—nay, that it has not always been apparent to all men.

Surely it is the beginning of all wisdom.

Not until we had discarded Atlas and substituted gravity, until we had forgotten Enceladus and learned the laws of heat, until we had rejected Thor and his hammer and searched after the laws of electricity, could science make any strides onward.

An irresponsible spirit playing with the world as his toy killed all science.

But now science has learned a new wisdom, to look only at what it can see, to leave vain imaginings to children and idealists, certain always that the truth is inconceivably more beautiful than any dream.

Science with us has gained her freedom, but the soul is still in bonds.

Only in Buddhism has this soul-freedom been partly gained. How beautiful this is, how full of great thoughts, how very different to the barren materialism it has often been said to be, I have tried to show.

I believe myself that in this teaching of the laws of righteousness we have the grandest conception, the greatest wisdom, the world has known.

I believe that in accepting this conception we are opening to ourselves a new world of unimaginable progress, in justice, in charity, in sympathy, and in love.

I believe that as our minds, when freed from their bonds, have grown more and more rapidly to heights of thought before undreamed of, to truths eternal, to beauty inexpressible, so shall our souls, when freed, as our minds now are, rise to sublimities of which now we have no conception.

Let each man but open his eyes and see, and his own soul shall teach him marvellous things.

THE END.

Printed in Great Britain
by Amazon